THE GURU

THE GURU LIES WITHIN…

MARK DAVID ABBOTT

*"With an open mind, seek and listen to all the highest ideals. Consider the most enlightened thoughts. Then choose your path, person by person, each for oneself." - **Zarathustra***

DO YOU WANT ADVANCE NOTICE OF THE NEXT ADVENTURE?

The next book is currently being written, but if you sign up for my VIP newsletter I will let you know as soon as it is released.

Your email will be kept 100% private and you can unsubscribe at any time.

If you are interested, please join here:

www.markdavidabbott.com
(No Spam. Ever.)

1

The young man stood beside the entrance to the tube station, watching the flow of commuters rushing past.

His leather jacket was zipped to the neck, and his hands were thrust into the pockets, but still he shivered, partly from the cold, partly from nerves. Taking a deep breath, he turned to enter the station, and caught a glimpse of himself reflected in the glass of a shop window. He paused and looked at the man staring back at him. He almost didn't recognize himself. For the first time in years, his cheeks were smooth and clean-shaven, the skin tone noticeably lighter than the rest of his face. His eyes were ringed with deep-set dark circles, and his cheekbones stood out prominently in a face made lean from lack of food and little sleep.

He had come a long way since his childhood in a country thousands of miles away, not just in distance, but in experience and spiritual growth. He was close to the ultimate goal. He had been chosen, and soon he would be in heaven, reaping the rewards of a life devoted to the almighty creator of the universe and the judge of humankind.

Turning, he walked through the entrance of the station and looked around. People pushed past as they rushed for the train, everyone in a hurry. He wouldn't do it here—it was too easy for people to escape. It was better to be somewhere enclosed. Crossing to the ticket machines, he bought a ticket, then moved through the turnstiles and rode the escalator down to the platforms. Pausing at the bottom, he glanced at the signs, deciding which platform to head to, but the decision was made for him. Most of the people were heading toward Central London, so with his hands still thrust in the pockets of his leather jacket, he joined them. No-one paid him any attention, all focused on their phone screens, many with headphones, tuned out from their surroundings, and unaware.

At the end of the tunnel, he turned left onto the platform and made his way through the crowd toward the center. The P A system announced the next train arriving in just over a minute, but he didn't worry. He had plenty of time to do what needed to be done. Stopping beside a glass panel covering an advertising poster, he stared at the picture of a young woman in a sleeveless blouse and a skirt that ended just above the knees. Her hair was loose and tumbled over bare shoulders, and she smiled at the camera through bright red lipstick.

The young man sneered. It was appropriate—the perfect place to start his journey to heaven. The poster represented everything wrong with the *Dar ul Kufr,* the land of unbelievers and their society, riddled with sinning and fornication. Still facing the poster, his back to the platform, he closed his eyes, and his lips silently moved as he prayed. Opening his eyes, he unzipped his jacket and removed the Glock 17 from his waistband. Turning, he stepped forward, raised the Glock, and pressed it to the back of the head of the man standing in front of him.

"*Allahu akbar.*" He pulled the trigger.

The man pitched forward and tipped off the platform. For a moment, there was no sound, as people all around stared in shock at the body on the track, then they erupted in screams.

The young man wasted no time. He turned to his left and started firing as the crowd ran for the exits, pushing and shoving, trampling over each other to save themselves. The man walked forward calmly, picking targets. It was easy, what the western crusaders called a 'target-rich environment.' He put a bullet in the back of a young lady in a grey tube skirt and heels, her falling body tripping over another older woman who fell on top of her, screaming. He walked past and shot her in the face as she looked back at him in terror. An elderly man with a walking stick sat frozen on a bench, his mouth hanging open in shock until a bullet to the chest made him slip sideways onto his wife, who was clinging to him with her eyes closed. He shot her, too, then turned to shoot a man in a pinstriped suit and a boy in a school uniform. He felt someone grab his arm from behind, and automatically, his instincts honed in combat, slipped free from the grip, turned, and put two bullets into another young man's chest.

The surrounding area had cleared as people fled, leaving the bleeding bodies of the dead on the platform. He continued walking toward the exit, firing into the backs of the retreating crowd, each bullet finding a target. He heard a whimper and glanced down at a middle-aged woman lying on her back, her eyes open wide as she coughed blood. "*Allahu akbar,*" he repeated and shot her in the forehead.

Stepping over bodies, he continued firing, finishing off

those who were still alive. As he neared the exit, he spotted a young woman huddled over an overturned stroller, her arms covering her head as her body shook in terror. Reaching out with his left hand, he grabbed her hair and pulled her away from the stroller, dropping her on the floor. He raised his right hand and shot her in the chest, a red stain spreading rapidly across her white blouse. Hearing a child's cry, he turned to the stroller, uprighted it, and looked inside. A girl was strapped inside, perhaps three or four, blond curls framing her face, her eyes and cheeks red as she cried out for her mother. The man felt a twinge of regret as he remembered a child of his own, a daughter he had loved with all his heart... until he found something he loved even more. He shook off the memory. He was the chosen one, and soon, he would be in Paradise.

"*Allahu akbar.*" He fired. The girl stopped crying.

He raised the Glock and looked back at the now-empty platform, then turned and pointed the weapon down the exit tunnel at the backs of the fleeing commuters. When he pulled the trigger, he felt the firing pin click on an empty chamber.

At the same time, over the ringing in his ears, he heard the rumble of an approaching train. He pressed the magazine release button and reached inside his jacket for a fresh magazine as the empty one clattered onto the platform floor.

Slotting the magazine in place, he chambered a round and walked back to meet the approaching train.

Constable Marion Johnson of the British Transport Police adjusted her LMT QCB Carbine on its sling as she glanced down the carriage. She had been a firearms officer for almost two months now but still couldn't get used to the sidelong glances and sometimes outright stares from the public. She understood why. She wasn't the usual image people had of a member of the armed police. She was small, only five feet five inches and slightly built, dwarfed by the muscle-bound frame of Sergeant John McWilliams, standing beside her. She reached up with a gloved hand and tucked a stray lock of hair back underneath her uniform cap. What people didn't realize was she had topped her batch in marksmanship, and while not able to match her male colleagues in physical strength, she regularly outran them on the obstacle course and the longer endurance runs.

She'd earned the respect of her classmates by the time she graduated but was still struggling to earn the same respect from colleagues in her new unit. Particularly the man towering over her in his matching black uniform and bulletproof vest.

She felt his huge hand on her shoulder, steadying her when she momentarily lost balance as the train went around a curve and reluctantly tuned back into his conversation. She had grown tired of his condescending remarks, but it was either that, or he was hitting on her. She couldn't understand men and their macho ways. They didn't think she was worthy of doing the same job, yet they never tired of wanting to get her out of uniform and into the sack. She had always known it wouldn't be easy. Her father had warned her. He'd been a policeman before her and had explained how hard it would be to make her way in what was predominantly a man's world, no matter how much the force spoke about inclusion and diversity. But, she wouldn't change her job for the world. It was far more exciting and rewarding than the lives these office slaves around her had chosen.

The train slowed as it pulled into the station, and there was a bustle of activity as people prepared to get off. She glanced down the train again from their position by the door.

Sergeant McWilliams finished some wisecrack she only half-heard, then turned as the doors slid open and stepped onto the platform. She was about to follow him when she saw a look of surprise on his face, and he fell backward onto the platform.

An instant later, her brain registered the sound of gunshots, and she turned her head and screamed. "Everyone, get down! Get down!"

The carriage filled with panicked screams and shouts, followed by the sound of gunfire and breaking glass.

With a glance at her fallen colleague, she poked her head out the door and looked down the platform. She felt rather than heard a bullet whizz past her head, and she ducked back inside. It had only been a second, but it had been enough—a lone gunman with a handgun, multiple casualties.

Time seemed to slow down, everything around her happening in slow motion as she stared down the carriage in a daze, frozen to the spot. All the training in the world never prepared you for actually being shot at. Then another shot rang out, and she saw a passenger on the far side of the carriage slump sideways in their seat as a mass of blood and gore splattered across the window beside them.

The longer she waited, the more people would die. At that moment, she made her decision. Marion leaped out the door, dropping to the ground and rolling away from the carriage. She brought her weapon to bear, flicked off the safety, held her breath, and squeezed the trigger—two shots, center mass—one more for luck.

The shooting stopped.

Marion was still for a moment, then exhaled. She glanced over at her Sergeant, lying to her left. He was staring up at the roof of the station, but he was blinking. A feeling of relief flooded through her. He was alive. Looking forward again, she kept her sights trained on the body of the gunman and got to her feet. She quickly walked forward, her finger covering the trigger, weapon pointed at the gunman, her eyes scanning the platform for any sign of another attacker. With bodies everywhere, she had to be mindful not to step on anyone or slip in one of the many areas made slick with blood. All she could hear was her breathing and the sound of her heart pounding in her ears. There was movement in the train carriage, but she kept her focus on the attacker as she neared his body. He was alive, but likely not for long. Air bubbles frothed red from one of the holes in his chest, and his lips and teeth were stained pink. Marion stepped closer, then moved the Glock away from his hand with the toe of her boot. Releasing her carbine to hang from its sling, she drew her own Glock, and keeping it trained on the shooter, she knelt down, and parted his jacket. No suicide vest. She checked his pockets for another weapon, but he was clear—no weapon, no I.D.

"Is there anyone else?" she asked.

His eyes locked on hers and his lips moved, but no sound came out, only pink spittle and a faint rasping breath. With a final gasp, the light went from his eyes.

3

J ohn jogged up the steps onto the top of the mighty
wall that ringed Galle Fort and stood with his hands
on his hips, gazing out across the vast expanse of the
Indian Ocean. Although it was still relatively cool,
sweat ran down his face, and his running vest clung to his
back. Despite any discomfort, it was preferable to running
later in the day with the temperature predicted to climb into
the low thirties Celsius and humidity as high as 80%.

To his left, the sun's rays were just peeking above the
horizon, and in the early morning light, he could make out
the beach across the bay at Unawatuna. Directly ahead, the
sea was calm, an incredible expanse of flat blue-grey as far
as he could see. Somewhere out there, thousands of miles
away were the islands of the Maldives, and off to the west,
the coast of Somalia.

The ocean always brought John an element of peace.
The vastness, the quiet, the lack of people helped him calm
his often-troubled mind.

The early morning was his favorite time with few people
around and a stillness in the air. It's when he liked to run, to

feel the blood pumping around his veins, the oxygen filling his lungs. His mind would quieten, and eventually, if he was lucky and the conditions were right, he would enter a flow state. A state where nothing mattered, nothing else existed, just him and the road, no past, no future... just now.

It didn't happen every time, but often enough for him to seek it out at every opportunity.

That morning, he had run four laps around the fort, almost ten kilometers in total, taking the internal road that followed the walls of the former Portuguese outpost. There had been no-one else around, only the sentry at the gate of the Sri Lankan Army garrison on the northern end, who, without fail, gave John a wave each time he passed.

John took a deep breath and sucked in a lungful of fresh sea air as the *muezzin* in the mosque behind him called out a summons to the faithful. Further afield, he could hear the rhythmic clang of temple bells, as if in competition. All that was missing were the bells from the nearby church. John shook his head. He could never understand the need to disturb the peace of the early morning with bells and loud-speakers. *If you believe in God, are you not allowed to sleep in?* Shaking his head, he placed his hands on the top of the wall and stretched his calves.

Religion wasn't for him. He'd seen too much hatred and cruelty to believe in an all-seeing benevolent being. John believed in taking matters into his own hands. If something needed to be fixed, he had to do it himself. Communing with an imaginary being got nothing done. The only one responsible for John's happiness or lack thereof was John himself.

Right now, John felt good. In fact, better than he had felt in weeks. Since his return from Syria several months ago, he'd been sleeping badly, his dreams haunted by the sound of gunfire and faces from the past, faces of people who no longer walked the earth. He had become irritable and withdrawn, filled with a restlessness, that no matter what distraction he sought, would not leave him alone. Days spent thrashing his classic Porsche through the hills and narrow roads around Sintra and evenings downing too many gin and tonics did nothing to help.

It was Adriana who suggested the trip. Two weeks away from the cold of Europe, somewhere bright, sunny, and warm. A change of location and routine would do them both a world of good, she'd said, and John readily agreed. Anything to get him out of his depressive funk, and within a week of her suggestion, they were on a plane to Sri Lanka.

John glanced at the rising sun and checked his watch. Almost seven. Time to head back to the villa and shower before Adriana woke up. He took one last look at the ocean, now changing from a flat grey to a mercury-silver tinged with red and orange, and grinned. It was going to be a good day.

4

He opened his eyes and gazed out across the darkened room. The flickering candlelight was just enough to make out the darkened shapes of the people sitting cross-legged on the floor before him—not a single movement, not a single sound, just slow rhythmic breathing.

The group was doing well, showing significant progress in the two weeks they had been with him. He had guided them into ever-deepening states of meditation without difficulty. Several of the students had commented to him privately about the breakthroughs they had experienced, both mentally and physically.

A slight movement in the right corner caught his eye as someone changed position. It was the young lady from Toronto. He narrowed his eyes to see her better.

Her eyes were closed, but her shoulders shook, and as he moved his head, he saw wetness on her cheeks, glistening in the candlelight. Was she crying? Her hand moved to wipe her cheek, confirming his deduction. As if sensing his attention, her eyes opened, meeting his in the dim light.

She was troubled. Something bad had happened in her past, and the meditation was bringing it back to the present.

Keeping his eyes locked on hers, he smiled reassuringly and raised his right hand, palm facing in her direction, then closed his eyes. He inhaled deeply, feeling the calm fill his body. He heard the girl sob, and as he exhaled, he felt the fingertips of his right hand tingling. Willing the energy toward her, he sensed her relaxing, the tension melting away from her, her mind emptying.

He took another long breath, then exhaled so slowly that he couldn't feel the air leaving his nostrils, then lowered his hand. Opening his eyes again, he looked at her. She had stopped crying, her forehead had relaxed, and the corners of her mouth turned up slightly as a blissful expression filled her face.

He nodded slowly. It would take longer for her, but she would get there. He would speak to her later, in private, and give her some guidance.

He cast his eyes around the room again, the light from the windows slowly increasing as sunrise approached. The rest of the group remained unmoving, lost in their own private contemplation.

In the distance, a peacock crowed, announcing the arrival of the day, and he closed his eyes. He took a slow, deep breath and exhaled, pulling his attention back from the peacock, into the room, then from the room into his body, until all external sensations ceased. There was no sound, no movement, no light, not even him. Nothing remained—only bliss.

5

Kiyomi smoothed down the front of her white skirt and knelt before the stupa. She placed the white frangipani flower, which she had plucked from the tree in the temple compound, at the feet of the idol, then lit a stick of incense from the oil lamp that flickered and spluttered in the gentle pre-dawn breeze. Clasping it in both hands, she closed her eyes, leaned back on her heels, and began to pray. She recited the *Buddha Vandana*, followed by the *Dhamma Vandana*, and then finished with a prayer of her own.

She prayed for the health of the world, for all mankind, then made it more personal. Asiri, her husband, had been in poor health and could not visit the fields or come to the temple. She prayed for his return to good health and prayed for a good harvest. Since Asiri had become ill, their savings had dwindled, and she had to pay her neighbors' son Nishant to help her work the fields. They needed a good harvest to have enough food and money to last the winter.

Kiyomi was tired. Tending to her husband and looking after their fields, although small, took all day and part of the night, but she wouldn't allow herself self-pity. Life was filled with ups and downs, and she had to face them as they came without attaching herself to the outcome. She believed the universe would provide for her, and this troubled time would pass as long as she continued to have faith. That was why, despite her exhaustion, despite the prospect of a hard day ahead, she still rose early every morning before dawn and came to the stupa to pray.

Finally, she said a prayer for her daughter, Nihinsa, and the thought of her brought a smile to her face. Nihinsa would never struggle in the fields as she had. She was blessed. She had been chosen. Chosen for a life in the service of a great spiritual being, and from Nihinsa, Kiyomi was confident, blessings would flow to her and her husband. She just had to believe. Although she only heard from her once a week since the foreign man had taken her away, she was confident everything was going well. Of course, she missed her, but what could be better than a life spent in the service of a man like him? A man who could speak to God as the great Buddha had done so long ago.

Kiyomi opened her eyes and placed the incense stick into the little brass stand beside her flower. She touched her fingertips to her lips, then placed them gently on the feet of the idol. She wasn't sure, but she thought she could feel a tingle of energy, something like an electrical current, run into her fingers. Her face filled with joy. Everything was going to be okay.

6

J ohn lifted the side of the mosquito netting and slid gently onto the bed, trying not to disturb Adriana. He propped himself on one elbow and gazed down at her as she slept. Despite the ceiling fan and the sea breeze wafting through the slats of the shutters, the room was warm, and she had partly thrown off the single sheet they used as a cover during the cooler hours of the night. The leg of her satin shorts had ridden up, exposing her shapely thigh and long slender calf. John admired her leg for a moment and grinned. He never tired of looking at her, and now, after just under a week in the Sri Lankan sun, her skin had turned a beautiful caramel color, contrasting against the crisp white sheets.

He reached out and ran his fingertip up her arm from her elbow to her shoulder, then leaned over and gently kissed her half-open lips. She stirred, and her eyes blinked open, a flash of emerald against tanned skin, then her lips responded. Her arms wrapped around him and pulled him closer, the softness of her breasts pressing against his bare chest. He groaned, and his heart rate quickened as the tip of his tongue slipped between her lips.

A while later, he lay on his back, spent, her head on his chest, watching the fan rotate slowly high above.

"I think I need another shower," he murmured.

Adriana giggled and raised her head, turning so she could look into his eyes, her hands on his chest, her chin resting on the backs of her hands.

"Perhaps we should have one together?"

John raised an eyebrow.

"To save water, of course," Adriana winked.

"Of course." John smiled and smoothed a lock of hair away from her face. "I've always admired your concern for the environment."

"We all have to do our bit."

"If this is how I can help save the planet, I'm all for it."

Adriana slid up his chest until her face was just above his, her eyes so close, he could see the flecks of gold in her irises. He felt her warm sweet breath on his face.

"Are you happy we came?"

"Very happy." John raised his head and kissed her on the lips. "Thank you."

"Sleeping better?"

"Like a baby." He wasn't, but he didn't want to ruin the moment. Adriana looked so happy, it wasn't fair to burden her with his troubles.

Adriana reached forward and placed a fingertip on his lips. "My baby." Tracing the shape of his mouth with her finger, she continued, "I was worried about you, John. Since you came back from Syria, you haven't been the same." She pinched his lips together between her fingertips and grinned. "But now, my old John is back."

John grabbed her hands and flipped her over onto her

back, moving astride her, pinning her hands to the bed. He looked down at her and grinned.

"John isn't going anywhere." Leaning forward, he kissed her on the forehead, the tip of her nose, and finally her lips. Releasing her hands, he slid off her, "Now, let's have that shower and some breakfast. I'm starving."

John watched Adriana walk naked across the polished wooden floor to the bathroom, admiring the sway of her hips, the cute tan line around her buttocks, and the shape of her toned calves. He was so lucky to have found a woman like her, and there was no way he would do anything to jeopardize their relationship. When Charlotte was taken from him, he had never hoped he would find happiness again, yet here he was. He felt a small twinge of guilt at the thought of Charlotte but deep down, knew she would have wanted him to be happy. A lot had happened since that awful day in Bangalore, and he would always have to live with the things he had done. The faces of the people whose lives he had taken still haunted him, but that was his problem, not Adriana's.

The past was the past and couldn't be undone, and John still believed that the people whose lives he had taken had deserved it.

So, what went on in his head was his problem and his alone.

7

J ohn and Adriana spent the morning wandering the lanes of the fort, visiting the small boutiques selling silk, gems, and local handicrafts. Adriana picked up a few souvenirs for her family and a few colleagues, but John was simply happy to spend time in her company.

By midday, it had become too hot to remain outside, so they walked into the restaurant of a boutique hotel to rest and refresh.

Converted from what would have once been a wealthy merchant's home, the building stretched back from the open-plan lobby and restaurant facing the road and opened out onto a lush tropical courtyard garden, with a swimming pool in the center. The interior was cool and a welcome respite from the baking heat outside, helped by the three feet thick walls, high ceilings, and the rattan fans lazily rotating above.

John guided Adriana to a table by the open window where they could look out onto the street and sat down. On the opposite side of the road, on a small patch of grass under an ancient banyan tree, a young Sri Lankan couple posed for wedding photos, both bride and groom sweating profusely under their ornate wedding finery.

John grinned. "The things we do for love, huh?"

Adriana didn't respond, staring at the couple with an unusual look on her face. John's smile faded, and he changed the subject.

"What would you like to drink?"

Adrian turned and studied his face for a moment before picking up the menu. "I'm craving something cold and sweet."

"Gin and tonic?"

She shook her head. "No, I'll be sleepy." She ran her finger down the menu. "I'll have this, ginger beer."

John nodded and looked around for a waiter. A young man caught his eye and hurried over.

"Good afternoon, sir."

"Good afternoon." John smiled. "Madam, will have a ginger beer, and do you have Botanist Gin?"

The young man shook his head. "No, sorry, sir, but we have Colombo No. 7, a Sri Lankan Gin. Have you tried it?"

"No, I haven't. Is it good?"

The young man smiled, exposing a row of glistening white teeth. "I don't drink, sir, but I'm told it's good."

"Okay." John smiled at Adriana and shrugged. "I'll try it, with tonic and lots of ice."

"Of course, sir."

John watched the waiter walk away, then turned back to Adriana. "Might as well sample the local specialty."

Adriana smiled, but her attention seemed elsewhere.

"Are you okay?"

"Yes, yes, sorry. I think I'm a little dehydrated and tired."

John reached across the table and took her hand. "Are you glad we came here?"

Adriana nodded. "It's a beautiful country." She glanced around the restaurant, empty apart from an Asian couple in the far corner, staring at their phones. "I wonder about the history of this building. It's hard to imagine it was a house once. It's so big."

"I know. It's hard to imagine it was a Portuguese outpost once as well. Maybe one of your ancestors was here."

Adriana chuckled. "I doubt it. My family has never been wealthy."

The waiter returned and set a tray down on a side table.

"Madam, your ginger beer."

"Thank you."

"Sir, your gin and tonic."

John looked appreciatively at the glass set before him. A large copa glass, just the way he liked it. "What's the garnish?"

"Sir, we put a slice of unripe mango."

"Interesting. Thank you." John picked up the glass, "What's your name?"

"Senthil, sir."

"Thank you, Senthil. We will order some food soon."

"As you wish, sir." He smiled at Adriana. "Madam."

John waited until Senthil walked away, then raised his glass. "Cheers."

"Cheers."

He took a sip, then licked his lips. "Nice, I like it. I can taste... cinnamon, I think. How's yours?"

"Yum. Do you want to taste?"

John reached over, took the glass from her, and took a sip. "Hmm, nice, but too sweet for me. Refreshing, though."

"Yes. This heat is draining."

"Let's go back to the villa after lunch and rest for a while.

Have a swim, a snooze, then we can come out again in the evening once it is cooler."

"Sounds like a good plan." Adriana grinned, then made a face. "I wish we had more time. Only two days left."

John shrugged. "We can always stay longer."

Adriana took another sip of her drink and licked her lips, then shook her head. "I can't. I only have so much leave I can take."

John leaned back in his chair and tilted his head to one side. "You don't have to work. You know that. We have money, more money than we can ever spend."

Adriana looked out the window, her eyes on the photo session across the road. The groom was fanning his bride's face with what looked like a magazine while the photographer changed lenses.

John waited, keen to know what was on her mind. Eventually, she turned back.

"It's not about the money, John. I just..." She glanced across the restaurant as if searching for the right words, "I want to do something on my own." Looking back at John, she reached over and took his hand. "I know you will always be there for me, but I want to do this for myself. I've always wanted to be a successful journalist, and now I have the opportunity I need to make the most of it."

"It's okay." John squeezed her hand and smiled. "I understand and will never stand in your way."

"I know."

John let go of her hand and reached for his drink, "The Syria story must have helped?"

"It has, but I'm only as good as my last story, so I need to keep going." She sipped her drink, then, her glass still in her hand, pointed her index finger at him. "That doesn't mean I want you risking your life again to get me a story."

John chuckled. "No way. Those days are behind me." His smile faded, memories of the recent trip to Syria filling his mind. The Yazidi women who were kept as sex slaves, and Karam, the young boy, forced to fight for the Islamic State jihadis, ultimately losing his life in a war that meant little to him. "Anyway, that was for Steve. I owed him."

"We owed him."

"Yes..." John looked across the table at the woman who meant everything to him. A stray lock of hair moved in the warm sea breeze blowing gently through the window. Reaching across with his spare hand, he tucked it behind her ear, and his fingertips brushed her cheek. She pressed her face into his hand, her eyes sparkling in the sunlight. John winked and sat back in his seat.

"Let's order some food. I'm starving."

J ust after placing their orders, a flurry of activity outside caught their attention. A small crowd had gathered in front of the hotel, westerners and Sri Lankans of mixed ages and gender, but all had one thing in common. They were all dressed in white.

"What do you think is going on?" Adriana asked.

John made a face. "Haven't the foggiest." He took a sip of his gin, rolling the liquid around in his mouth, savoring the taste. "Maybe a tour group or something."

The crowd slowly grew, and by the time their food arrived, they filled the space in front of the hotel. John was about to ask Senthil what was going on when the crowd parted and lined up on each side of the road. A black Range Rover pulled up in front of the hotel, and a burly-looking man, also dressed in white, climbed out of the passenger side and opened the rear door. The crowd surged in, surrounding the car but leaving a space clear in front of the hotel entrance.

Adriana and John watched, forgetting their food as a man stepped out of the rear of the Range Rover, and a buzz of excitement spread through the crowd. He, too, was dressed in white, a linen shirt, open to the chest, and matching loose pants. He was tanned and fit looking, his hair swept back from his face, his features suggestive of a Mediterranean or Middle Eastern descent. In fact, he looked as if he would be more at home on a yacht in the harbor of St Tropez.

Pausing, he turned and took time to smile at the crowd on both sides, his right hand held against his chest, then jogged up the steps into the hotel, closely followed by the large man and two women.

John looked back at Adriana and raised an eyebrow, then noticed Senthil, still standing beside them, his eyes on the crowd outside.

"Who's that Senthil?"

Senthil looked over his shoulder to where one of his colleagues was seating the group at a table.

Turning back, he leaned forward, lowering his voice, "He is a... how do you say... a man of God."

"A man of God?" John glanced at Adriana, who was watching the group with equal curiosity. "What do you mean?"

"He has a house near here and another place up in the hills. People come from all over the world to learn from him."

"Learn what?"

"Meditation, how to find God." Senthil shrugged, "That sort of thing. He comes here a lot."

John glanced over to the man's table. He sat facing the room with the two women sitting either side of him and the bulky man with his back to John. He caught John's eye and smiled. John nodded, returned his smile, then turned back to Senthil.

"Thank you, Senthil. The food smells great."

"Please, enjoy your meal."

"We will. Oh, and I'll have another," John replied, pointing at his empty glass. He looked over at Adriana, but she shook her head. John waited until Senthil had left before picking up his cutlery.

"Obviously, the meditation business pays well," he muttered before slicing into his fish.

Adriana glanced over at the man's table as she chewed. "Perhaps he's like Tony Robbins, more of a life coach."

"Maybe." John swallowed. "My fish is superb. How's yours?"

"Delicious."

John reached for his water glass and took a sip, "Senthil said he's a man of God, whatever that means."

"That could just be his interpretation."

"Hmmm, maybe. If he's helping people find peace in their lives, giving them guidance, it's great. I have nothing against that. What annoys me are these guys who make money from promising special access to God. You saw his Range Rover? It's the long-wheelbase Vogue. They're not cheap, and in Sri Lanka, with the import duties, it would be even more expensive."

"It could be a gift." Adriana shrugged. "He might be independently wealthy, could be many things. Why should we judge?"

John grinned as Senthil returned with a fresh gin and tonic. He thanked him, raised the glass, and winked at Adriana.

"You're right. It's none of our business. Let's enjoy the few days we have left here."

J ohn was about to signal for the bill when Senthil appeared beside him with a tray holding two drinks. He set a gin and tonic down in front of John, then picked up the other glass.

"These are from the gentleman over there." He nodded toward the man in white. "He said, please accept his apologies for any disturbance his people outside may have caused."

"Oh." John glanced out the window to where the crowd in white was sitting quietly on the grass or talking in small groups. "They've been no trouble at all."

Senthil placed the other glass in front of Adriana. "I took the liberty, Madam, of changing your ginger beer to a gin and tonic." He grinned. "I hope you don't mind."

"Not at all, thank you." Adriana gave him her biggest smile, and Senthil's face reddened. "That's very kind of you."

John raised his glass, looked across the restaurant to the other table. Waiting until he caught the man's eye, John nodded, raised the glass a little higher, and smiled.

Turning back to Adriana, he grinned. "Perhaps he is a man of God after all."

Adriana chuckled and took a sip. "Whatever he is, I think a nice long siesta by the pool is called for after this."

"Why not?"

A short while later, John helped Adriana with her chair, then they walked together across the restaurant toward the exit, his fingertips resting on the small of her back as they made their way between the tables. John could feel eyes on him, and as they neared the table of the party in white, John stopped.

"Thank you very much for the drinks, but you didn't have to."

The man in white smiled, dabbed his lips with his napkin, and said, "It was nothing. I just hope my people outside didn't disturb your lunch. I'm sorry, but they follow me everywhere."

He had an accent John couldn't place. Southern European was the best he could think of.

John smiled. "Not at all, but thank you for asking." John looked around the table at the others. The two women, both attractive, tanned, and perhaps in their mid to late twenties, smiled back. John glanced at the large man, who had turned in his chair to look at him, a slight frown on his forehead. He smiled briefly at John before resuming his frown.

Turning back to their leader, John said, "You seem to be a very popular man."

The man grinned and shrugged, then pushed his chair back and stood. He was of a similar height to John, broad-shouldered but lean.

"People call me Atman," he said, holding his hand out to Adriana.

"Adriana."

Still holding her hand, he cocked his head, an eyebrow raised. "Español?"

"Portuguese," she replied, her eyes flicking to her hand and back to his face.

"A beautiful country." He smiled again. "Beautiful people." He released her hand and turned to John.

"John." John shook his hand. The man's grip was firm, and his eyes locked with John's as if he was looking deep inside his head.

"John." Atman nodded slowly. "English, no?"

"Yes, and yourself?"

Atman didn't answer but continued staring into John's eyes. John felt uncomfortable and tried to look away, but it was as if his eyes couldn't move. Atman frowned and reached out with his left hand, his fingertips touching John's chest.

"You carry a lot of pain... sorrow. You blame yourself." He dropped his hand and released John's right hand, then smiled, his face softening. He placed a hand on John's shoulder, and when he spoke, his voice was low, gentle. "It's not your fault."

John went to say something, his mouth opening, but couldn't think of what to say. He closed his mouth again, swallowed, then glanced over at Adriana, who was watching the exchange with considerable interest.

Atman turned to Adriana. "Will you both join me for lunch tomorrow? I have a house near here. It would be my honor to host you."

Adriana looked at John.

"That's very kind of you, but we..." John protested.

Atman turned to John. "I won't take no for an answer."

John glanced at Adriana and shrugged. "If my partner has no objection..."

"Good, it's settled."

John's eyes flicked back to Adriana, who still hadn't said anything, but the corners of her eyes and mouth twitched with a hint of amusement.

Atman continued. "Where are you staying? In the fort?"

"Yes, in the old Ambassador's Villa."

"Good. I know it." Atman turned to the bulky man, who nodded back. Looking from John to Adriana again, Atman smiled broadly. "My car will come for you at twelve-thirty." He reached out his hand again, grabbing John's, then turned it over, placing his other hand on top. "I'm sure we will have a lot to talk about."

10

"What did you think of that?" John murmured as they walked down the steps of the hotel onto the street outside.

"I'm not sure," Adriana replied slowly. She smiled at a group of young western women standing on the edge of the steps, then stopped.

"Hello," she said to the nearest woman, a blonde dressed like all the others in white, her outfit a long flowing linen dress that fluttered in the sea breeze.

"Hi," the woman said brightly. "Are you also here for Atman?"

"Ah, no." Adriana smiled and shook her head. "We just met him inside."

"Isn't he wonderful?"

"Yes," Adriana replied and glanced at the woman's companions, who were listening in, their faces beaming with happiness. "You are all here to see him?" She gestured to encompass the other groups gathered on the grass on the opposite side of the street. "All of you?"

"Yes, all of us."

"But why have you come here?" John asked.

The woman giggled. "He is a great being. We want to see him all the time, but..." She smiled at her companions. "He's a very busy man, so we grab whatever chance we can get."

"Hmmm, okay." John smiled. "But how did you know he was here?"

"He told us, of course." One of the other women spoke up. She was a little older than the others and sounded English.

"He told you?"

"Yes," the woman replied as if John was an idiot. John was about to say something but felt Adriana's hand on his arm.

"You said he's a great being," she asked the first woman. "Why do you say that? What makes him different?"

"You've seen him, right?" The woman seemed to blush and reached out to touch Adriana's arm as if she was sharing a confidence. "He has a presence. When he looks into your eyes, you feel like nothing matters, that everything will be okay. He fills us with an amazing... ah..." She looked up and to the right as if searching for the word. "Peace."

"Yes," the other women chorused, nodding in support.

"When I first came to him, my life was terrible," the English woman shared. "Full of suffering and sadness. He made me feel whole again."

"How did he do that?" John asked.

"His teachings... he's full of wisdom... and his energy. When you sit for meditation in a room with him, he takes you so deep, and it fills you with such bliss, you don't want it to end."

"Really?" John raised his eyebrows but tried not to appear too skeptical. He had heard of spiritual masters during his time in India, teachers who could transport you to different realms and induce altered states of mind but had never experienced it for himself. The closest he had felt was a deep flow state while on a long run, but that was fleeting and didn't happen often enough.

"Yes," the lady continued. "But just being in his presence can be enough. Many of us have experienced healings just being around him."

"That's why we always follow him around," the first woman piped up. "You should visit his ashram, ah... retreat centre. It will change your life."

"His ashram?" Adriana asked. "Where is it?"

"In the hills, near Ella. It's beautiful there."

The others murmured agreement.

There was movement in the periphery, and the women glanced toward the hotel entrance.

"He's coming," someone called out. Everyone gathered around the bottom of the steps, pushing and jostling for a view.

John guided Adriana away from the crowd. They watched as Atman appeared at the top of the steps, the large man standing to his left and the two women who had dined with him standing behind them.

He smiled at the crowd and raised both hands, palms facing the crowd, and a buzz rippled through the crowd. He stayed like that for a moment until his Range Rover pulled up at the entrance. Dropping his hands, he made his way down the steps, the large man moving aside anyone who got too close.

As they reached the Range Rover, the driver opened the rear door, and Atman climbed inside while the large man climbed into the front passenger seat. The driver hurried around to his side as the crowd surrounded the vehicle, many holding their hands to their chests or their palms together in the *namaste* position. Once the driver was inside, the vehicle edged slowly forward until it was clear of the crowd, then accelerated down the street.

John watched the crowd disperse slowly, then looked at Adriana.

"Well?"

She shrugged, "He's like a pop star."

"I know. Did you see their faces?"

Adriana nodded. "And how they spoke about him?"

"Yeah," John sighed. "It was a bit weird." He took Adriana's arm, and they slowly walked away from the hotel toward their villa.

"Do you think he can do what they say he can do?"

"I don't know." John made a face. "When I lived in India, I heard of many people like him, but so many of them turned out to be frauds."

"But if he is, how are these people so... what's the word?"

"In love with him?"

"Yes! That's it. Those women were like teenagers in love."

"There were men there, too."

"I know." Adriana pulled John closer and squeezed his arm. "What is it about him?"

"I don't know. I mean, he does have a certain... charisma. He oozes confidence and looks the part—tanned, successful."

"Did you feel anything?" Adrian turned her head to look at his face.

"No, not really." John narrowed his eyes and frowned slightly. "I mean, when he locked eyes with me... it was as if he was looking inside... I couldn't really look away." John smiled down at Adriana. "It was uncomfortable, actually. No-one makes eye contact for that long."

Adriana nodded thoughtfully. "What about the things

he said? You have pain and sorrow inside, that you blame yourself."

John said nothing for a while as he thought it over. They turned into the narrow cobble-stoned lane that led to their villa.

"A party trick. Show me one person who doesn't have pain and sorrow in their memories. I would guess you could say that to anyone and be right nine times out of ten." They stopped beside the high gate of their villa, and John turned to Adriana, holding her in both arms. "If I said that to you, would you find something in your past you are unhappy about?"

Adriana looked up at him, her forehead slightly creased. He could see her eyes moving as she searched her memories, and then she smiled.

"Ok, Mr. Guru, you got me." She giggled. "Now, let's go inside where you can continue to bless me."

"Sir?" The elderly watchman called out from the wide, open verandah at the front of the villa.

John looked up from the table, and when he met the watchman's eye, the old man called out, "Good morning, sir," and held a newspaper in the air.

"Oh, thank you." John placed his coffee cup back on the table, dried his lips with his napkin, and stood. He walked barefoot across the large open living room, filled with antique furniture, and onto the verandah that overlooked the walled garden at the entrance. Smiling at the watchman, he took the paper from him, then held out a handful of rupees. The watchman protested, shaking his head, but John pressed the notes into his hand.

"For your family."

The watchman smiled and reluctantly put the money in the breast pocket of his shirt, slipped his rubber flip-flops back on, and walked back to his seat by the gate.

John waited until he sat down, then looked up at the sky. Clear and blue, with not a cloud in sight, it hinted at another hot day. The buzz of a rickshaw, passing in the street on the other side of the compound walls, mixed with the distant sound of temple bells and the cawing of a crow on the rooftop gable. He smiled to himself and turned to go back inside the villa. It was going to be another lovely day.

He unfolded the newspaper, glancing at the front page as he made his way back to the dining table, then stopped dead when he saw the face that took up most of the front page above the fold.

"What is it?"

John didn't respond, his eyes scanning the article.

"John?"

John looked up. He hadn't noticed Adriana coming downstairs. She was standing on the bottom step, her hair still damp from her shower.

John crossed the room and held out the paper.

Adrian looked at the front page and frowned, then looked up at John.

"You never met him," John explained, "but he's the guy who took Mia to Syria."

"Ahhh... Naeem?"

"Yes. Read the article."

Adriana looked back at the paper and started reading aloud.

"Naeem Emwazi was shot dead by London Transport Police after he killed twenty-seven people and seriously wounded five others on the London Underground yesterday morning. Emwazi, a second-generation Lebanese Australian, was believed to have left Australia four years ago to fight for the Islamic State in Syria. In a statement yesterday, the Islamic State's Amaq News Agency claimed, *The brave warrior who carried out the attack on the London Underground was a member of the Islamic State and carried out the attack on the instructions of a senior IS leader to take the jihad*

directly to coalition countries." She stopped reading and
looked up, her mouth open, a deep crease in her forehead.

John stood with his hands on his hips, staring back at
her, a million thoughts running through his mind. Was it his
fault? Should he have handed Naeem over to the authorities? But what authorities? When they had been captured by
the Turkish Army, Naeem had somehow disappeared, either
escaped or... let go. Perhaps John should have put a bullet in
him? No, they had needed his help to escape. John exhaled
loudly and shook his head.

Adriana, watching him closely, walked over and placed a
hand on his arm. "What are you thinking?"

John took a deep breath, then slowly exhaled. "I'm just
wondering if I could have prevented this?"

Adriana jerked her head back and frowned. "How? How
is this your responsibility?"

"I was with him, Adriana, right until the Turkish Army
found us."

Adriana grabbed both his arms and looked up into his
face. "Hey, this is not your fault. You couldn't possibly have
known what he was going to do."

John nodded, but he still had a nagging doubt.

"Twenty-seven people, Adriana..."

"Baby, it's awful, horrific, but there is nothing you could
have done." She stood on her toes and kissed him on the
lips, then tilted her head back to look into his eyes. "Don't
forget the good you did. You saved that little girl's life. She
can now grow up to live a full and free life. What if she's the
next Mother Teresa or Marie Curie? You saved her mother's
life too, and rescued those Yazidi women from a life of
slavery."

John gazed at her beautiful face, her skin a warm
cinnamon tan, her large, expressive eyes... his very own

angel. She was right, but her words didn't completely dissolve the ball of anger and despair in the pit of his stomach.

"Don't let this ruin your day." She smiled and squeezed his arms. "Look where we are. A beautiful villa to ourselves in a beautiful country, filled with wonderful people."

"You're right." John allowed himself to smile. "Let's have breakfast. I've only had coffee so far, and I'm starving." He leaned forward and kissed Adriana on the forehead, then guided her to the table.

The cook poked his head out from the kitchen, "Ready, sir?"

"Ready, Chaminda. What's on the menu this morning?"

"Egg curry and hoppers, sir." Chaminda grinned, exposing brilliant white teeth against his dark skin. "Madam, tea, coffee?"

"I'll have tea, please, Chaminda. Same as usual."

Chaminda grinned even wider, then disappeared back into the kitchen.

Adriana turned the newspaper over, so they couldn't see Naeem's face and picked up her napkin, unfolding it and placing it on her lap as John sat down opposite her.

"Maybe I should warn Mia? Her story got a lot of press when you rescued her. It won't take long for the news agencies of the world to track her down."

"I think you should." John picked up his coffee and took a sip. It had gone cold. He made a face and put the cup back down. "Do you still have her number?"

Adriana nodded. "I'll call her after breakfast."

Chaminda came out with a Noritake teapot, ornately decorated in pinks and blues, and placed it in front of Adriana.

"Chaminda, I'll have some fresh coffee, please, when you have a moment."

"Of course, sir."

John waited until Adriana had poured herself a cup of green tea before asking, "You don't want to do a story about this? Your newspaper would love to run something, I'm sure. Especially since, thanks to you, they led the stories about Mia's rescue."

Adriana picked up the teacup and held it with both hands just in front of her. She gazed at the fine tendrils of steam rising off the surface, her eyebrows narrowing slightly, then looked up.

"No." She shook her head and set the cup back down. "They might do it, but I won't. I don't want to give that man any more attention. There's enough negativity and hatred out there in the world, and a twisted organization... or belief system the Islamic State embodies should not get any more publicity."

John watched her, a half-smile on his face. Her voice was calm and level, but her eyes blazed with visible passion.

"You're right." He smiled and reached out for her hand.

Adriana took a deep breath and smiled, squeezed his hand, then picked up her teacup and took a sip, just as Chaminda came out with their breakfast.

He set a large white porcelain tureen in the middle of the table, paused for effect, then removed the cover. The fragrant scent of spices, fried onions, and tomatoes filled the room.

"Wow!" Adriana exclaimed and fanned the aroma towards her. "That smells fantastic."

"Thank you, madam." Chaminda hurried back into the kitchen, returning with a plate piled high with what looked like discs made of white noodles. "These are string hoppers, madam, made from rice flour. You eat them with the curry."

"Great, thank you, Chaminda," John replied and gestured to Adriana to help herself. He waited while she loaded her plate, then did the same.

"Do you have any story to work on when we get back to Lisbon?" John asked as he scooped the tomato-based gravy onto the hoppers and loaded his spoon.

"Well..." Adriana grinned. "What do you think about this guy Atman?"

John paused, his spoon halfway to his mouth, and raised an eyebrow. "What do you mean?"

"You saw how those people were flocking around him yesterday, obviously so... what's the word...?"

"Enamored?"

"Enamored..." Adriana repeated thoughtfully. "Does that mean in love with?"

John moved his head from side to side as if weighing up his answer. "In a way, yes."

"Good. They are enamored with him." Adriana took a mouthful of egg curry and rolled her eyes. "Mmm, this is so good." She licked her lips. "I am enamored with this breakfast."

John chuckled, his mood lightening.

Adriana swallowed, then pointed her spoon at John.

"Why don't I use today's lunch invitation as a way into Atman's... organization... and do a story on him and his followers? What attracts people to him? How he has such a hold on them?"

John nodded thoughtfully as he chewed, then swallowed.

"I think it's a good idea. Perhaps it can be a lesson in the dangers of blindly following these so-called religious teachers." He pointed at the newspaper. "It's people like him who create situations like that."

"Naeem?"

"Yes. He blindly believed everything the leaders of the Islamic State told him. He questioned nothing, no matter how awful, how evil, or how twisted. He and thousands like him believe killing people who think differently from them is the right thing to do. That it will put them on the fast track to meeting,"—John made quotation marks in the air with his fingers—"God. That they will be rewarded in heaven. He thought keeping sex slaves was a divine right!" John ran out of steam and shook his head.

Adriana sat back in her chair and was watching him.

"The Islamic State is a bit of an extreme example, though. I don't think Atman is training an army of spiritual warriors to wage war on the rest of us."

"No." John put down his spoon. "But he could be equally dangerous. When people dress in funny clothes, believing they are different from everyone else, I'm always worried. It's one of the classic signs of cultish behavior."

"Yes." Adriana sat forward and leaned her elbows on the table. "But equally, if he is a genuine teacher and is really helping people find... peace... It will be a nice story, a good counterbalance to awful news like that." She gestured toward the newspaper.

"Only one way to find out."

Adriana grinned, her eyes sparkling with excitement, and picked up her spoon. As John watched her, a warm feeling spread through his chest. He loved it when she got her teeth into a story.

12

At exactly twelve-thirty, there was a honk outside the gate, and the watchman got to his feet and peered out through the viewing hatch. He exchanged words with someone, then pressed the button on the wall, and the gate slid slowly open. Atman's black Range Rover rolled into the parking space in front of the villa, and a young Sri Lankan man dressed in a crisp white shirt and matching white pants climbed out.

John watched from the upstairs window as the man engaged the watchman in conversation. He turned to Adriana, who was standing in front of the mirror, adjusting her earring.

"Our ride has come. The Range Rover from yesterday."

Adriana tightened the fastener on the back of her earring, brushed her hair back, then did a quick twirl. "Okay?"

"More than okay." John grinned. "One look at you and this Atman guy will give up his search for God to explore more earthly pleasures."

Adriana giggled and walked barefoot across the polished wooden floor of the bedroom and kissed him on the cheek.

"Don't worry," she murmured in his ear. "I only have eyes for you."

John wrapped his arms around her and pulled her close. "Why don't we cancel lunch plans and stay here. Forget this guy and his fan club."

Adriana looked up into his eyes, and studied him for a moment, a mischievous glint in her eyes. Leaning forward, she kissed him on the lips then tipped her head back.

"We can continue this later." She pulled away, "I'm curious to find out more about him. I really think there's a story there."

"I think you've got your priorities wrong, but never mind." John sighed and made a face, but his eyes were smiling. "Let's go." He winked. "The sooner we get there, the sooner we can come back."

Adriana picked up her bag from the bed and smoothed down her dress. "I'm ready."

"I see you got the memo about the dress code." John nodded approvingly "You will fit in nicely."

"It's a strategy." Adriana glanced at herself in the mirror again and fiddled with a button at the front of her sleeveless white linen dress. She glanced over her shoulder at John. "If I make myself look more like them, they will feel comfortable, as if I'm an insider, and might be more open to questions."

"Clever." John looked down at his clothes and grimaced. He had dressed for comfort in a pair of loose khaki pants and an olive-green cotton shirt he had picked up in one of the fort's boutiques. "I'm going to stick out."

"Don't worry. It's better this way." Adrian walked over

and placed a hand on his arm. "Imagine if you were also wearing white. It would look as if we're trying too hard."

"Yes, you're right." John gestured toward the door, "Shall we?"

"Let's go, Mr. Hayes."

13

A part from an enthusiastic "Good afternoon," the driver didn't say much, just beamed a huge smile as he opened the passenger doors.

John settled into his seat and looked around the luxurious interior as the driver backed out of the gate into the lane. He started fiddling with the buttons on the center console, then glanced over at Adriana and winked. "Watch this."

There was the faint whirr of an electric motor, and the back of the seat reclined while a footrest rose slowly from the floor.

The driver finished reversing, and before setting off, he turned in his seat, still smiling. "Sir, Madam, there is some water there in the fridge." He pointed to a compartment in the center console.

"Thank you," Adriana replied while John returned his seat to the upright position.

"You are welcome."

"What is your name?" John asked.

"Lasith, sir," the driver replied.

"Good afternoon, Lasith. How long will the journey take?"

"Around thirty minutes, sir."

"Thank you."

The driver guided the Range Rover up the narrow lane, squeezing past a row of rickshaws parked on the corner.

John looked over at Adriana. "Being a man of,"—he mouthed the word 'God'—"is obviously quite lucrative."

Adriana frowned and shook her head, her eyes flicking to the driver and back. John shrugged and settled back in his seat.

"Hey, did you phone Mia?" He glanced across at Adriana again.

"Oh, no, I didn't." Adriana looked at her watch. "What time will it be in Australia now?"

John did a quick calculation, "Around six p.m., I think."

"I'll call her now."

"Say hi from me."

"I will." Adriana scrolled through the numbers on her phone, then held it to her ear.

John glanced out the window as the Range Rover skirted the cricket ground outside the fort, then paused at the traffic signal. John heard Adriana speak but tuned it out, his mind wandering back to Syria when he first saw Mia.

She had looked nothing like the photo Steve had shown him, the one taken when she was happily living in Australia—before the boyfriend brainwashed her into converting to his religion and following him across the world to the so-called *Dar al-Islam*, the land of the faithful. He remembered the shock he felt when he saw her malnourished frame, the exhaustion and strain on her face, making her look ten years older, and the squalor she was living in. His fingers tapped a restless beat on the armrest as images flashed before his mind's eye and his heart began to race.

He could hear the distinctive and rapid 'clunk clunk clunk' of AK47s firing, the acrid smell of propellant and scorched metal, the screams and cries of the wounded and dying. He was back, pinned down behind the pickup truck as rounds passed overhead or thudded into the body of the vehicle. He'd curled into a ball, trying to make himself as small as possible, his face pressed into the dirt, his eyes clenched tight. Hearing a shout nearby, he lifted his head a little, opening one eye, and watched terrified, his limbs numb and unable to move. The young boy, Karam, stood and with a defiant yell, emptied his magazine at the IS fighters attacking them before spurts of blood erupted from his back and the back of his head exploded before he slumped to the ground.

Someone shook his arm. "John, John." But he shook them off. He didn't want to die.

"John, hey."

He felt the hand on his arm again and blinked. He was back in the car, Adriana's hand on his arm. He took a deep breath and released his grip on the armrests.

"John, are you okay?"

John forced a smile and nodded.

"You're sweating."

John turned to look at her. She was leaning toward him, her forehead creased, her eyes searching his. He smiled again, this time genuinely.

"I'm okay."

"Sir, if you are hot, you can adjust the air conditioning."

John looked toward the front and met the driver's eyes in the mirror.

"Thank you, Lasith." John popped the hatch on the

console fridge, took out a small plastic bottle of water, and unscrewed the cap. He took a swig, then wiped his forehead with the back of his spare hand. His heart still racing, he took another deep breath, willing himself to relax. He looked back at Adriana, who was still watching him closely.

"Sorry, I... just had a flashback."

Adriana's frown deepened. "Syria?"

John nodded.

Adriana sighed, then squeezed his arm. She smiled with her mouth, but something troubled her eyes.

"I know you won't admit it, John, but you are suffering PTSD. Maybe today will do you some good."

John made a face and shrugged, then took another sip of water.

"How was Mia?"

Adriana chewed her lip, not answering, still watching his face.

"John, it's serious."

John nodded, replaced the cap, and set the bottle down in the cupholder. Turning to face her, he gave a reassuring smile. "It's okay. I can handle it. Now tell me, how was Mia?"

Adriana studied his face for a moment before replying. "She was good. She already knew about it, so she's keeping a low profile. She said she doesn't want to relive that part of her life."

"Makes sense. Still tough, though. He was the father of her child."

"Hmmm." Adriana settled back in her seat and stared out the window. "She didn't seem too affected. At least on the phone." She turned back to look at John. "I get the impression she's put up a wall as a defense mechanism. To keep those memories out."

"Yup," John sighed as he turned back to the front and

gazed out the windshield. An oncoming bus filled the lane in front of them as it pulled out to pass a slower-moving vehicle. It loomed large in the windshield before swerving back onto the correct side of the road, missing them by just a matter of feet, but Lasith didn't hesitate, maintaining a constant speed and direction as if nothing had happened.

John realized he hadn't reacted either, as if it was only a movie he was watching. He mulled over what Adriana had said. He understood what Mia was going through. He had built walls and locked memories away. It was the only way to survive.

The only problem was when those walls began to crack.

14

As Lasith had promised, about thirty minutes later, after a drive inland from the coast along narrow country lanes, the Range Rover slowed and pulled up outside a large double-width gate. He gave a short toot on the horn, and a hatch in the gate opened briefly and closed again. The gate slid open, pushed by a young Sri Lankan man dressed in what seemed to be the uniform of white linen. Lasith wound down the window, exchanged a few friendly words in Sinhalese, then drove in.

Inside was a large gravel parking area surrounded by lush tropical foliage. Lasith parked alongside a Land Cruiser and a row of motorbikes, turned off the engine, then ran around the front of the vehicle to open Adriana's door.

John climbed out his side and looked around. It was warmer and more humid than near the coast, but the air was filled with the sound of birds and insects and the faint sound of musical instruments, a flute and something else. John searched his memory. He'd heard it before, some kind of Asian instrument, but he couldn't place it. John took a breath and inhaled, his mind trying to label the multitude of unfamiliar scents—flowers, foliage, and the soft sweet smell of incense.

"This way, sir." Lasith gestured toward a pathway leading from the carpark into the garden. On the left side of the path was a stone Buddha, flowers placed at its feet and twin sticks of incense smoldering in a brass stand.

John smiled at Adriana and let her take the lead past the Buddha and up the pathway. The path led through a stand of broad-leafed tropical plants onto a large lawn that sloped up to a low-set colonial-style bungalow. They could see figures in white moving around on the wide verandah that wrapped around the house, where the sound of music was coming from.

Lasith hurried ahead while John and Adriana took their time, enjoying the well-kept gardens and getting their bearings.

"Oh," Adriana squealed. "Look, a peacock!" She tugged on John's arm, and they both watched as a peacock spread its iridescent green and blue tail feathers in a broad fan. "This place is beautiful."

"It really is," John agreed.

The peacock finished its display, closed its tail feathers, and strutted proudly across the grass before disappearing behind a tree. John looked up toward the house and saw Atman standing on the top step, watching them, a broad welcoming smile on his face.

"Come, the God-man is waiting for us," John murmured.

"Shhhh," Adriana admonished. They continued their walk up to the verandah.

"Welcome." Atman placed his right hand on his chest.

"Thank you," John replied. "You have a beautiful home."

"It is beautiful." Atman removed his hand from his chest, turned it palm up, and looked up at the sky with a smile.

John looked up but couldn't see anything.

"But it's not my home." Atman beamed at them both. "I am blessed to be surrounded by generous people."

John frowned slightly, and Atman noticed.

"The house is owned by one of my students, and he generously allows me to stay whenever I am here."

"That's very nice of him."

"Yes." Atman nodded, still smiling. "Now, where are my manners? Please come in." He took a step back and gestured toward the verandah.

John looked at Atman's bare feet and the collection of shoes beside the bottom step, then slipped off his loafers and glanced at Adriana to do the same.

Atman watched them as they removed their footwear, then stood back further as they climbed the steps. The verandah was wide, and on the right, a long wooden table was laid out with cutlery and napkins, an arrangement of white orchids in the center of the table. To the left, several white calico sofas were arranged at right angles to either side of a large white armchair.

"Please," Atman waved toward the sofas.

John followed Adriana toward the sofas, skirting a low coffee table, and took a seat on the farthest sofa, where they could look back toward the entrance and the dining table.

"I will join you in a moment." Atman smiled, then walked inside the open door of the house.

John reached over and gave Adriana's hand a squeeze. "Okay?"

"Yes." She smiled. "This place is beautiful."

"Hmmm." John looked around. Lush cascading ferns in hanging pots hung from the roof of the verandah, and along the wall of the house were occasional tables supporting potted orchids and brass and bronze statues of Buddha and assorted Hindu gods and goddesses.

"What do you think that says?" Adriana pointed toward a large copper panel on the wall, engraved with an ornate script. "It's Arabic?"

"Yes." John nodded. "I've seen something like that before... when I was in India. I think it's the ninety-nine names of Allah."

"That is correct," said a soft female voice from behind them. John turned to see a young blonde woman holding a wooden tray. "Please, take a refreshing towel."

John waited for Adriana before taking one for himself. It was cool and moist, and he dabbed the sweat from his fore-head and neck before wiping his hands. The young woman held the tray out for the towels, and once they had put them back, she nodded toward the copper panel.

"Atman honors all religions, as you can see. He teaches that all religions offer a path to God."

"That's nice," John replied noncommittally. He turned his head to look at the woman and smiled. "Thank you for the towels. Where are you from?"

"Canada," She smiled. "Toronto specifically."

Now that she said it, John could hear it in her accent.

"You must be happy to be here at this time of the year."

"Oh, yes. It's snowing there." She glanced out across the garden. "Here, it's so... beautiful."

"What's your name?" Adriana asked. "I'm Adriana."

The woman turned back and smiled. "I'm Sarah. Welcome."

"If you don't mind me asking, Sarah, what brought you here?"

Sarah smiled even wider, then looked down at the tray, her mouth moving slightly as if she was thinking of what to say. John thought he imagined it at first, but a pink flush spread across her cheeks. She looked up toward the entrance to the house and then back at Adriana.

"You've met him, right? He's wonderful."

Adriana reached out and touched her hand, lowering her voice as if sharing a secret, "I know. He's so..."

"You've experienced it, too?" Sarah interrupted with excitement. "It's as if he can see right into your soul."

"Exactly," Adriana agreed.

John struggled to keep a straight face.

"I spent my entire life searching for something, but I didn't even know I was searching. There was just a void in my life. Then I met Atman." She lowered her voice to a whisper and leaned toward Adriana, "He's transformed me." A noise by the entrance made her look up. Her smile widened again, and the pink flush grew deeper. Looking back at Adriana, she said, "Maybe we can talk later."

Adriana squeezed her hand. "I'd like that, Sarah."

John glanced toward the entrance and saw the large man they had seen yesterday, standing by the front door deep in conversation with Atman as two young Sri Lankan girls bustled around the table.

The large man looked in John's direction, and John smiled. The man didn't respond. Turning back to Atman, he leaned his head closer as Atman spoke, nodded, then Atman placed a hand on his shoulder. He nodded again and disappeared inside the house.

When John turned back to look at Sarah, she had gone.

15

"You must be hungry," Atman called out. "Please come and join me at the table." He stood with his arms open, palms turned up, then gestured toward the table with his left hand.

John and Adriana stood, and as they walked toward him, John noticed Atman looking past them toward the coffee table. A flicker of irritation flashed across his face, so briefly John thought he had imagined it, then the smile was back.

"Did no-one offer you a drink?" He shook his head in mock exasperation. "Please forgive me." He turned and caught the eye of one of the girls beside the table. "Anika, please bring some water for my friends here."

She nodded, smiled, and hurried into the house.

"Adriana, will you do me the honor of sitting here, please?" Atman guided her to a seat. "And John, will you please sit there?" he said, pointing to the chair on the opposite side of the table.

John walked around to the opposite side and pulled out a chair. He waited until Adriana sat down before sitting.

Atman took the seat at the head of the table and smiled at them both.

"Thank you so much for being my guests today."

"Thank you for inviting us," Adriana replied.

John smiled but said nothing. In his mind, he was pondering a tactful way to ask why they had been invited, but before he could say anything, the young girl, Anika, returned with a jug of iced water and filled their glasses. John thanked her and was about to say something when Atman spoke again.

"You must be wondering why I invited you?" He looked at John for a little longer than John felt comfortable, then smiled. "I spend a lot of time in my retreat centers around the world and meet the same type of people all the time." He leaned toward Adriana and lowered his voice. "I get bored." He winked at her and started laughing, loud and unrestrained. Despite John's cynicism, he felt himself smiling.

Atman's laugh subsided to a chuckle, and he grinned first at Adriana, then John.

"So, when I come here, I try to meet different people, talk about different things. I hope you don't mind?"

"Not at all," John replied and reached for his glass. He took a long pull of ice-cold water and set the glass down. "So, what is it you do exactly... ah... Atman. Can I call you that?"

Atman chuckled. "That's what everyone calls me, but..." He shrugged and winked at Adriana. "It's just a label."

John frowned, not sure if that was a yes or no.

Atman studied his face for a moment, his head tilted to one side, then smiled again. "Atman is easiest. I have been known by many names, but Atman is what I go by now."

John was about to ask what his other names were, but

Atman continued, "In answer to your first question, what do I do? Well..." He exhaled loudly, then spread his hands and shrugged. "I teach love and acceptance, but most of all, I help people find their true self."

"What does that mean exactly?"

Atman chuckled. "Where do I start?" he shrugged. "But that's not a conversation for right now. Let's eat first." He reached forward and picked up a tiny brass bell John hadn't noticed. He shook it, sending a brief tinkle across the verandah, and the two Sri Lankan girls appeared in the doorway. Atman nodded, and they disappeared back inside.

John glanced toward the other place settings. "Will someone else be joining us?"

"Yes, any minute now. I have students and some people who have been very helpful to my mission as my guests."

As if on cue, they heard voices, and a portly, middle-aged man and a tired-looking woman in her early thirties walked through the doorway. They stood beside Atman and smiled at John and Adriana.

"This is Robert, the owner of this lovely property, and Line, who is a guest of mine."

The two placed their hands on their chests in what John was beginning to think of as the 'Atman handshake' and smiled.

"Welcome," they said, almost in unison. Line moved to sit next to Adriana while Robert took the seat next to John. There were still two seats free, which were quickly taken by Sarah and the large man, who Atman introduced as Georges, pronounced in the French way with a soft 'g.'

The table remained silent while the two girls brought platters of food out and laid them in the middle of the table.

"I hope you don't mind, but we are all vegetarians." Atman looked from John to Adriana. "But, I think you will find our cook has prepared such delicious food, you won't even miss meat."

"It smells good," John replied politely, hiding his disappointment. He inspected the food as his stomach growled, hoping there would be enough to fill him up. He'd been for his usual early morning run, which gave him a big appetite, but he had eaten little during breakfast after reading the news about Naeem.

He waited, making polite small talk while the others served themselves, then helped himself to several curries and some rice. He took a mouthful and breathed a sigh of relief. He would survive until dinner time.

Turning to Robert on his right, he said, "You have a beautiful place here, Robert."

Robert swallowed and smiled. "Thank you. Sorry, I didn't get your name."

"John."

"Thank you, John. I'm happy you like it. I've been very fortunate."

"Yes. Do you live here permanently?"

Robert nodded and smiled at Atman, who was listening quietly. "I do now."

"Robert is a very generous patron with a kind soul," Atman explained.

Robert dipped his head in appreciation and placed his right hand on his chest.

"And you, John? Do you live in Sri Lanka or are you just visiting?"

John swallowed a mouthful of curry and rice, reached for his glass, and took a sip before replying.

"Just visiting." He nodded toward Adriana, who was deep in conversation with Line and Sarah. "Adriana and I have been here for a week, but we go back tomorrow."

"Back?"

"To Lisbon."

"Ahhh." Robert chewed thoughtfully. "A beautiful city. I was there about ten to fifteen years ago." He smiled at Atman again. "I think you have been there, too."

"I have indeed, Robert. I remember the place with great fondness. Very warm people."

John nodded, chewed, and had a quick glance around the table. Adriana seemed to be getting on well with the two ladies. There were plenty of smiles and even a few laughs. He looked at Georges, who had said nothing so far, apparently concentrating on his food, but John got the impression he was listening to everything.

"So, John, forgive me for being curious. You're not Portuguese, so what do you do in Lisbon?" Atman asked.

John scooped another spoonful of food into his mouth to give himself time to answer. He never liked to give away too much, especially to strangers, but it was also hard to give an answer people understood since he didn't really do anything.

Atman chuckled. "I'm sorry, John. My timing was unfortunate. Please enjoy your food." He gestured to Robert. "Robert was a film producer in Los Angeles before he settled down here." Robert nodded and grunted agreeably, his mouth full. "Line was, in fact, still is a famous DJ from Norway."

Line, hearing her name, looked up, her eyebrows raised, and Atman made a gesture with his hand and smiled as if to say, "It's okay, we are talking about you, not to you."

She looked away and rejoined the conversation with Adriana.

Atman leaned toward John and in a stage whisper, said, "I think we are both too old for her music... at least Robert is." He burst into laughter, and the others stopped what they were doing and laughed as if they were all part of the joke, everyone except Georges, who remained as serious as ever.

John waited until the laughter died down, then nodded toward Georges. "And Georges?"

"Ah, Georges," he exclaimed with a hint of mischief. Atman sat back and placed both hands on the table. "What do you do, Georges?"

Georges looked a little uncomfortable. He glanced around the table, then down at his plate.

"My friend Georges is my right-hand man," Atman answered himself. "I can't manage without him. Isn't that right, Georges?" Georges remained silent, his focus on his plate, his jaw moving silently as he chewed. Atman sat forward and grinned. "Georges is shy, but without him, I wouldn't be able to do half the things I do."

John nodded, took a quick look at Georges again.

"Have you known each other long?"

Atman smiled. "Georges has been with me forever."

16

Lunch pleasantly surprised John. He sat back, his stomach full, his plate empty, stifled a burp, and smiled at Atman.

"The food was excellent. Thank you."

"You have Robert to thank for that. His cook, Sansuka, is a genius." He winked at Robert. "I keep trying to steal him to have him cook for me at the ashram."

"Any time, Atman," Robert replied. "I'm sure he would be honored."

Atman waved away the offer with a grin. "He knows I'm only joking. That's why he made the offer. He will never let him go. A cook like Sansuka is worth his weight in gold."

Robert chuckled and nodded in agreement.

"Come, we'll let them clear up." Atman pushed back his chair and nodded toward the girls hovering in the doorway. He walked across the verandah, stepped down into the garden, and looked back at John as if waiting for him to follow.

John stood and looked toward Adriana.

"It's okay John, Adriana is in good company. You come with me."

John shot a questioning look at Adriana, and she gave a slight nod and smiled, so John turned away and joined Atman on the lawn.

"Come, leave your shoes. Walking barefoot on grass is good for your immune system." Atman smiled and started walking across the grass. John glanced back to see Adriana walking to the sitting area with Sara and Line, and Robert and Georges were talking to each other by the front entrance.

"Robert and Georges won't be coming with us?"

"No, no, they have work to do." Atman paused and looked back. "Robert says he's retired, but he can't let go of his old life." He continued walking, his hands held together behind his back, and John kept pace beside him. "But he's slowed down a lot. The film business can be very stressful."

"I'm sure."

"Line, too." Atman pursed his lips and shook his head. "Burned out, John, and she's only young. These people have all the external trappings of success. People aspire to be like them, follow them on Instagram, Facebook, almost worship them." He shrugged. "The reality, John, is they are lost. Hollow inside. They've discovered, chasing the things they thought would make them happy didn't actually make them happy once they got them."

The lawn sloped down from the house toward a large frangipani tree, its branches filled with white flowers. Atman paused at the foot of the gnarled trunk, placed a hand on it, and looked up into the branches.

"They come to me, John, to find peace." He looked back at John and locked him in his laser beam-like gaze. "As have you."

John frowned. "I didn't come to you. You invited us for lunch."

"Yes, John." Atman's eyes bored into him. "But don't you think the universe conspired to make it happen? Why did we meet yesterday? Why did we talk?"

"You believe that?" John's frown deepened, and he shrugged. "Coincidence."

"Do you deny, John, that something troubles you?"

The intensity of the continued eye contact was making John uneasy, but he didn't want to be the first to look away.

"Isn't everyone troubled?"

"Perhaps, John, but you have seen great pain and suffering. You have stared death in the face."

John blinked, breaking eye contact, and looked away. He felt a prickling sensation at the back of his neck. Conscious of not giving too much away, he looked back at Atman.

"What makes you say that?"

"I can sense it, John. I can feel it."

John made a face and shrugged, then looked up into the branches. The conversation was getting a little too personal for comfort. A movement caught his eye, and he watched a pair of bright green parrots alight on a branch high above him. They squawked and screeched as they hopped from branch to branch. Feeling a hand on his arm, he dragged his attention away to look at Atman, who was smiling gently.

"You should come to my ashram, John. You would benefit a great deal. Spend some time in silence. You can't carry this burden around with you."

"What makes you think I'm carrying a burden?"

"I'm talking about the burden you keep locked down inside you, but it haunts you, John. I can see that. It comes out at night and prevents you from sleeping."

John scoffed half-heartedly.

"You will only find peace, John, when you learn to go within."

"I've never been one for religion."

Atman laughed and removed his hand from John's arm.

"This is not a religion, John. Religion is to control the masses. What I teach is how to find freedom. None of you are truly free until you go within and find truth."

"What is truth? What does that mean? Surely, it would be different for everyone?"

"Yes, John, you are right." Atman's smile deepened. "Which is why you have to do it for yourself. No-one else can do it for you."

"Then..." John paused, choosing his words carefully, "Please don't take this the wrong way, but why do people come to you if they need to do it themselves?"

"Ha," Atman laughed. "I like you, John. You ask good questions." He moved away from the tree. "Let's keep walking." He led John slowly across the grass, moving further from the house toward a lush stand of foliage that bounded the lawn at the bottom of the slope.

"Think of it like this, John. When you came to Galle, did you come by taxi or did you drive yourself?"

"I drove."

"I assume you used something like Google Maps to find your way here?"

"Yes."

Stopping by a large hibiscus, Atman reached out to touch one of the large red flowers. "The tea made from these flowers is very good for lowering blood pressure." He smiled at John. "But I don't think you have a problem with blood pressure, do you?"

"No."

Atman plucked a flower, then strolled on, stopping to

look at a plant, to sniff a flower. John walked beside him, still waiting for an answer to his question. He looked up toward the house, wondering how Adriana was doing, but from where he was, he couldn't see the verandah clearly.

"Think of me, John, as Google Maps." He stopped and stared intently at John. "Without it, you would eventually have found Galle, but it might have taken a long time. You would have taken wrong turns, gone in the wrong direction. I mean, just getting out of Columbo would have taken you all day." He broke off his stare and laughed. "With Google Maps, it was so much easier, wasn't it? Did you waste any time or effort? No! You came the right way."

John nodded thoughtfully, but before he could say anything, Atman extended his index finger and waggled it at John.

"But don't make the mistake of thinking that only I can show you the way. You can do it yourself." He lowered his finger and shrugged. "Anyone can." He winked and started walking again. "But it's a lot easier with Google Maps."

At the far corner of the garden, nestled in the foliage, was a large stone statue of the elephant-headed Hindu God, Ganesha. Atman stopped in front of it and closed his eyes, his features relaxed, and an almost blissful expression of contemplation spread across his face. His body swayed back and forth, then his eyelids fluttered. In the silence at the foot of the garden, John heard Atman exhale, then lift the hibiscus flower he had plucked earlier to his lips. He kissed it, then opened his eyes and leaned forward to place it at the foot of the statue. Turning, he grinned at John.

"Ganesha. He's one of my favorites. The Hindus always pray to him first since he's known as the remover of all obstacles."

"I thought you said what you do is not religion."

"That's correct, John, but I can still respect the religions of others." He gestured toward the house. "Let's see what they are doing."

They continued their slow walk along the western boundary leading up the sloped lawn.

"So, you say you can help me find inner peace, but to continue your analogy, how do I know you're the right app? How do I know the app even works?"

Atman smiled and placed a hand on John's shoulder as they walked.

"For that, John, you need to come to the ashram."

17

Reaching the house, they climbed the steps to the verandah. Adriana and the two other women, sitting in the nest of sofas, looked up as Atman and John arrived.

"Are you having a good time, Adriana? I hope the ladies have been looking after you."

"Yes, thank you. They have."

"Good, I'm happy." Atman turned to John. "Now I'm afraid I must leave you. We return to the ashram this evening, and there are some things I must attend to before we leave." He looked from John to Adriana. "You are my guests, so please stay as long as you like."

John threw Adriana a look, and she nodded almost imperceptibly. "That's very kind of you, Atman, but I think we will make a move. We are leaving tomorrow as well."

"As you wish." Atman tilted his head. "Don't forget what I said. Come to my ashram. It will help you."

John nodded without committing. "Thank you."

"Sarah will give you the address. We have a program starting in two days. The timing would be perfect for you."

"Well, we are due back in Lisbon tomorrow, so maybe next time."

"We'll see." Atman smiled. "My driver will take you back to your villa." He reached out and took John's hand in both of his. "It's been a pleasure. I know we will meet again."

John smiled, not so sure. Atman released his hand, placed his right hand over his chest, closed his eyes for a moment, then turned and entered the house.

John watched him go, then walked over to the sofas, just in time to hear Sarah telling Adriana, "You must come to the retreat. It's beautiful there. High in the hills, much cooler than here, and the energy is amazing."

"It's fabulous," Line agreed.

Adriana nodded. "It sounds wonderful. I don't think we can this time, but please let me have the address so we can find it later."

Sarah took a notepad from the table and wrote the address before tearing off the top sheet of paper and handing it to Adriana.

"I've written the address and the website. All the information is on there. There is a retreat fee to pay, but it's worth it for what you will receive."

Adriana scanned the page, then folded it in half and slipped it into her pocket. "Thank you, but maybe next time."

"But you must come," Sarah pleaded. "The next program starts soon. It would be such a shame to miss it. See if you can change your flights."

"Okay." Adriana chuckled. "John and I will talk about it when we get home."

"Yes, yes." Sarah clapped her hands together in delight and did a little jump. "You will love it."

Adriana looked at John, half-shrugged, then smiled.

John also shrugged, then looked around.

"Excuse me, I'll just use the bathroom before going."

"It's down the corridor, the third door on the right." Sarah pointed toward the front door.

"Thank you." John gave her a smile and walked toward the entrance. Stepping inside, he hesitated, getting his bearings. He was in a large, full-width living room. The ceiling was high and pitched, the rafters painted white, and below, the timber floors were dark and highly polished. The white walls displayed large colorful canvases of modern art, and the wooden furniture was tasteful, not too ornate.

A collection of white calico sofas, like the ones on the verandah, made up several seating areas, the decor of the verandah continuing inside. Immediately ahead, a corridor led from the living room, and John followed it, counting the doors on the right. He could hear voices from a room at the end of the corridor, and his curiosity getting the better of him, he continued walking, stopping outside an open door at the end. Inside, in a leather office chair behind a large wooden desk, sat Atman, his back to the door, a phone held to his ear. Georges stood near the desk, and noticing John outside, frowned and walked toward him.

"I'm looking for the bathroom?"

Georges' frame filled the doorway, and without a word, he pointed to the correct door.

John gave him a smile. "Thank you."

He turned around, went back to the correct doorway, and opened the door. As he walked in, he looked back to see Georges going back inside and closing the door behind him.

18

J ohn walked back outside and stood with his hands in his pockets, watching Adriana, Sarah, and Line, leaning on the verandah railing looking out over the garden. They were talking softly, and he could only make out brief snatches of conversation.

His mind wandered back to his own conversation with Atman. He didn't know what to make of him. Was he a genuine teacher or a conman? He was charming, intelligent, and said things that seemed perceptive. When he fixed John in his gaze, it was like a tractor beam. John hadn't experienced anything like it before. But he wasn't one to blindly trust what another man was saying. He believed in finding his own way, solving his problems himself, but if he was completely honest, a part of him was intrigued. He was looking forward to hearing what Adriana had to say.

As if she could read his thoughts, she turned around, and her face lit up in a dazzling smile. His heart did a little jump.

"Ready?" he asked.

"Yes." Adriana turned to her companions and kissed

them both on their cheeks as John waited on the top step, wondering how to say goodbye to the women. A hug? A European-style kiss on each cheek? Would they prefer something more formal, like a handshake? In the end, they saved him from a decision by raising their hands and giving him a brief wave. He smiled back, waiting for Adriana to join him. When her arm looped through his, they descended the steps and walked down the path toward the car park.

"Well?" John asked. "Did you have a good time?"

"I did. You?"

"It was interesting."

Adriana turned her head to look at his face. "What do you mean?"

"I'm not sure if he's a con man or the real thing."

"Well, they think he's genuine."

"Sarah and Line?"

"Yes. They seem to think he's the next... um... messiah."

"Ha," John laughed. "I'm not sure I agree with that. He seems to have something, though. But..." John shrugged. "He could just be a charming guy who makes intelligent guesses and can read body language."

"Have you always been so cynical, Mr. Hayes?"

"No. Just call it experience." John leaned over and kissed her forehead. "People are rarely what they first seem."

"Sarah and Line told me some amazing stories. You might change your mind after hearing them."

"Hmmm, we'll see." John nodded toward Lasith, who was standing beside the open rear door of the Range Rover. "Let's not discuss it in front of him. Wait until we get back to the villa."

"You don't trust him?"

"I'm sure everything we say will be reported back, if not

to Atman, then to Georges," John said in a low voice, then beamed at Lasith. "Thank you, Lasith. How did you know we were coming?"

"Mr. Georges told me."

"Of course." John smiled and waited for Adriana to climb in before walking around the Range Rover to the other side. As he opened the door, he nodded at the security guard who had come out of the small concrete guardroom to open the gate. John climbed inside and sat down, and as he pulled the door shut, something caught his eye. The door to the guardroom was half-open, and he could see inside on the rear wall what looked like a rack of... weapons. He craned his neck to get a better look, but the Range Rover edged out the gate, and he could no longer see inside.

19

They remained silent on the journey back, both lost in thought. After a freshen up and a change of clothes, John fixed a couple of Botanist and tonics, and they sat down in the shaded area beside the pool.

John took a long pull on his drink, licked his lips, and let out a satisfied sigh.

Adriana smiled. "Sounds like you needed that."

"I did." John grinned. "And that's enough vegetarian food for this trip."

"I thought it was very good."

"It was," John agreed, reaching for his glass again. "But let's not make a habit of it."

Adriana chuckled. "Sarah and Line are vegans."

John shuddered. "I knew there was something wrong with them."

Adriana giggled. "So..." She took a sip of her drink. "Tell me what you thought of the experience."

John exhaled, frowning slightly as his fingertips played with the condensation on the glass.

He made a face. "I don't know."

Adriana waited.

"He seems nice enough... When we walked through the garden, he told me I carry a lot of guilt and sorrow."

"Okay."

"But you can say that to anyone, and they will find something they are guilty or sad about."

Adriana nodded.

"He also said I had stared death in the face."

Adriana raised her eyebrows. "Really?"

"Yup."

"That's interesting."

John nodded, still frowning as he gazed across the pool.

"What else did he say?" Adriana prompted.

"He said I should visit his ashram. That he could help me find the inner peace I'm searching for."

"Are you?"

"What?"

"Searching for inner peace?"

John was silent for a while. He looked at Adriana, studied her face, the line of cheekbones, the way her hair tumbled onto her shoulders. She returned his gaze, her eyes filled with concern.

John shrugged and smiled. "Not consciously."

"Subconsciously?"

John screwed up his face but said nothing. They sat in silence, watching the sunlight reflected off the surface of the pool, making patterns on the rear wall of the courtyard garden.

"You know what I've been through, Adriana," John said, eventually. "The things I've done. I have to live with that. I made choices, and I have to live with the consequences. So let's be realistic. No man in white pajamas is going to change that, whether or not he's the new messiah."

"I know that, John." Adriana sighed. "But perhaps he can help you deal with the memories in a better way?" She leaned forward and gazed into his eyes. "I've seen how it affects your sleep, John, and..." She looked away and swallowed. "It's getting worse. Since you came back from Syria, you've been... distant, even irritable."

John reached over for her hand. "I'm sorry."

"John, I know I've said it before, but you do have PTSD."

John shook his head and scowled, letting go of her hand.

"John, look at me."

He did.

"John, I've seen it with some of my colleagues. Remember Jorgé? I told you about him."

John nodded.

"He's not been the same since he came back from Iraq." Adriana reached out and took John's hand. "I see some of the same things in you. I've seen you when you think you are alone. You're not there but reliving some traumatic experience. I see it in your face. And so often at night, your sleep is disturbed. You talk, shout, even cry."

"I'm sorry." John took a deep breath and squeezed her hand. "I didn't realize it was affecting you."

"John, I love and care deeply about you. How did you think I wouldn't notice? That's why we're here now. I thought it would help."

"I'll try harder." John shrugged and forced a smile. "Yes, it has helped. The last week here with you has been wonderful."

"For me, too, John. But what happens when we go back?"

John looked away again. He thought he had everything under control, but the reality was he struggled with the memories and flashbacks. The gin helped a little, so did the morning run and the fast drives in the Porsche. It all helped to distract him, but for how long?

"How do we know this guy can help? What if he's a fraud?"

"What if he isn't? What if he really can help you, John?"

Letting go of Adriana's hand, he reached out for his drink and drained the glass.

"Anyway, there's no point in this discussion. We have a flight to catch tomorrow." He stood and pointed to Adriana's glass. "Another one?"

"No, I'm good."

John walked inside, poured himself a large Botanist, and took the lid off the ice bucket. "Chaminda?"

"Yes, sir?"

"Can you please bring me some ice? This has already melted."

"Yes, of course, sir."

John opened a bottle of tonic, taking it and his glass back to the poolside, and sat down.

"I have an idea," Adriana said as soon as he sat down.

"Hmmm?"

"Why don't you change your flight and delay your return. Go up to the ashram and spend some time there. See for yourself what it's like."

"By myself?"

"I have a job to go back to."

Chaminda appeared with the ice. "Shall I put it for you, sir?"

"No." John smiled up at him. "Just leave it here, and I'll do it. Thank you."

John filled his glass with ice, topped it up with tonic, swirled it around, then took a sip before sitting back in his chair.

"What do you think?" Adriana asked.

"I don't know."

"I think it could really help you."

John exhaled loudly. "What if he's a fraud?"

"If he's a fraud, I have a good story. If he isn't, you might benefit."

John grimaced. "That's why you should come, too. Tell them you're here doing research and working on his story."

"I can't. It was hard enough getting this time off. Besides, I can research him from outside, and you can be my source inside." She smiled. "With the benefit for you of finding mental peace."

"A win-win?"

"Yes."

John sat for a moment, staring at his glass, tilting it side to side, clinking the ice cubes against the side of the glass.

"Okay."

"Okay?" Adriana raised her eyebrows, surprised he agreed so readily. "Are you sure?"

"Yeah." John shrugged. "Why not? But I think you will get the benefit from this one."

"Why?"

"Well..." John took a sip of his drink. "That Georges guy is a bit strange."

"Maybe he's just shy?"

"Huh." John snorted. "Maybe, but when I went inside to the toilet, Atman and he were in an office. Atman was talking on the phone, and when Georges saw me, he closed the door."

"Okay..." Adriana nodded slowly. "So, he was having a private conversation."

John smiled. "When we left, I'm sure I saw a gun rack in the guardroom."

Adriana looked surprised.

"But the house is Robert's, right?" she countered. "Perhaps he feels the need for extra security? There were security cameras on the verandah, one at each end, set in the roof. "

"See what I mean?"

"Perhaps you're just too negative? The house is full of expensive things. Tempting for the people who live around here."

"Maybe."

"John, the girls told me many stories—how he has transformed their lives, brought them happiness, helped them deal with their own traumas. Sarah had an awful life, sexually abused when she was a child and violent relationships since. She said Atman saved her."

"That's good, very good." John took a breath. "But I have a natural distrust for this kind of people and religion in general. It causes nothing but problems. Look at what it did to Mia and Naeem. Those killings yesterday were all in the name of religion."

"What Atman is teaching isn't religion. At least, that's what I understand from speaking to Sarah and Line."

"Yes, I'll give him that. He told me the same thing."

"So, give him the benefit of the doubt. Try it out. If you don't like it, you leave. What have you lost?"

"I'll have to eat vegetarian food."

Adriana burst into laughter.

———

The next day, after a late lunch, they said goodbye to the villa staff, checked out, and took the Southern Expressway northward toward Colombo. The road was smooth and wide with barely any traffic, but John set the cruise control of the rental Toyota Camry to just under the speed limit. They weren't due at the airport until early evening, so they had plenty of time.

The previous evening, John had changed his flight with only a minor penalty and extended the lease on the rental car. Then he went online and registered for the two-week meditation retreat. The course fee of $5,000 U.S., surprised him. At almost 100,000 Sri Lankan rupees, it was a substantial amount in local terms, leading to an animated discussion with Adriana.

John grumbled there was no way the actual running costs would be anywhere near that amount, but when Adriana reasoned that staying in the villa for just a week cost a lot more, John reluctantly agreed. However, he remarked that paying that much and not being able to have a gin and tonic and being forced to eat vegetarian food wasn't an attractive proposition.

The website didn't tell them much about Atman and his background. Pages of vague references and gushing platitudes weren't any help and gave little indication of what to expect when he got there.

That night, John had slept badly, a recurring nightmare where the faces of the people he had killed flashed before his eyes. He woke around three a.m., soaked in sweat. He lay for a while, staring up at the rafters, conscious of not disturbing Adriana, then slowly slipped out from under the mosquito net and changed his t-shirt for a dry one.

When he eventually got back to sleep, he dreamed of a figure in white standing before him. He couldn't see the face, wasn't sure if the figure was even human, but the figure radiated safety and calm. When he woke for his morning run, he felt more rested than he had in a long time.

Now, as Adriana dozed in the seat beside him, John had to admit he was becoming intrigued about the experience ahead. Either way, whether or not Atman was a fraud, the next two weeks could be interesting.

It was a little over two hours before they reached Colombo's International Airport and pulled up outside the departure terminal. John had originally planned to help Adriana check-in, but security restrictions meant only ticketed passengers could enter the building.

Standing on the pavement, in the noisy chaos outside the terminal, John held Adriana's hands and felt a lump in his throat as a wave of melancholic gloom swept over him. He wasn't sure why, but he felt more nervous now than when he had left Adriana to enter Syria.

"You'll call me when you land in Dubai?"

"Yes,"—Adriana smiled up at him—"and as soon as I land in Lisbon."

John nodded and forced a smile.

Adriana frowned. "Is everything okay?"

"Yes, don't worry about me." John smiled wider and squeezed her hands.

Adriana studied his face for a moment. "It's only a meditation course..."

"I know," John sighed. "I don't know why... perhaps it's because we've had such a great time in the last week. I just..."

"Hey..." Adriana leaned forward and kissed him gently on the lips. "It will be fine. You'll come back a new man."

"Hmmm, I guess so."

"What's the worst that could happen? If you don't like it, you leave early."

John nodded and this time, gave her a genuine smile.

The repeated blast of a whistle that had been part of the background noise became more insistent and louder. John turned his head to see a police officer standing beside his double-parked car, gesticulating angrily and looking for the driver.

"Looks like I have to go," John said and jerked his head in the car's direction.

"Okay." Adriana gulped and forced a smile.

John pulled her close, kissed her on the forehead, then pulled her head to his shoulder.

"I love you," he murmured into her hair.

The flashing lights of a tow truck reflected off the terminal doors, and John released Adriana from his embrace.

"Call me," he said, squeezed her hands once again, then ran off to rescue his car.

21

J ohn's phone vibrated on the table, and he reached for it, eager to take the call.

"Hey. In Dubai?"

"Yes."

John's face broke into a smile at the sound of Adriana's voice.

"How was the flight?"

"It was okay. I slept for most of it."

John nodded, forgetting she couldn't see him. He stared from the verandah of Colombo's venerable old Galle Face Hotel, across the lawn to the flat blue waters of the Arabian Sea. Somewhere out there, over three thousand kilometers away, was the woman he loved.

"How long are you there for? An hour, hour and a half?"

"An hour and a half." Adriana sounded tired. "Just enough time for me to stretch my legs."

"Okay..." A waiter in a white shirt and bow tie approached John's table, but John waved him away with a smile. "I miss you."

"Me, too."

John heard Adriana sigh.

"I can always cancel and come back to Lisbon."

"No," Adriana replied forcefully. "John... this will be good for you... for both of us. Just give it a try."

John took a deep breath. "Okay, I will."

They remained silent for a moment, John listening to the sounds in the background of the call—voices, airport announcements, music.

"What are you doing now?" Adriana asked.

"Just having breakfast."

"On the verandah?"

"Yes."

"I loved that hotel." John and Adriana had stayed at the Galle Face Hotel on their first few nights in Sri Lanka.

"Yes," John said, looking around him. "It's not bad. My last bit of comfort for a few days."

"It won't be that bad."

"I hope not." John chuckled. "I just wanted a bit of sympathy."

"Sympathy?" John heard the amusement in Adriana's voice. "I bet you were in the Traveller's Bar last night, having a few gin and tonics."

"Who, me?" John feigned innocence.

"I know you too well, Mr. Hayes."

"You certainly do, Ms. D'Silva."

"I love you, John."

"Me, too," John replied, conscious of the people sitting at the next table.

"I have to go. I want to visit the washroom before they call the flight."

"Okay," John sighed. "Hey, message me when you land in Lisbon. I'm not sure what the signal will be like in the hills, so I'll call you back whenever I can."

"Okay, will do."

John felt a lump in the back of his throat.

"Bye, John."

"Bye." John kept the phone to his ear until it went silent, then slipped it back onto the table. He bit his lip and reached for his coffee to give him something to do. Raising it to his lips, he stared unseeingly out to sea, imagining Adriana boarding her flight. He hated being away from her, more so since the time he'd spent in Syria. He hoped this visit to the ashram wouldn't be a complete waste of time.

22

I t was just under a five-hour journey to Ella if he took the highway south, back past Galle, then along the coast before heading into the hills. There was a more direct route, but the state of the roads meant it added another two hours to the journey, and John wasn't in the mood for an unnecessarily long journey. He wasn't due at the ashram until the evening, so he delayed his departure for as long as possible, requesting a late checkout and having an early lunch before climbing into his rental Toyota and setting off through the suburbs. It took over forty minutes to exit Colombo, the traffic heavy and the roads narrow, but once he was on the Southern Expressway, he made steady progress. Three and a half hours later, he turned inland onto the A2 for the journey into the hills. The route skirted the Lunugamvehera National Park, the road on one side lined with thick tropical jungle and emerald-green rice paddies on the other. Wildlife was abundant, and he had to slow occasionally as a mongoose or a slow-moving monitor lizard crossed the road in front of him. Eventually, the road started climbing, the air getting noticeably cooler, and he turned off the air conditioning and wound down the windows. As he climbed higher, the vegetation changed as the jungle gave way to acres and acres of the low, close-cropped bushes of the tea plantations—all the same color, all the same height.

Before the town of Ella, he turned off the main road and followed a narrow, single-lane road, which climbed higher and higher. At times, the hairpin bends were so sharp, John had to make a three-point turn to make the corner. At one corner, he stopped on the verge, climbing out to stretch his legs and take in the view. From his viewpoint, the hillside plunged down into a deep valley before rising up an equally steep hillside on the other side. Here, the land was too steep for tea, and the slopes were thick with lush jungle. A dog barked in the distance, but otherwise, it was quiet.

The view was breathtaking, and not for the first time that day, John wished he had convinced Adriana to stay with him. Inhaling a lungful of cool crisp air, he allowed his mind to wander, thinking about giving everything up in Lisbon and settling down with Adriana in a small cottage in the hills.

John smiled to himself. It sounded idyllic, but could they actually do it? How long would it take before they got bored and started fighting or spent their days drinking themselves into a stupor? Perhaps he was too cynical. Maybe they could come to Sri Lanka and buy a tea estate. That would give them something to do while living in these beautiful surroundings.

A honk of a horn brought him back to the present, and he turned to see a jeep laden with tea pluckers careening around the bend on its journey downhill. The tea pluckers stared in apparent surprise at the westerner standing on the roadside, but when John raised a hand, they smiled broadly, exposing brilliant white teeth against their dark sun-scorched skin.

John watched the jeep disappear down the road, then returned to staring at the view. An eagle soared easily above the valley at his eye level, and he watched as it circled higher and higher until finally disappearing from sight over the hill behind him. He checked his watch—time to get going.

About ten minutes later, the GPS showed he needed to turn down an even narrower lane, lined on one side by a high chain-link fence topped with barbed wire.

John peered at the fence and pursed his lips. "That's a serious fence," he mumbled to himself before taking the turn. After three hundred meters, the road ended, but on the left was a steel gate about seven feet high with the name Pramodaya painted across it in an ornate orange script, and to the right of the gate was a guardhouse. A young Sri Lankan man stepped out with a clipboard in his hand and bent down to look in the window.

"Name, please?"

"Hayes."

The guard ran his finger down the list. "John Hayes?"

"That's correct."

"Thank you, sir." The guard made a tick. "Please park inside on the left." He reached into the guardhouse and flicked a switch. The gate slowly and silently slid open, revealing a parking area and a low-slung white building at the rear. John could see the Range Rover parked in one corner beside a battered pickup, a few small Japanese cars, and several motorbikes. John drove in slowly and pulled the car into an empty space. Turning off the engine, he opened the door to see the guard standing beside the car.

"Sir, please take your bags and register at the building over there." He turned and pointed to the white building.

"Okay, thank you."

"And sir, please leave your car keys with me."

John frowned. "Why?"

"Just in case we need to move it, sir."

"Ahh." John frowned. "Okay."

John popped the trunk, then walked around and unloaded his bag before handing the keys to the security guard.

"Please keep them carefully."

"Don't worry, sir." The guard smiled. "We have a key safe in there." He gestured toward the guardhouse. "They will be perfectly safe. Even Sir keeps his keys there."

"Sir?"

"Atman, sir."

"Okay." John nodded. "Thank you." He picked up his bag and nodded toward the white building, "Over there, you said?"

"Yes, sir."

As he walked toward the building, John looked around and spotted a security camera above the gate and another by the office building. To his left, a security barrier blocked the entrance to a single-lane road that led into the ashram, and next to that was a stone-walled building, with a soot-covered steel chimney rising out of the corrugated iron roof. The word 'Generator' was written across the green double doors in bright yellow script. To his right, thick foliage obscured all view beyond the carpark.

John reached the building and followed a path around the side to a set of steps leading to an open door, signposted 'Reception.' John set his bag down on the path and walked inside. A wooden counter ran the length of the room on the right, and a row of chairs was against the wall on the left. A middle-aged western woman dressed in white stood behind the counter and peered at him over the top of a pair of reading glasses.

"Mr. Hayes?"

"John."

"Welcome, John." The woman made a note on her pad, then looked up again. "Welcome to Pramodaya. My name is Gayatri."

"That's a pretty name. Indian, isn't it?"

"Yes." Gayatri's expression softened. "It's the name of a goddess. Atman chose it."

"He *chose* it?" John raised an eyebrow.

"Yes, when you have been with Atman for a while, and he sees you have made enough progress, he picks a spiritual name for you. It brings forward certain qualities that will help you on your path."

"Okay." John nodded as if that made sense.

"Anyway, welcome. You are so lucky to be here at the same time as Atman. He travels a lot these days, so your timing is very fortunate."

"Good." John grinned, "It's good to be lucky."

"Indeed." Gayatri continued, "Can you please deposit any valuables with me?" She said it as a command, not a question, and held out a large Ziplock bag. "We'll keep them for safekeeping here in the office. There are many people here for the retreat, and unfortunately, we have had thefts in the past. So, it's safer this way."

"Really?"

Gayatri nodded, waiting for him to take the bag from her.

"I have nothing valuable."

"Your passport and wallet? We have no need for money here, Mr. Hayes. Everything is provided for."

John hesitated.

"Please do not worry. It's all kept in a safe, and no-one else has access except me and Atman."

"Okay." John went outside and brought his bag in, then removed his wallet and unzipped his bag to remove the pouch containing his passport, slipping them into the Ziplock bag.

"Your phone, too. Atman doesn't want you to have any distractions while you are here."

Thinking fast, John shook his head. He glanced over his shoulder then leaned forward as if sharing a secret,

"Actually, Gayatri, please don't laugh, but I don't have a cell phone. I'm a little old-fashioned, and I don't like them. "

"That's very good." Gayatri almost smiled. "Atman says they are sucking the life out of us."

"Yes, I agree," John replied. "He's so right."

Gayatri wrote John's name on the bag, sealed it, and walked over to a large safe in the corner. She shielded the keypad with her body as she punched in the code, then opened the door and put the bags inside. John craned his neck to see inside, but she closed it before he could see anything.

Coming back to the counter, she picked up a small brass bell and rang it.

A door at the end of the room opened, and a tall, thin man in his sixties poked his head out. He was deeply tanned, and his long grey hair was tied back in a ponytail, giving him the appearance of an aging rocker. Unlike Gayatri, he was smiling.

"Maruti here will show you to your room. You will share with him."

"Oh, great." John forced a smile. Sharing! He wished he hadn't listened to Adriana.

Maruti led him along a stone pathway, lined on both sides with tea bushes separated from the path by a low hedgerow. A set of keys jiggled in his hand as he tossed them up and down. John breathed deeply to quell his irritation. He hadn't paid five thousand dollars to spend two weeks shacked up with a hippy, trying to find himself.

"This was a working plantation once," Maruti explained, looking out over the hedgerow. "But the owner went bankrupt, and Atman bought it from him." He nodded at the tea bushes closest to him. "*Camellia Sinensis.*"

"I'm sorry?"

"The Latin name for the tea plant." He again gestured over the hedgerow. "We keep these just to show the history of the land, but we are allowing the jungle to regenerate on the rest of the property. Tea cultivation is quite destructive to the environment."

"Really?" John asked. "Why is that?"

"Well..." Maruti stopped and looked back at John as if it

was obvious. "It's a mono-crop, of course. All other vegetation has to be cleared and all trees cut down. It's not like coffee, which needs shade trees." He half-smiled at John. "You'll see while you're here. The birds and animals that visit this place aren't found on the tea estates."

"How big is the ashram?"

"About twenty acres, I think." Maruti started walking again, nodding to a long single-story building on his left. "That is the dining hall and the kitchen, where all the meals are served. Breakfast at eight, lunch at twelve, and dinner at five." He smiled at another western male, who was splitting wood with an axe and piling it against the wall.

"We cook all our food on a wood fire, and the vegetables are organic. We grow a lot of it here on the property. But you will see all of that tomorrow." He stopped again and looked back at John. "Atman teaches selfless service is very important for your spiritual growth, so while you are here, you'll be expected to help in the kitchen and in the gardens."

John waited until Maruti looked away, then shook his head. It was going to be a long two weeks.

"That is the meditation hall." Maruti jerked his head toward a much larger building with stone walls and a high-pitched tiled roof, set back behind the dining hall on the highest part of the property. "We will have an orientation there at five-thirty, so settle into your room, freshen up, and wear something comfortable... something you can sit on the floor in." He started walking again. "We pair up the new people with an experienced student, a buddy system, which is why you're rooming with me. So, if you have any questions, feel free to ask."

The path led between two buildings that looked as if they had been converted from stables or whatever the

equivalent would have been on a tea estate. There were
about ten doors with a window on either side along each of
the rough stone frontages. Some doors were open, allowing
John a glimpse of beds and walls decorated with pictures
and colored cloth.

"What are those buildings?"

"The women's dormitory," Maruti said without stopping.

A door at the end opened, and a figure in white stepped
out. There was something familiar, and as John got closer,
he realized why.

"Sarah."

Sarah looked up in surprise, and Maruti stopped in his
tracks and turned around.

"We met the day before yesterday at Robert's place. In
Galle," John said, and Sarah half-smiled, glancing at Maruti
then looking over John's shoulder.

"Yes, hi. Adriana didn't come?"

"No, she had to go back to Lisbon."

"Oh." There was an awkward silence for a moment,
Sarah not making eye contact, but then she said, "So good
you could come."

"Thank you," John replied, smiling broadly. "Good to see
you again."

Maruti cleared his throat. "John, your room is this way."

John nodded at Sarah, who was looking down at her
feet, then followed Maruti, who was already heading up the
path. He frowned. Sarah had been much friendlier in Galle.

Maruti turned his head. "Atman prefers us to remain
focused on our practice while we are here," he said over his
shoulder. "So, men and women are discouraged from
mixing together."

John shrugged but said nothing as he followed Maruti
along the path to another building similar to the women's

blocks. Maruti led him to the last door in the block and unlocked the door.

"I don't snore... much." He winked, then pushed open the door. "But my room is bigger than all the others." He shrugged. "So, there are some benefits."

24

J ohn dumped his bag on the empty bed to the right of the door and looked around the room. On the left was another bed, covered in a tie-dyed purple bedcover, and pinned on the wall were photos of a woman of similar age to Maruti.

"My wife," said Maruti in a quiet voice, noticing the direction of John's gaze. "She died two years ago. Cancer."

"I'm sorry."

Maruti shrugged. "We all die in the end."

John watched his face for a moment but couldn't think of a suitable reply.

"The bathroom's at the back." Maruti pointed to a door in the rear wall. "Water is solar heated, so it's only hot in the evening, but cold water is good for waking you up."

"Great."

Maruti pointed to a small steel cabinet at the end of John's bed. "That's empty if you want to put your clothes away, but I wouldn't bother. They will give you something like this to wear while you are here." He pointed at his own outfit—loose white linen pants and a long white linen, Indian style shirt.

John frowned slightly, and noticing, Maruti continued. "It's to stop people judging you by what you wear. We all wear the same, so we are ostensibly equal." He gave a wry smile. "It suits me. I don't have to decide what to wear in the morning."

"How long have you been here, Maruti?"

He looked up at the ceiling as if calculating, "Three and a half years, give or take a few months."

"Three and a half years! Wow."

"Yeah," he sighed. "Matilda was here with me." He nodded toward the photo. "She loved it here, but cancer got the better of her in the end."

John played with the zip on his bag, a question on the tip of his tongue. In the end, curiosity and perhaps misplaced mischief got the better of him.

"Could Atman not do anything for her?"

Maruti stared at him, and John wondered if he had crossed the line. He turned his attention to his bag, removing the clothing and stacking it on the bed.

"You know he's not God, right?" Maruti said after a moment.

John looked up and saw Maruti still watching him. His face was gentle, kind even, but his eyes were sharp and intensely focused.

"Yes, of course." John smiled. "I didn't mean to offend you. It's just the other day my partner, Adriana, was told stories about how he had healed people." John shrugged, "So I thought... perhaps..."

"Huh," Maruti scoffed and dismissed him with a wave of the hand. "Don't believe everything you hear."

"Okay." John turned his attention back to his bag.

"John, what you will learn here can help you greatly. So much of what we experience is colored by our mental state. So, what you learn here can change your life." Maruti's tone had changed, less gentle, more forceful. "But remember one thing. It's not magic, and your journey is your responsibility." He grinned, "That's two things." His face became serious again. "You have to do the work, put in the effort. Do you understand?"

John turned to face him. "I think so."

Maruti's eyes drilled into him with an intensity John had only seen once before. He pointed a finger at John.

"Question everything. Find your own answers." He turned his finger back on himself and pointed at his chest. "Listen to the voice in here." His face softened, and he dropped his hand. "I have some work to do. You have just under an hour to freshen up, then I'll see you at the meditation hall."

"Okay... and thank you."

"No problem. Make sure you lock the door when you leave." He nodded toward a bookshelf overflowing with books in the corner. "I don't want anyone taking my books. They never bring them back."

John nodded as Maruti walked toward the door.

"Oh, and if you've brought any contraband, lock it away in your bag."

"Contraband?"

"Chocolate, cookies, whatever. If you leave it out, the rats will get it."

John shook his head. "I don't have anything. They told us not to bring anything."

Maruti chuckled and stepped out the door. He turned back and with a grin.

"Don't listen to everything they tell you, either."

25

John fiddled around with his bag until he no longer heard Maruti's footsteps, then walked over to the door and poked his head out.

He could just see Maruti turning the corner at the end of the path. A plume of smoke rose straight into the still air from the kitchen, but otherwise, there was no sign of human life. John scanned the other doors in the dormitory block, but they were all closed, although several open windows hinted at the rooms being occupied. John switched his attention to the view. Directly in front of the room, the land sloped gently away, the tea bushes gradually giving way to thicker, lusher vegetation as the jungle slowly reclaimed its rightful place.

The sun was low in the sky and threw long shadows across the gardens. As John became more in tune with his surroundings, he noticed the bird song. Chirps and tweets of all kinds filled the air, and the trees and bushes became alive with movement as birds flittered and flew from tree to tree. Looking up, he watched as a group of house martins swooped back and forth, feasting on insects in the cooler evening air. High above them, a solitary bird of prey circled effortlessly in the updrafts.

John took a deep breath, filling his lungs with the crisp, sweet country air, then turned and went back inside.

He took his phone out of his pocket—it had vibrated while he'd been talking to Maruti—and checked the screen. *Landed.* He smiled, walked back to the window, checked no-one was around, then hit dial. It took a little while to connect, but he grinned when Adriana answered, sounding a little out of breath.

"Are you running?" he joked.

"No." Adriana chuckled. "I'm just rushing to Passport Control before the rest of the plane catches up."

"All okay?"

"Yes, tired but okay."

"Good. I just got here."

"Oh, how is it?"

John turned and looked back at the room—the peeling paint, the narrow single beds, the concrete floor—and smiled.

"Good, very good."

"That's a relief. I was worried it might be horrible."

"No, no." John turned and looked out the window again. "It's nice. On a converted tea estate up in the hills. It's much cooler up here."

"Have you met anyone yet?"

"Yup. I have an old guy as a roommate."

"Roommate?"

"Yeah." John grinned, trying to sound as happy as he could. "They pair the new people up with the experienced students. He seems nice enough. Not too... ahh... evangelical."

"That's good. At least you'll have someone to guide you

and talk to."

"Yes, that's true, but hey, ahh, I'm not supposed to have a phone. I hid mine."

"Already breaking the rules?"

"Well, not all rules should be followed." John laughed. "Anyway, I don't know when I can charge my phone without getting caught, so I'll keep it off most of the time and only turn it on when I can talk to you."

"That's okay, John. Don't worry about me. I want you to get the most out of it."

"I will, don't worry."

"Good. Okay, I have to hang up. I've reached Passport Control. I love you."

"Love you, too."

When the phone went dead, John turned it off and thought about where to hide it. He didn't think Maruti was the type to go through his bag, but erring on the safe side, he decided to hide it under his mattress. He selected a loose shirt and baggy cotton pants, then stowing the rest of the clothes in the cupboard, he zipped up his bag and placed it on top. Tucking the change of clothes under his arm, he walked toward the bathroom, stopping in front of Maruti's bookshelf, running his eyes over the shelves.

Books on Christianity, Hinduism, and Buddhism filled the shelves. There was even a Koran next to a Bible, both showing signs of being well-read. On the bottom shelf were a couple of books that made John grin. Several paperbacks by Lee Child, Wilbur Smith, and David Baldacci occupied space next to a biography of Nelson Mandela and a book on UFOs.

John looked at the top shelf, which held a small, framed portrait of Atman, next to a picture of the Hindu God Shiva. In front of the two pictures were a small brass statue of

Buddha, several crystals, and a brass incense stand surrounded by ash.

Apart from a battered guitar leaning against the rear wall, there was little else in the way of personal possessions. John switched his attention to the photos on the wall. One in particular caught his eye—Maruti in a colorful sleeveless shirt, his arm around his wife, both grinning at the camera. She had a kind face, soft blue eyes, and mousy hair turning to grey in a short bob. They looked happy and very much in love. There was another photo of her alone, sitting in the sun in a garden. She appeared much thinner, her eyes surrounded by dark smudges. She no longer looked happy, only exhausted, just a shell of the woman who was in the earlier photo.

John sighed, suddenly depressed. Walking into the bathroom, he looped his clothes over the towel rail, then stared at his reflection in the dirty, cracked mirror above the sink. What was the point? Everyone you loved was going to die sooner or later. Why did people bother chasing things, setting goals, accumulating possessions? Everyone ended up in the ground, pushing up daisies. Damn. He exhaled loudly. Coming here was supposed to make him feel better.

He turned on the tap, leaned down, and splashed water on his face, then realized he hadn't brought a towel in with him. Taking off his shirt, he dried his face with it, then changed into fresh clothes. Walking back into the bedroom, he checked his watch. There was plenty of time before they expected him at the meditation hall. Glancing at the photos on the wall again, he made a decision. If he stayed in the room, he would sink further into depression. He needed movement, sunshine, and fresh air.

26

J ohn stepped outside and locked the door behind him, then looked left and right, deciding which way to go. He had come from the right, so he took the path left to find out where it went. The path led past a large vegetable garden on the left, filled with various greens, rows of tomatoes under shade cloth, and patches of bare soil where crops had already been harvested. There was no-one around, and John wondered when he would be called upon to help. He wouldn't mind if he got to work in the garden. A bit of fresh air and sun would do him a world of good, but he didn't feel like working inside the kitchen. He'd washed enough dishes for a living when he was a teenager. It wasn't his idea of fun, especially when he'd paid five thousand dollars for the privilege. He walked on, passing a composting unit and a large water tank, toward a stand of trees. He recognized some of them from his time in India—Jackfruit, mango, silver oak. They were filled with birds, and pairs of squirrels chased each other up and down the branches. Passing through the trees, the land sloped up toward a large, colonial-style bungalow, similar to the one owned by Robert in Galle. John guessed it must have been the original Tea Planter's house. It was beautifully restored, with crisp green window frames, what looked like a newly tiled roof, and baskets overflowing with flowers hanging from the verandah which wrapped around two sides. It looked significantly smarter and far more luxurious than the accommodation John was staying in. He walked closer, keen to get a better look, when a figure in white appeared on the verandah and jogged down the steps, heading down the path toward him. He was a young western man, well-built, hair trimmed short, the complete opposite of Maruti's ageing hippy look. He smiled without warmth and held up a hand as if to say, 'stop where you are.' John kept walking, a matching smile on his own face.

"You can't come up here. This area is not for the public." The young man called out, his accent hard to place, but John would have guessed European, with English not being his first language.

"I'm here for the retreat," John replied.

Behind the man, John noticed another figure watching from the verandah, similar to the man who had now stopped and was blocking the path. The young man's body language wasn't aggressive, but it was clear John could go no further.

John played dumb. "Isn't this the meditation hall?"

"No." The man shook his head, his demeanor visibly relaxing. "You've come the wrong way." He pointed back over John's shoulder. "It's back that way, the large building on the right after the dormitories."

"Ah, okay," John smiled and spread his hands, making his posture unthreatening. "I got confused. It's my first day here."

"No problem."

John looked over the man's shoulder toward the bunga-low, where the other figure was still watching.

"What is that building? It looks very nice."

"That is Atman's private quarters."

"Ahhh." John nodded slowly. He smiled again at the young man. "I'll head back. I don't want to be late on my first day."

The man smiled back, a little more warmth in his expression. "You still have time, don't worry."

"Thank you." John turned and started walking back the way he had come. Just as he entered the stand of trees, he looked back over his shoulder. The young man was walking back to the bungalow, but the figure on the verandah still watched him.

Once through the trees and out of sight of Atman's bungalow, John stepped off the path, over the low hedgerow, and made his way through the tea bushes into the secondary growth jungle. He walked slowly and carefully, mindful of where he placed his feet. He couldn't remember if there were snakes in Sri Lanka, but he didn't want to take any chances.

While looking at the ground, he walked straight into a large spider web and halted abruptly to peel the sticky strands off his face. A movement in his peripheral vision caught his attention, and he spotted a spider almost as large as the palm of his hand scuttle away to safety. Suppressing a shudder, he walked on, even slower now, having to watch his feet as well as look ahead.

After about five minutes, the light getting dimmer as the jungle grew thicker, he walked out into a cleared patch with the boundary fence running through the middle. The foliage had been cleared back about two meters on each side of the chain-link fence as far as John could see to the left and the right. He looked up at the fence, the top of which was at least two feet higher than his head, and topped with barbed wire. John frowned. Why did a meditation center need such a big fence? Was he being paranoid? He glanced at his watch. He still had fifteen minutes before he was due back for the orientation.

Turning right, he followed the fence line until it turned at right angles. On the corner post were two cameras, one pointed in each direction. John deliberately avoided looking at them and kept walking. He was bound to have been spotted, but he didn't know why he was feeling guilty. He wasn't doing anything wrong.

The sun was low in the sky as the jungle came alive with the sounds of insects and birds preparing for the night. John didn't fancy fighting his way back through the foliage in the falling light and figured if he followed the fence line, he would end up back at the front of the property.

About five minutes later, he saw the car park ahead. Leaving the fence line, he made his way through the vegetation and stepped out near the guardhouse. His car was still where he left it, but the Range Rover was gone. He walked over to the guardhouse and peered through the open door. Inside, the guard sat, leaning back in his chair, watching a movie on his phone. He seemed to sense John in the doorway and sat up with a start, almost dropping his phone.

"Sir?" He looked over John's shoulder, then back at him, his face a mask of confusion. "You are supposed to be up at the hall."

John smiled to put him at ease. "Yes, I am lost. Which way is it?"

The guard relaxed and stepped out of the booth, pointing down the path. "That way, sir. It's the large building on the left. You can't miss it. Do you want me to come with you?"

"No, it's okay. I'll find it." He winked at the guard. "Enjoy your movie."

The guard looked away, embarrassed, then smiled. "Thank you, sir."

John walked away, checked his watch again, then picked up his pace. He was going to be late on the first day.

———————

27

T he door to the meditation hall was closed, and the only sign people were inside was the pile of footwear scattered on the ground outside the door. There was a sign saying, 'leave your footwear here,' but most seemed to have ignored the almost empty rack beneath it, leaving their shoes lying on the ground. John slipped off his own shoes and placed them neatly on the rack, then brushed down his shirt and pants, removing the stray leaves and remnants of the spider web.

Taking a deep breath, he pushed open the door and stepped inside, pausing for a moment to allow his eyes to adjust to the lower levels of light in the room. Someone had been speaking when he entered, and the sound stopped. John looked toward the front of the hall, where a full-width platform was lit with soft, warm lighting. In the middle of the platform stood Gayatri, the woman from the registration office, who now glared at him over her reading glasses like an angry schoolteacher. John felt more eyes on him and noticed the rest of the students, sitting cross-legged on cushions on the floor, turning to face him. He smiled and gave a brief wave to no-one in particular, while looking around for somewhere to sit.

The women were sitting on the left, and he spotted Sarah sitting near the front. He grabbed a cushion from a pile near the door and found a space at the rear of the men's section. As he settled himself, he noticed Maruti watching impassively from the rear corner. John nodded, then got his bearings as Gayatri resumed her introduction. John did a rough headcount, estimating thirty-five to forty people in the hall, two-thirds of them women. Half were dressed in white, while the others were dressed like him in normal, comfortable clothing. John shifted his position again, adjusting the cushion under his butt, and tuned in to what Gayatri was saying. She appeared to be reading off a list of dos and don'ts, so John tuned out again and instead studied the main stage at the front.

Occupying the center of the stage was a large armchair covered in white cloth, and seated on the floor on each side was a young Sri Lankan girl dressed in a red sari. Their hair was tied back in tightly plaited ponytails, and they looked like they were in their early teens. They sat with their eyes closed, an expression of calm contemplation on their faces.

To the left was a large amethyst cave, almost five feet in height, and on the right, an altar lit with candles and decorated with flowers. John narrowed his eyes and craned his head to get a better look. On the altar was a stone statue of a seated Buddha, a cross, and a brass Natraj, the dancing form of the Hindu God Shiva, which John had seen during his time in India. Multiple sticks of incense sent spirals of sweet-scented smoke into the air. The room was warm, not too warm but pleasantly so, and it felt calm and peaceful.

John switched his attention back to what Gayatri was saying.

"We start at five a.m. here in the hall. Please don't be late." She looked pointedly at John. "Breakfast will be served at eight a.m., followed by *seva*. *Seva* means service, and Atman requires you all to take part. Without unconditional service, you will not make progress, and your spiritual growth will be stunted." She looked around the room, pausing for effect. "Please check the roster on the whiteboard outside the kitchen every morning for your service assignments. At eleven a.m., we have another meditation here in the hall, followed by lunch at twelve p.m. You have another hour of *seva* at two p.m., then free time from three until five p.m. We have a light supper at five p.m., and the evening meditation begins at six. Lights out at nine." She stared around the room again. "No exceptions."

John glanced over at Maruti, but his eyes were closed.

"You will get out of this retreat what you put into it," Gayatri continued. "Please value this time. We are blessed to have Atman himself leading the retreat, so please make the most of his divine presence."

A door opened to the side of the stage, and Gayatri's body language changed immediately from bossy headmistress to teenager in love. She folded the paper she was reading from, slipped her reading glasses off her nose, her face visibly flushed even in the low light of the hall, and placed both hands together in front of her chest.

A murmur rippled through the hall, and those dressed in white jumped to their feet and stood, holding their hands in the *namaste* gesture. The new students followed suit, getting to their feet, staring at the stage in eager anticipation.

John stood, sneaking glances at the people around him, those in white, staring at the stage in rapture. Maruti stood as well, but unlike the others, he stood with his eyes closed and hands down by his side. John raised his hands in *namaste* but felt self-conscious and dropped them to his side.

The first person to come through the door wasn't Atman but the familiar figure of Georges. He took a quick look around the hall, then stepped back. Atman followed him out, and a collective gasp could be heard.

He raised his right hand in the air, a broad smile on his face. He walked over to the armchair, nodded at the two Sri Lankan girls, then turned and faced the hall again. This time, he raised both his hands in the air, palms facing the hall, fingers spread wide. He closed his eyes and stood like that for almost a minute, then opened his eyes, placed both hands on his chest, nodded toward the hall, then sat down on the armchair.

Gayatri hovered beside him, with a silver tray holding a silver cup. Reaching for it, he took a sip, then placed it back on the tray. Gayatri moved away, and Georges stepped closer, bent down, and placed a white shawl over Atman's shoulders before he stepped away and stood a little to the side, gazing out over the students.

Atman made a motion with his hand, and the students in white, followed by the newcomers, sat down on their cushions.

John made himself comfortable, shifting slightly, so he had a clear line of sight to Atman and waited.

The two Sri Lankan girls in red sat down again on the stage on each side of his chair and closed their eyes. Gayatri sat cross-legged on the right side of the stage, and Georges pulled up a chair from the rear of the stage and seated himself just behind Atman, near his right shoulder.

Atman said nothing for a while, a smile on his face, his eyes roaming the faces of the seated students. His gaze found John and locked on him for a moment before passing on. John felt an unusual tingle in the back of his neck and prickling along the hairs on his arm, but he dismissed the sensation, putting it down to nerves. He had done nothing like this before and wasn't sure what to expect.

Then he heard Atman's voice, soft, calm, but somehow filled with power. "Sit up straight and close your eyes."

28

J ohn's right leg was numb. He tried wriggling his toes, but they wouldn't respond. He had a burning pain somewhere in the muscles surrounding his left shoulder blade, and he needed to pee badly. How long was this going to continue?

The hall was silent and still, and John began to wonder if he was alone. He slowly opened one eye and saw the hall was still filled with people. Atman was now sitting with his legs up and crossed on the armchair, a blissful smile across his face. The two girls and Gayatri all sat with their eyes closed, not moving, but from where John was sitting, he couldn't see Georges.

John opened the other eye and looked around the hall. The man closest to John on his left appeared to be asleep. He was slumped forward, his chin on his chest and what looked like a long string of saliva dangling from the corner of his mouth. Others sat unmoving, some straight, others hunched over. Near the front, on the ladies' side of the hall, he heard a sniff and what sounded like muffled sobs. He leaned to one side, trying to see Sarah, but couldn't make her out among the seated meditators.

He turned to look at Maruti. The old guy was sitting ramrod straight, his legs crossed in a full lotus position, the backs of his hands resting on his knees, fingers spread except the thumb and forefinger, which were joined at the tips forming a circle. His head was thrown back as if he was looking up at the ceiling. At first glance, his eyes appeared to be open, but as John peered closer, he could see Maruti's eyes were rolled back into his head, exposing just the whites of his eyeballs. He didn't appear to be breathing, no movement in his chest. John was fascinated and couldn't tear his eyes away. He forced himself to look to the front again and closed his eyes, but after a moment, he couldn't resist taking another peek at Maruti.

How did he do it? How could anyone sit so still for so long? What was he experiencing that made his eyes do that?

John sneaked a look at his watch. It had been an hour since Atman had walked onto the stage and sat down, and there was no sign of movement happening any time soon. John grew irritated. Would anyone notice if he sneaked out? Would he even be able to stand?

Slowly, as quietly as he could, he eased his legs apart, stretching his right leg as much as he could in the confined space around him. The blood flowed back to his feet, bringing with it an unbearable prickly crawling sensation. He stifled a gasp and leaned forward, gripping his toes in his hand and squeezed them, massaging them, anything to get rid of the pain of the pins and needles. Fuck! He cursed silently and then rocked his right knee up and down, but nothing was helping. Biting his bottom lip, he sat back and exhaled slowly through his nostrils.

He glanced at the stage, and his heart jumped as he

noticed Atman watching him with that eerie laser-like stare of his. Fuck. John mentally cursed again and closed his eyes as his right foot twitched and spasmed.

How am I going to last two weeks of this? I can't believe I paid five thousand dollars for it!

As the tingling in his foot eased, he heard Atman's voice from the front.

"Slowly, gently, bring your awareness back. Back to the room. Back to your body. Feel the love and joy you just experienced flowing out from your heart center and filling the room, blessing everyone here. Then imagine it flowing out of the building and filling the ashram, then further, filling the whole countryside, the beautiful island of Sri Lanka. The love and joy are continually expanding and now cover the entire planet, blessing every living being.

"Now take a long slow inhalation, hold it for a count of three, then exhale slowly. Offer a prayer of thanks to the universe, then gently wiggle your fingers, your toes... rub your hands together, create heat between your palms and place them on your face, then slowly open your eyes."

John breathed a sigh of relief. "About bloody time," he muttered.

29

A tman stood and looked around the hall as the students scrambled to their feet. A broad smile spread across his face as he placed his right hand on his chest. All around John, people did the same, smiling, happy faces, as if they had just been asked out by their school sweetheart. John craned his neck and looked toward the ladies' section, where he saw at least one woman wiping tears from her face. Was John the only one who didn't enjoy himself? Was there something wrong with him?

John turned and looked at Maruti, who remained seated, his eyes now closed, apparently still deep in meditation. John frowned, feeling a little envious. Movement on the stage distracted him. Georges escorted Atman out the side door, followed by the two young Sri Lankan girls, while the crowd of students talked among themselves excitedly.

Gayatri hurried to the front of the stage and gestured for everyone to quieten down.

"There will be a light meal in the dining hall for the new arrivals, but starting tomorrow, please remember the mealtime will revert to five p.m. And please pick up your retreat clothing from the table at the dining hall entrance. All colors have a vibration, and white is the highest and most pure. It will help you make progress." She reverted to head-mistress mode and glared out across the hall. "You will not be admitted to the hall tomorrow unless you are wearing the correct clothing. Do not be late. Five a.m. sharp."

John bent down, picked up his cushion, and moved toward the rear door, his right leg still tingling. He placed the cushion on the pile, opened the door, and walked out. Now dark outside, he climbed down the steps, retrieved his shoes, and moved slightly away from the hall. He stood just on the edge of the shadow thrown by the lights that lined the footpath, where he could see the front door as the other students came out. A few nodded at John as they passed, most of the older students in their own groups, a few of the newcomers looking nervous, while others glowed with evident excitement.

Sarah, one of the last to exit, came out with Gayatri. She spotted John immediately and smiled at him. Gayatri, glancing in his direction, said something, and Sarah's expression changed slightly. John couldn't quite figure out what, but it was noticeable. He stored the thought away for later and nodded a greeting to them both.

Gayatri again said something to Sarah, and she nodded, glanced in John's direction, then walked away toward the dining hall. Gayatri stopped in front of John, and raised a haughty eyebrow.

"Did you forget the timings?"

"I'm sorry." John grinned. "It wasn't a good start, was it?"

"Hmmm, please be on time tomorrow."

"Scout's honor," John replied, standing to attention.

Gayatri didn't look impressed.

The door of the hall opened again, and Maruti walked

out. He stood on the top step, rolled his shoulders back, and looked up at the night sky for a moment, then took a breath and jogged down the steps with the agility of a man half his age. Slipping on a pair of flip-flops, he spotted John and Gayatri and walked over.

"I wouldn't hang around here, John, if you want something to eat." He jerked his head toward the dining hall. "Those hyenas will finish everything off before you get there." He smiled conspiratorially at Gayatri, lowering his voice as if sharing a secret. "Always be the first to the dining hall, isn't that right?"

Gayatri, even less impressed with Maruti's comment, made a disapproving shape with her mouth, turned around, and walked off after Sarah.

Maruti watched her go then grinned at John. "Gayatri likes to be mother hen."

"Yes, I'm learning that. I feel like I'm back at school."

Maruti shrugged. "Takes all types... Anyway, how was your first session?"

John looked at him, wondering what he should say. He liked his new roommate. There was something about him that made him feel comfortable, unjudged.

"Honestly?" John made a face. "Pins and needles. Boredom. Nothing else."

"Don't worry about it." Maruti nodded sympathetically and placed a hand on John's shoulder. "It's normal." He smiled. "It's a practice, not a miracle."

John studied his face for a moment, looked around to make sure no-one was in earshot, and lowered his voice anyway.

"I thought there was something wrong with me."

"You'll be fine. Each day will be better. Now, go and get something to eat."

"Yes." John ran his hand over his stomach. "I'm starving! Are you coming?"

"No, I had something earlier." He patted John on the shoulder. "I'll see you back at the room. Now get going before there's nothing left."

30

Once inside the hall, John noticed the genders were separated again, the women sitting on one side at two long tables, the men at a separate table on the right.

The segregation was irritating John. He didn't see why it was necessary. Some long-termers seemed to take it too far, avoiding eye contact, even refraining from speaking to the opposite sex. Thankfully, the new intake still behaved normally, but John wondered how long it would take to rub off on them.

Westerners dressed in white moved around the room, serving food and water, and one young man guided John to an empty seat at the end of the men's table. He sat down, nodded a greeting at the man sitting next to him, and waited as another westerner poured a glass of water for him and yet one more placed a plate of rice and what looked like lentils in front of him.

John suppressed a groan and started eating. The food was tasty, but half the quantity John needed, and he finished it in no time. The man next to him said nothing the whole time, chewing silently and staring at his plate, and John wasn't in the mood to force a conversation. He washed it down with the glass of water, then stood and carried his glass and plate to the serving hatch at the end of the dining hall. A pair of anonymous hands reached out from inside and took them from him with a muttered 'thank you.'

John turned and surveyed the hall. Some were still eating, while others sat quietly, contemplating empty plates. Few were talking. John sighed. Two more weeks! He shook his head and wandered over to where Sarah was sitting, ignoring the disapproving look from one of the female volunteers. Sarah was talking to the middle-aged lady sitting next to her. She had a kind face, and when she saw John standing next to the table, she smiled warmly. John stood next to Sarah, and she stopped talking and turned to look up at him.

"Hi. All okay?" he asked.

"Yes, ah..." Sarah looked around nervously, then continued, "This is Katrina, from Berlin."

John smiled at her. "I'm John, pleased to meet you."

"Hello." She smiled back.

"This is Katrina's first time, too."

"Oh, really. Good, so we're not the only ones." John looked at Katrina. "I hope you were more comfortable sitting on the floor than I was."

She raised her eyebrows and shook her head. "No, I have stiff knees."

John nodded in sympathy. "Perhaps we can ask them for a chair?"

Sarah nodded. "That's a good idea. I'll arrange it for the morning."

One of the female volunteers appeared beside them, cleared her throat, and looked meaningfully at John.

John fixed her with his biggest smile. "Hello."

She ignored him, addressing Sarah and Katrina, "Have you finished?"

Sarah shot John a furtive look, then turned to face the volunteer. "Almost, thank you, Marsha."

The woman looked at John again, turned up her nose, then walked away.

John exhaled loudly. "I guess that's my cue to leave. Pleasure to meet you, Katrina." He smiled at Sarah. "Good night."

Sarah's mouth twitched as if to smile, then looked away, her eyes sad.

John looked around, winked at the volunteer, and walked out of the hall.

31

J ohn stood outside and stared up at the sky. The air was cool, the sky clear, and despite the light pollution from the ashram, thousands of tiny points of light visibly twinkled and sparkled in the inky blackness.

The door opened behind him, and he stepped to one side, nodding at the two women who came out. They nodded back—one smiled, but neither said anything, hurrying down the path to the accommodation.

John checked his watch. It was still relatively early, and even though lights out was at nine, he was in no hurry to rush back to the room. Deciding to take a walk, he turned right toward the front gate. The administration block was dark, the windows and doors closed, and the only sign of life was the yellow light leaking out from under the closed door of the guardroom beside the gate.

John walked over to the gate and leaned on it to slide it open, but it didn't budge. He tried again, shaking it in case it was jammed, but there was no movement, just a metallic clanging from the end near the guardhouse. John walked closer, and in the faint light from the guardhouse, he saw the gate was secured with a heavy padlock. John frowned and scratched his head. Turning, he knocked on the guard-house door.

After a moment, an elderly Sri Lankan man, different from the one John had met when he arrived, opened the door and looked out.

"Good evening." John gave him a wide smile.

The man looked puzzled. He looked over John's shoulder toward the office then back at John.

"Good evening, sir."

"Can you please open the gate? I want to go for a walk."

The man was shaking his head before John had even finished speaking. "No, sir. No, sir. You cannot go out."

John raised his eyebrows. "Why not?"

The guard looked uncomfortable. "I'm sorry, sir. I'm not allowed to open the gate." He glanced nervously over John's shoulder again. "Sorry, sir."

John smiled again, leaned forward, and lowered his voice. "It's okay. I won't tell anyone."

"No, no." The guard shook his head violently. "I will lose my job."

"Who will know?" John asked.

The guard looked around, then stepped back inside the guardhouse and pointed to his left. John frowned. What did he mean? In a sudden moment of clarity, he understood. He nodded, smiling again, and made a placatory movement with both his hands.

"It's okay. Don't worry, I understand."

The guard's face relaxed.

"You have a good night."

"Thank you, sir." The guard finally smiled.

John quickly scanned the interior of the guardroom, noting the open cabinet on the wall filled with keys, the computer monitor on the built-in desk showing multiple camera feeds, a walkie-talkie standing upright in a battery charger, and the flickering screen of the guard's own telephone.

"Enjoy your movie," John said, nodding to the phone, then turned away. He glanced up at the camera above the gate—he had forgotten about it until the guard had pointed in that direction—then walked back toward the office. Why did they need so much security?

Sri Lanka was a safe place, much safer than many other countries John had been in. The civil war was long over, and it had never really touched the south of the country. Foreigners were welcome, the locals unfailingly friendly and helpful. So, what were they worried about? John continued past the dining hall. Through an open window, he could see someone mopping the floor, and light spilled out from the kitchen, where he could hear voices and the sounds of pots and pans being moved around. Perhaps it was like the Berlin Wall, designed to keep people in, not out.

John chewed his lip. Maybe he was just paranoid, reading too much into things. Perhaps it was just a place for lost and lonely people to feel a sense of community, a sense of belonging to something. He walked past the ladies' dorm. All the doors were closed, but cracks of light were visible behind the curtains. He walked on to the men's block, paused outside the door to his room, and took one last look around.

The insect and bird noise from earlier had died down, and apart from the distant bark of a dog and muffled voices from the other rooms, the evening was quiet and still. John gazed up at the stars again. He tracked the blinking lights of a high-flying aircraft as it moved slowly but steadily across the sky. When it disappeared from sight, he pushed down on the door handle and went inside.

32

Maruti was stretched out on the bed, his head propped on a pillow, his legs crossed at the ankle. He looked up from the book he was reading.

"Walking off dinner?"

"Tried to. The front gate was locked."

"Yup, every night."

John sat down on the bed, leaned against the wall, and brought his legs up, crossing them in front of him.

"Why?"

Maruti shrugged and turned his attention back to his book. "Our own safety, they say."

"You've never wanted to go out at night?"

"Go where?"

"I don't know." John poked out his bottom lip. "An evening stroll... visit the village... get some chicken curry?"

Maruti chuckled.

John watched him for a while, but it looked like he wasn't getting an answer.

"What are you reading?"

Maruti held up the cover, so John could see it. "It's about an Australian guy who gets caught up in the pro-democracy protests in Hong Kong."

"Any good?"

"So far, yes."

"Hmmm." John stared down at the floor for a while. "I used to live there."

"Where?"

"Hong Kong."

"Really?" Maruti raised an eyebrow but kept reading.

"It's sad to see a great city being destroyed."

Maruti lowered his book and looked over at John. "By the protestors or the government?"

John shrugged. "Depends on which side of the fence you're on."

Maruti watched him for a moment. "And which side of the fence are you on?"

"Does it matter?" John pushed himself off the bed, walked toward the bathroom, and stopped in the doorway. "It's not like I can make a difference from here."

"That's true."

John splashed water on his face, brushed his teeth, and changed into a t-shirt and a pair of loose boxers.

When he walked out again, Maruti looked over and said, "You can always send them love and healing during the next meditation."

"Hmmm, I'll be sure to do that," John muttered and sat down on the bed. He heard a noise and realized Maruti was laughing.

"Was that a joke?"

"Maybe."

John laid down on the bed and stared up at the ceiling.

The paint was flaking in patches, and a crack ran from above John's bed across the ceiling toward the front door.

"How long does it take before sitting on the floor stops being painful?"

Maruti grunted. "It's always painful."

"My leg went numb."

"Yup."

"Does it get better?"

"You get used to it."

John sighed.

"Hey, don't stress about it." Maruti put his book down, turned on his side, and propped his head on his elbow. "The first few sessions are torture. In time, your body will adapt, but that's not important. With practice, your mind will quieten down, and you'll experience a state where you won't even feel your body."

John turned his head to look at him. "Is that what happens to you? I saw you this evening."

"Something like that." Maruti smiled, "Better get some sleep. We have to be up at four-thirty." Reaching up, he turned off the light.

33

J ohn's eyes snapped open. It was still dark, but his heart was racing, and his t-shirt was soaked. He had been dreaming about something, but now that he was awake, he couldn't remember what. Sitting up, he peered across the room. He could just make out the sleeping form of Maruti and the sound of his slow and deep breathing.

John shivered. He needed to change his shirt. Swinging his legs off the bed, he stood slowly and stepped over to the cupboard containing his clothes. He eased the door open, pausing halfway as the unoiled hinge squeaked. John waited, worried he had woken Maruti, but his breathing remained steady and even. Reaching inside, he fumbled around until his fingers touched what felt like a t-shirt. He pulled it out and swapped it for the damp one he was wearing.

Sitting on the bed, John closed his eyes and slowed his breathing. Long slow inhalations followed by equally long and slow exhalations. His heart rate slowed, but now he was wide awake. He glanced at his watch. One-thirty. He felt like he'd been asleep for hours, then realized he had been. Maruti had turned the lights out at around eight-thirty, and John hadn't taken long to drift off to sleep. But now sleep seemed a distant prospect. He stood and walked over to the window and looked out.

The moon was just off full and bathed the tea bushes and trees in a silvery light. A large black shape flashed past the window, and John jerked his head back, his breath caught in his throat. *What was that?* He saw it again, then breathed out as he recognized the wing shape and movement of a bat. He leaned his elbows on the windowsill and watched as it and another smaller bat flitted back and forth, hunting insects in the night air.

Easing the window out further until it was open wide, he stuck his head out, breathing in a big lungful of crisp and cool night air. He looked up at the sky again, marveling at the millions of stars above him, more than he could count. Was there anything else up there? Was there another planet just like this one? Perhaps someone else looking at their own sky, asking the same question he was?

Was there an old man with a beard, sitting up there on a cloud, maybe Morgan Freeman's twin, watching him, judging his actions, deciding whether what he ate or what he wore was worthy of allowing him into heaven? If so, why could some people eat pork and not beef and vice versa?

John grinned as he gazed up at the night sky. It was all nonsense if you thought about it logically, but so few people did. They blindly believed whatever they were told, following along like sheep, committing atrocities in the name of some imaginary, supposedly benevolent being. John thought back to what he'd experienced so far at the ashram.

He understood why they were supposed to eat vegetarian food. He'd read about it before when he was in India and Thailand. Reaching deeper states of meditation was apparently aided by a vegetarian diet, but John wasn't so sure. This evening during the meditation session, he'd been so hungry, and all he'd thought about was sinking his teeth into a juicy steak or a nice piece of roast chicken. At least it had taken his mind off the numbness in his leg for a while. And making women sit on one side and men on the other was stupid. How did that help things? Anyway, everyone had their eyes closed.

John's stomach growled again. He sighed and looked down at the gardens. Hopefully, breakfast would be more substantial than dinner had been.

He saw something move in his peripheral vision. He ignored it at first, thinking it was just another bat, but it happened again, and something made him turn and look closer. Down near the stand of trees, between the dormitory and the bungalow, was a dark shape in the middle of the path. John looked closer but couldn't make it out. It moved again. What was it? An animal? A stray dog? No, it was too big. Maybe a leopard? John continued watching until it moved again. It grew in height, and John realized it was a person. What were they doing out so late? A security guard?

John moved his head back inside the window, slowly, so as not to attract attention, and stood just back from the window, watching the figure approach. As the person got closer, John could make out more detail in the moonlight. It wasn't a man, the frame too slight, the height just over five feet. It was hard to make out more since a shawl covered their head and most of their body. John leaned forward, eager to see who it was. He heard a sniff and watched the person wipe their face with the back of their hand. He craned his neck, trying to get a better view. His shoulder brushed against the window frame, nudging the window open a little more, and the hinge creaked.

The figure stopped, startled by the sound, their head whipping around. At that moment, the moonlight fell on her face. It was one of the Sri Lankan girls who had been sitting on the stage. Her eyes widened in fright as she saw John, and she gasped, frozen to the spot. John was about to say something to reassure her when she ducked her head down, pulled the shawl tighter around her head, and hurried off toward the women's dormitory.

John frowned. What was that all about?

34

John lay on the bed for a long time, wide awake, thinking about what he'd seen. Who were the Sri Lankan girls? Why were they here, and why was one of them out so late at night? She appeared to have been crying, although John realized it was possible he had imagined that. What he hadn't imagined was she was obviously returning from the bungalow. That thought deeply troubled him and kept him awake for a long time before eventually, sleep got the better of him.

When his watch alarm sounded at four-thirty, it took him a moment to remember where he was and why he was getting up so early. He sat up and glanced over at Maruti's bed, but he had already gone, the bed made and the tie-dyed cover sheet folded at the foot of the bed. John hadn't heard a thing. He climbed out of bed, stumbled to the bathroom, and ran the tap, splashing cold water on his face, then tamed his hair with his wet hands. Leaning on the wash-basin, he stared into the mirror as memories of what he had seen during the night came back to him. He frowned. He would speak to Maruti about it as soon as he got the chance.

Straightening, he went back into the room and flicked on the light, then cursed. He'd forgotten to pick up his white meditation clothing when he left the dining hall the previous evening. He shook his head and sighed. No doubt he would receive a telling-off from headmistress Gayatri. Slipping on the clothes he'd worn the evening before, he stepped outside, locking the door behind him, and made his way through the cool early morning air to the hall.

John was one of the first to arrive, but after grabbing a cushion from the pile, he reserved his spot in the back row. He had no desire to sit near the front. There were several others already sitting, including Maruti, who was in his regular place in the corner, eyes already closed.

John remained standing, putting off sitting down until the last minute and watched the others slowly filter in.

On the stage, a volunteer adjusted the white covering on Atman's armchair, while another arranged flowers on the altar and lit sticks of incense.

Sarah walked in just before five, and John mouthed, "Good morning," but she looked away and hurried toward the front. The hall steadily filled, most sitting immediately, but a few like John remained standing, some with their arms crossed or hands in their pockets, while others limbered up and stretched.

Gayatri appeared on the stage from the side door and ran her eye over Atman's chair, tugging on one side of the covering, making an adjustment before walking to the altar. Watching as the volunteer made last touches to the flowers, she said something to the young lady, who nodded, then stepped off the stage, moving to a place somewhere in the front among the seated students.

Gayatri stood in front of the altar and raised her hands in prayer, staying like that for a moment before turning and looking over the hall. Her eyes met John's, then looked him up and down, her expression changing to disapproval as she observed his non-regulation clothing. John smiled and waved, then looked down, adjusted his cushion, and sat down. When he looked up again, he could see Gayatri glaring at him with undisguised contempt.

The side door opened, and her face transformed from one of intense dislike to the exact opposite. She raised her right hand to her chest, and a smile spread across her face, her body visibly relaxing. John chuckled and wriggled a little, trying to find the most comfortable spot on the cushion, his eyes still on the show on stage. Gayatri's smile faltered a little as one of the Sri Lankan girls walked out, but she recovered and nodded a greeting as the young girl sat down next to Atman's chair.

John waited, but the next figure through the door was Georges, who stood back as he had done the previous evening as Atman followed him through. John sighed as everyone stood again. He had just gotten comfortable.

Atman didn't wave to the crowd this time, moving quickly to his chair and sitting. Georges placed the shawl on his shoulders, and Gayatri hurried over with the tray and water glass in what appeared to be a regular routine. John moved slightly so he could see past the man in front of him and watched Gayatri's face drop as Atman dismissed the offered glass with a wave. She backed away as Atman closed his eyes. He still hadn't said anything, and the students in the hall remained standing, waiting. After a moment, he blinked his eyes open, almost surprised that everyone was still standing and gestured for them to sit.

It took a minute for everyone to settle, Atman watching, his face expressionless. Once the hall was still, he closed his eyes again.

"Sit up straight and close your eyes." His voice was commanding and forceful in the silence of the hall. John ignored the instruction and continued watching the stage. There were two things different from the previous evening. This morning, only one girl sat at Atman's feet, and Georges was no longer on the stage.

———

John couldn't get into it.

Atman's voice filled the hall with instructions as he guided the students into a meditative state, but it was just background noise to John. His mind raced back and forth, wondering about the missing Sri Lankan girl. Was the one he saw last night the one who was missing? What was she doing out at night, anyway? Had she been crying? How about Atman? His mood seemed off this morning. Where had Georges gone? So many questions. Eventually John gave up and opened his eyes.

He looked over at Maruti, who sat completely still, his back straight, his face a mask of contentment. John looked back to the front. Atman's eyes were closed, his face relaxed, his verbal instructions becoming slower, the gaps between them longer, his voice lower. To John's right and a couple of rows ahead, one of the men started shaking, let out a gasp, then his body stilled again. Someone on the left giggled, then burst out laughing. No-one paid her any attention, and after a minute, she lapsed into silence again.

John sighed, adjusted his position, and closed his eyes again. Perhaps he was just imagining things, projecting his own frustration and irritation, making up stories in his head. Maybe there was only ever one girl in the morning. Maybe the other one was up late, so she slept in. Perhaps they did shifts. And Atman, maybe he wasn't a morning person.

John took a deep breath, held it for a count of three, and slowly exhaled. He may as well try to get something out of the retreat. He scanned his body, relaxing each muscle from the top of his head, working his way down to the tips of his toes. He slowed his breathing, trying to remember the instructions Atman had given the previous evening. Every time his mind wandered, he brought his attention back to his breathing. Slowly but steadily, he stopped being aware of the physical sensations in his body, the hardness of the floor against his ankles, the stiffness around his left shoulder blade. It was still there, but it didn't seem to affect him, as though he was observing the sensations from outside his body. His breathing slowed on its own until it was barely noticeable, and he felt his head slump forward.

"Slowly come back, move your fingers and toes..."

What? John frowned, lifted his head up, but kept his eyes closed. Was that it? He had just started to feel like he was getting it. Why did the session end so quickly?

"Rub your palms together, place them over your face, and slowly open your eyes."

John blinked his eyes open, still irritated, and looked toward the stage just as Atman opened his eyes. He looked straight at John and nodded.

What was that about? John exhaled, rolled his shoulders back, and stretched his legs out, rubbing his calves as the blood rushed back toward his feet. He took a quick look at his watch, then looked again. It was seven am. He'd been sitting for two hours.

36

J ohn rose with the rest of the students as Atman stood and made his way out the side door. He felt a little spaced out and would have killed for a coffee. He was still confused about the meditation. Had he fallen asleep? How else could he account for the loss of time? He studied the faces of the student. What did they experience? Some looked blissed-out, while others, mainly the women, avoided eye contact as if a look from him would sully their reputations or deny them a place in heaven.

As soon as the side door closed behind Atman, the students began talking among themselves and moving toward the rear door.

Gayatri moved to the front of the stage, held up her hands, and called out, "One moment, please." All heads turned toward the stage, and she waited until the hall was quiet again. "Atman has requested that for the next five days, we observe silence wherever possible. He wants us to focus on and observe our internal dialogues and not to be distracted by external conversation."

John could see heads nodding in agreement as if what she was saying made perfect sense. He held up his hand.

"Yes, Mr. Hayes."

"John, please call me John."

Gayatri didn't reply, her mouth set in a thin straight line.

"How are we supposed to communicate?"

"Communication must be kept to a minimum."

"But..."

"That will be all, Mr. Hayes. Can you please stay behind? I wish to speak with you privately."

John shrugged and looked at the people around him as they turned to leave. Not a single person met his eye, all avoiding him except for the German lady, Katrina, who gave him a warm smile as she passed.

John waited until the hall emptied, just a few people remaining, then made his way to the stage. Gayatri was talking to one of the students, gesturing toward the altar but stopped when she saw John approach. She walked to the back of the stage and came back with a pile of folded white clothing.

"Good morning, Gayatri," John greeted her cheerily. Gayatri glared for a moment, then thrust the clothing at him.

"We require you to wear these for the meditation."

"We?"

Gayatri cleared her throat. "Atman."

John looked down at the white shirt and pants she had given him, then looked up, smiling broadly.

"Thank you very much."

"Mr. Hayes..."

"John."

Gayatri's mouth twisted. "Can you please change before attending breakfast?"

"Of course. Will you be joining us?"

"Do I have to remind you to keep communication to an absolute minimum?"

"Not at all." John made as if to zip his lips shut and winked. He turned around and walked toward the rear of the hall, a big grin on his face. He was enjoying needling Gayatri.

37

Back in the room, John could hear water splashing in the bathroom, so he stripped off and changed into the white clothing Gayatri had given him. The pants were too short, as were the sleeves, leaving his wrists and ankles exposed, and when he moved his arms around, the shirt stretched taut across the shoulders. He was still rolling his shoulders back and forth when he heard a chuckle behind him. He turned to see Maruti standing in the bathroom doorway, drying his hair with a thin cotton towel.

"One of the side effects of meditation is that you get taller."

"Very funny."

"I'll find you something that fits. I think I have something here." He dropped the towel on the bed, opened a drawer in the cabinet beside his bed, and pulled out another shirt. "Try this." He tossed it over to John, then rummaged around until he found a pair of pants. "These should fit. We're a similar height."

"Thanks. Gayatri obviously doesn't know my size."

"Huh," Maruti scoffed. "I'm sure she knows your size very well."

John arched an eyebrow, wondering if Maruti would elaborate, but when he remained silent, John nodded and went into the bathroom to change. The clothing fit much better. He folded the other clothing before walking out.

"What do I do with these?"

Maruti was sitting at the end of the bed in a patch of sun streaming in through the open door. He nodded toward the bed beside him. "Leave it here. I'll sort it out."

"Thanks." John placed the clothing on the bed, then stood staring out door, his hands on his hips. He hesitated, then just as he opened his mouth to speak, Maruti said, "You're doing fine, don't worry about it."

"Ahhh... I'm sorry?"

"Your meditation. It's fine. Don't stress. Let it happen."

John frowned. That wasn't what he was going to ask, but while they were on the subject. "I think I fell asleep."

Maruti grunted. "Everyone does. Even Atman."

"Really?"

"Yup. Sometimes he snores like a freight train."

"Oh." John scratched his head. "But..."

Maruti looked up at John, "I told you he's not God, didn't I."

John nodded. He had, and John agreed with him. What was God, anyway? That led to another question.

"Then why do—"

"People worship him?" Maruti shrugged, then leaned against the wall and stretched his legs out, crossing them at the ankle. "People always want to believe in something outside themselves when the real power is actually within them."

John nodded slowly, moved over to his bed, and sat

down. "So..." He searched for the right way to say it, cautious of offending Maruti. "Is Atman a genuine... ahh... teacher?"

Maruti stared at John, his eyes unblinking. Despite his advanced years, his eyes were clear and intense, his gaze unwavering. John forced himself to maintain eye contact for as long as possible, but in the end, looked away.

"Oh, he's a genuine teacher, alright, but he's human."

The last comment made John look back, but Maruti was gazing out the doorway again.

"The two Sri Lankan girls, Maruti, on the stage."

Maruti nodded slightly.

"Who are they?"

"Atman says this life is their last incarnation. That they won't be born again. When they leave this body, they will ascend."

"Ascend where?"

"I'm still trying to find out myself." Maruti shrugged and chuckled at the same time.

John fiddled with the edge of his bedsheet while he thought over what he'd just heard.

"How does he know?"

Maruti sighed. "You have a lot of questions today."

"Sorry, but I'm curious."

"Hmmm." Maruti said nothing for a while, and John thought he had pushed too far. Eventually Maruti said, "He told us he had a vision during meditation, and after that, he searched the countryside until he found them. Apparently, if he hadn't, they would have lived an ordinary life, never realizing their potential. All their previous lifetimes of spiritual practice would have been wasted."

"So, he saved them."

"Yes."

"You believe that?"

Maruti turned to look at John again, and John once more was struck by the intensity of his gaze. Maruti said nothing, then smiled and looked away.

"I saw one of them last night while you were sleeping."

Maruti remained silent.

"Outside here, on the path."

Now he turned to look at John again, waiting for him to continue.

"I couldn't sleep and was looking out the window, one-thirty, maybe a little later, when I saw her coming from up there." John pointed toward Atman's bungalow.

Maruti didn't comment, his expression giving no clue as to his thoughts.

"I think she was crying."

Maruti still said nothing.

"And she wasn't on stage this morning."

Finally, Maruti nodded. He shifted forward on the bed and leaned on his hands, turning his head to look out the open doorway. John waited for an answer, a comment, anything, but Maruti remained silent. Eventually, John heard him sigh, and he stood up.

"Come. Breakfast should be ready."

38

G ayatri seemed disappointed when John walked into the dining hall. She was by the serving hatch, supervising the distribution of the food. Looking him up and down as he found an empty seat, she frowned, then turned back to the hatch. John pretended not to notice.

He nodded a greeting at the man sitting next to him as Maruti sat opposite.

A volunteer placed a plate of steaming hot rice noodles and a bowl of potato curry in front of him, and John waited until Maruti was also served before he started eating. The food was delicious, but John was so hungry, he would have eaten anything. Once he was halfway through the plate, he thought back to his discussion earlier. He wanted to question Maruti further, but when he looked up and opened his mouth to speak, Maruti shook his head.

Immediately after breakfast, John was assigned to washing dishes in the kitchen and didn't see Maruti again until the eleven a.m. meditation. This time, Atman was escorted onto the stage by the young, well-built man John had met near the bungalow, Georges nowhere to be seen. Neither was the Sri Lankan girl.

John struggled through the meditation, unable to relax or get comfortable. The hall was hot and stuffy, the midday sun beating down on the roof, and the ceiling fans did little to dispel the accumulated body heat inside. John grew increasingly irritated and fidgety, and the end couldn't have come quick enough. As soon as Atman told them to open their eyes, John grabbed his cushion and was out of the hall as fast as his numb right leg could carry him.

A black mood descended, and he didn't even wait for Maruti. What was he even doing there? It was all a waste of time and would never change the things he had done. All the other students, except perhaps Maruti, were a bunch of loonies. He stood in the middle of the pathway, undecided. He wanted to walk, but which way? He chose right and walked off as the door opened behind him and the other students started to come out. Walking down past the dining hall, he paused outside the administration building. He peered in the window, but there was no-one inside, and the door was closed. Attendance at the meditation appeared to be mandatory for everyone.

He walked on toward the gate. With the guardhouse door open, he could see the guard napping inside. John ignored him, pulled the gate open, and walked out, turning right toward the main road. He was perhaps twenty meters down the road when he heard a shout.

"Sir, where are you going?"

John didn't bother turning around, just raised a hand in the air to show he'd heard and kept walking. He was a free man. He could go where he wanted.

He walked to where the lane joined the main road and stood at the junction. There was no-one around, no sound of traffic, no sign of any other humans. The only sound was that of cicadas buzzing away in the trees. A trickle of sweat ran down the side of John's face, and he looked up at the sky. There was no wind, and the sun was burning into the top of his head. John looked around and found a patch of shade. Clearing the ground, he sat with his back against a tree. His stomach rumbled, and he was thirsty. He couldn't believe he had paid five thousand dollars to sit on a hard floor for hours at an end, half-starved on lentils, and not even be able to have a decent coffee or even a nice, chilled glass of gin and tonic.

His mouth watered, and he closed his eyes, visualizing rivulets of condensation running down the side of a large glass of gin. He imagined tilting the glass, hearing the clink of ice cubes as they touched the side of the glass, the slightly bitter taste of quinine in the tonic, the fragrant botanicals in the gin, the coolness of the liquid flowing down his throat. He smiled, his eyes still closed, and giggled—giggled, not chuckled. He could see himself doing it as if there were two Johns, and the other John was definitely giggling. The giggling intensified, and his shoulders shook as it turned into laughter. Throwing his head back, he laughed out loud, his eyes still closed, a part of him still separate, observing what was happening to him. Then the laughing subsided, and he began to sob.

An overwhelming sense of grief filled his being as tears streamed down his face. Faces flashed across the screen behind his eyelids—they seemed familiar as if he should know who they were but not clear enough to be sure. As each one appeared and disappeared, he felt as if a layer of skin was being shed from his body, and he felt lighter, younger... clearer. He stopped crying as the faces slowed, then disappeared altogether.

He sat motionless, unable to move, unable to open his eyes, though a part of him was still observing. It noticed now that he was empty—empty of a weight he had been carrying around for years without realizing.

Another face formed in his mind's eye. The light was softer, warmer, and seemed to be filled with emotion. Was it love? It was a face he had not seen in a long time—too long—a face he thought he would never see again. "Charlotte," he whispered out loud. She smiled, then slowly faded away.

John's eyes blinked open, and it took him a moment to get his bearings. He was still sitting on the side of the road under a tree. What had just happened? Had he imagined it? Did he have a heat stroke?

He took a deep breath, then stood up, steadying himself against the tree when a wave of dizziness threatened to overcome him. He shook his arms and legs, tipped his head from side to side, and took another long deep breath. When he exhaled, a broad grin spread across his face. Whatever had happened, he now felt fantastic!

---

ohn walked back in the direction of the ashram, gazing around him at the trees, the plants, the sky. The colors seemed clearer, more vibrant. Even the barbed wire on top of the ashram fence seemed to sparkle in the sunlight. Had they put something in the food? His stomach growled. No, he hadn't eaten enough food. Maybe he was delusional because of hunger, or it was an allergic reaction to lentils.

Reaching the gate, he slid it open, stepped inside, waved to the guard, and kept on walking. He couldn't wait to share his experience with someone—Maruti, maybe even Sarah— then remembered the new rule about remaining silent, and his shoulders sagged.

He passed the admin block, the door now open, walked around the corner, and as he passed the window, he heard someone tapping on the glass. He stopped, turned to look, and saw Gayatri gesturing at him. Walking over, he waited until she opened the window wide and gave her a huge grin.

"Isn't it a wonderful day, Gayatri?"

She blinked in surprise, then reaffixed the frown she

seemed to reserve for John. She held her index finger in front of her lips, reminding him to be quiet.

"Atman wants to see you. Up at the house."

"Really?"

Her face tightened, and her lips pinched together.

"Yes."

John grinned and leaned closer. "Don't worry. I'll tell him how much you've been looking after me."

Gayatri blinked in surprise, then her face flushed. Before she could say anything, John turned and walked down the path, the grin fading from his face, his feelings of joy and peacefulness evaporating. What did Atman want with him? John thought over his actions since he had arrived. Had he done something he shouldn't have?

John frowned and shook his head even though he was alone. No, he'd not done anything wrong, and if it was because he had gone for a walk outside, he would have a thing or two to say about that. He was here of his own free will and could leave of his own free will. It wasn't a boarding school. He passed the dining hall, now full of the students, and his stomach rumbled again. Hopefully, Atman would give him something to eat.

As John passed through the stand of trees and climbed the gentle slope toward the house, a figure in white appeared on the top step.

How the hell did they always know he was coming?

As he got closer, he saw it was the young man he had seen the day before and on stage this morning. John studied him more closely. He had broad shoulders, his face was lean, and his hair cropped short at the back and sides, almost a military haircut. He looked nothing like the other students John had seen. The man nodded as John reached the bottom step.

"Atman is expecting you. Please come in." Standing back, he gestured with his left hand for John to come inside.

John climbed the steps, noticing the security camera above the entrance. Now he knew how they saw him coming. He gave the empty verandah a quick scan—no furniture or artwork, just the hanging baskets of flowers and... the small black dome of a camera at each corner of the ceiling. John entered the house and paused just inside the door. The layout was similar to Robert's bungalow in Galle, with a seating area on the left and a dining area on the right. However, unlike Robert's home, which had been filled with furniture, artifacts, and artwork collected over a lifetime of work and travel, this area was stark and more functional. On the rear wall of the sitting area was a large smiling portrait of Atman. A garland of flowers hung from the frame, and three sticks of incense smouldered in a brass holder on a table beneath it.

A large armchair, a twin of the one on the stage, was set at the far left of the room, with two sofas positioned at right angles. The sofas and armchair were white, as were the walls. Apart from Atman's portrait and the flowers, an expensive-looking Persian rug, which covered most of the wooden floor, was the only other hint of color in the room.

"Please take a seat." The young man gestured toward the sofas. "Atman will be with you shortly."

"Thank you." John moved to the sofa and sat down. The man was still watching him, and John smiled. "What is your name?"

"Max."

"Max? You don't have a... ahhh... spiritual name."

"Just Max."

"I'm John, just John."

"Yes."

John gave up trying to make conversation and leaned back on the sofa, making himself comfortable. Max stayed in the space between the sitting area and the dining area, his back to the hallway, legs slightly apart, his hands held together in front of him.

John stared at him, and he looked away, focusing on a spot on the wall. After a minute, he stepped to one side at some unseen command, and Atman appeared in the hallway. He beamed at John and raised his hands.

"John, why are you sitting there?" He nodded toward the dining table. "Come, have lunch with me."

"Thank you." John smiled and stood.

"Max, have another place set for John."

"Yes, sir." Max backed away, then turned and walked over to the kitchen, disappearing inside.

Atman waited for John to join him by the doorway, then reached out for his hand, taking it in both of his. He tilted his head to one side and stared into John's eyes. He said nothing for a moment, his face serious, and then he nodded. "You are making progress. Good." He let go of John's hand and waved toward the dining table, where an elderly Sri Lankan man was setting two plates with cutlery to match.

"Have a seat. You must be hungry."

"Very."

Atman chuckled. "We keep the meals smaller. I don't want people falling asleep when they should be meditating." He winked at John. "Don't worry, here you can eat as much as you like. Duminda here is an excellent cook, isn't that right, Duminda?"

Duminda looked up from the table and bobbed his head, said, "Yes, sir," then slipped away past Max, who was standing in the kitchen doorway.

"That will be all, Max."

"Yes, sir." Max nodded and retreated into the kitchen as John pulled out a chair and sat down.

John waited for Atman to sit opposite him.

"Bodyguard?"

Atman nodded and sighed. "Yes. I know it seems over the top, but sometimes, people feel my personal time belongs to them."

"Really?" John raised his eyebrows. "You've had problems?"

"Nothing for you to worry about, John." Atman waved away the question. "Now, tell me about you." He leaned forward and fixed John with his piercing gaze. "You seem... lighter."

John reached for the water jug and poured himself a glass, giving himself time to respond. He offered to fill Atman's, but he shook his head, his eyes still fixed on John. John took a sip, set the glass down, and sat back.

"It's going okay."

"That's not an answer."

John sighed and looked down at the tabletop, tapped the wooden surface with his fingers, then looked up.

"Okay, I'll tell you the truth."

Atman nodded, his face still serious.

"Yesterday, I was extremely uncomfortable. I lost the feeling in my toes, my shoulder ached, and I was bored. This morning, I fell asleep, and just now, in the last session, I was angry."

Atman nodded, the hint of a smile in the corners of his mouth. "And?"

John made a face and shrugged. "And nothing."

"John," Atman admonished. "You said you would tell the truth."

John frowned. What truth did he mean? That he still

didn't trust him? That he was sure something fishy was going on? That he thought many of the students were nice but delusional? He reached forward for his glass and took another sip.

"I know you felt it. I can see it in your eyes."

Ah, that.

"Yes, I felt something, but not during the meditation."

"John, it doesn't matter where it happens." Atman shrugged and sat back, a pleased smile on his face. "It matters that it does."

Duminda walked out with a large bowl of rice and another bowl filled with a fragrant curry.

Atman smiled at him, then nodded to John. "Please help yourself."

John loaded up his plate, waited for Atman to do the same, then picked up his spoon. Before he could take a bite, Atman asked, "So explain to me what happened."

John paused, his spoon close to his mouth. Where should he start? How much could he tell him? He spooned the curry into his mouth to give him time to think. He had no intention of sharing his past, the things he had seen and done with someone he hardly knew or didn't really trust, but he wanted to understand what he had experienced. He chewed his food, swallowed, and nodded his approval to Atman.

"Delicious. Much better than what we are eating down there." He jerked his head in the direction of the dining hall.

Atman burst out laughing.

John took another mouthful of food, avoiding answering the question for as long as he could.

"I like you, John. You are not afraid to say what you mean."

John grunted, his mouth still full of food.

"Most people who come to see me, they..." He shrugged. "They tell me what they think I want to hear or what they think is the right thing to say."

John swallowed and studied Atman's face for a moment. He looked almost wistful.

"Are they afraid of you?"

"No." He shook his head and gazed down at his plate. "It's not that. It's more like..."

"They want to impress you."

Atman's head snapped up. "Yes." He nodded vigorously. "They think I will judge them by what they say." He spread his hands, his spoon dripping curry onto the tabletop. "I love everyone equally. I don't judge people by their actions but by their hearts."

John loaded his spoon again, then asked, "How can you know what's in their hearts?"

"When you meditate deeply, John, your mind clears of all the dross that stops you from truly seeing."

John thought about this while he chewed.

"Okay, let's say I believe you..."

Atman started laughing again.

John waited until he stopped.

"Let's say I believe you," he repeated. "That's what's happening to you. What about the others? People have been laughing, crying, and shaking while meditating in the hall."

Atman nodded, his expression serious again.

"If I'm honest," John continued, "I've not heard you say anything I couldn't download on a meditation app or see on YouTube. You know, a couple of times, I've thought I could have saved myself five thousand dollars and done this at home."

Atman looked amused and made a dismissive gesture with his hand. "The money is not important, John. Don't focus on it. I don't need it. It doesn't interest me. And you are right. Everything I teach can be had for free."

"Then why charge? You can't tell me it costs you that much to run this place."

"Energy, John. It's all energy."

John arched his eyebrows and waited for Atman to explain.

"The money makes the students feel invested and ensures they value the teachings I give them. If I didn't charge, they wouldn't take things as seriously."

John leaned back in his chair and crossed his arms, making no effort to hide his skepticism.

"I know you don't believe me, but it's true." Atman smiled. "Think of,"—he looked around the room—"a car, for example. You buy a cheap car. What's the world's cheapest car... that Indian one?"

"Tata Nano."

"Yes. It costs what, two thousand, three thousand dollars?"

John nodded.

"Okay, now name an expensive car."

"Porsche 911."

"Good. Now, they both do the same thing, right? Admittedly, the technology is different, the materials are better quality, but at the end of the day, they both basically do the same thing. They are a form of transport. Yes or no?"

John moved his head side to side as if weighing up the argument and grudgingly agreed. "Yes, I suppose so."

"But one is valued more, right? If you had both in your garage, you would take much more care of one than the other? Treat one as more precious than the other?"

John nodded.

"Now that rather crude example is what I'm getting at. I

need to charge a fee. Yes, it's much more than the actual costs to run this place, but I want serious students, who will come here, learn, then put my teachings into practice."

"It's almost a hundred thousand Sri Lankan rupees, so you are obviously aiming at westerners. Locals can't afford that."

"Locals can attend for free."

John suppressed a frown at this contradictory statement. Locals valued the teachings if it was free? John spotted an opening.

"The two Sri Lankan girls, on the stage?"

Atman's eyebrow twitched, but then he smiled.

"Ah, my two young protégés. I found them, you know." He looked proud of himself. "In their village. No-one there even knew their potential, but they are very advanced beings." His face became serious. "This is their last incarnation. They are ready to ascend."

John watched his face, not sure if he was serious. He gave him the benefit of the doubt.

"Ascend?"

Nodding, Atman put down his spoon, leaned his elbows on the table, and steepled his fingers in front of his chin.

"Do you believe in God, John?"

"No."

"Why not?"

John exhaled. "If there was a God, the shitty things that go on the world wouldn't happen. I think God is just a concept people made up because they want to believe in something bigger than themselves."

"And heaven is just a concept as well?"

"I believe so. Have you met anyone who has been there and came back with proof?"

"Ha!" Atman laughed and sat back in his chair. "You are

right, John." Atman studied him for a moment. "When I say ascend, I'm not talking about heaven. I am talking about energy and vibrations. These two girls have reached such a high vibrational frequency, they will no longer have the need for the human body. They will shed this physical form and ascend to a higher plane."

John shoveled another spoonful of curry into his mouth before he could say anything rude. The guy was a nutcase.

Atman watched John chew his food.

"I'm sure you don't believe me, but that's okay. You see, you asked me earlier about the people crying, laughing, and shaking in the hall. That's all energy. The three of us on the stage... through our deep meditation, we raise the frequency in the room, freeing all of you from the mental blocks, prejudices, and misconceptions you store in your subconscious. The crying, laughing, physical movements... those are all blockages dissolving, releasing... freeing you to realize your true self."

John put down his spoon, picked up his napkin, and wiped his mouth, then sat back in his chair and slowly nodded as if agreeing.

"It doesn't matter if you don't believe me." Atman smiled. "Ask yourself this. How do you explain the experience you had? Today, while sitting under the tree beside the road?"

John looked up with a start. "How did you know that?"

Atman's smile widened. "I told you. I can see things."

40

J ohn slowly walked away from the bungalow, his brow wrinkled, deep in thought. He'd wanted to take the conversation further, but Max had entered the room and whispered something in Atman's ear.

Atman excused himself, followed by Max, leaving John alone in the room. He hadn't even been able to ask more about the Sri Lankan girls. What were their names? Where did they stay?

After sitting alone for five minutes with no sign of Atman returning, or indeed anyone else, John got up and made his way back to the dormitory.

The fact was, John was confused. Atman was a charming, charismatic person, easy to talk to, comfortable to be around, but some things he said made John doubt his sanity.

John had a deep-felt mistrust of anything to do with religion. He had seen it cause so many problems in the world. All it seemed to do was create division. Despite Atman talking about all being equal in his eyes, the men and women were segregated, and all had to wear white. His justification for charging high fees for his retreats was utter nonsense. John was convinced it was all a moneymaking racket, and there was much more going on than met the eye. The security cameras, his bodyguard, the secrecy... it didn't add up.

He walked on a bit further.

But then, if the guy was a fraud, how did John explain what he'd experienced? The loss of time could be explained away by falling asleep. In fact, he was sure that was all that happened. But today, under the tree? What was that? Had he been dehydrated? He needed to find Maruti. He was the only one who might give him an honest opinion.

The men's dormitory block was deserted, and John's room was empty, so he walked to the dining hall. The hall looked quiet as he approached, and he checked his watch. Lunch had been over for thirty minutes, which meant the students had dispersed for their service assignments. John couldn't remember what his was and couldn't be bothered to find out. This whole selfless service thing was nonsense, too. What better way to keep running costs down than to convince your students that doing the work for free would help their progress. That way, the retreat center didn't need staff and could still charge the students for their attendance. It was pure profit for Atman.

John kicked off his shoes and jogged up the steps into the hall.

That was probably the real reason for serving small vegetarian meals. Why spend money on meat when you didn't have to? John smiled. It was the perfect business model, only bettered by a fasting retreat. There you paid and didn't get any food. John chuckled as he crossed the empty hall to look at the roster on the notice board next to the serving hatch. He ran his finger down the list until he found Maruti's name, then across to the column for the afternoon. *Laundry.*

John bent down, poked his head through the hatch, and looked into the kitchen. A student was washing the dishes, while another stacked them in a stainless-steel draining rack. Another was spraying the worktops with something and wiping them down.

"Excuse me, where's the laundry?" he called out.

The student with the spray bottle, a man of about John's age, looked up in surprise.

"We're not supposed to be talking."

"I know, but where's the laundry?"

The student sighed, looked at the others, then replied, "Back near the office."

"By the gate?"

"Yeah..." The man frowned. "Aren't you John? You're supposed to be helping us in here, brother."

John made a sympathetic face. "I'm sorry... ahhh... brother. I was just with Atman. Something's come up."

At the sound of Atman's name, the man's face relaxed, and the two doing dishes turned around to look.

"No worries, no worries," the man said. "We'll manage."

John winked. "Thank you."

He pulled his head out from the hatch, straightened, and headed off in search of the laundry.

41

"Atman is very pleased with you."

Gayatri's head jerked up in surprise. She turned to look at John, standing in the open doorway of the office building.

"Oh." She blushed.

John gave her a big smile. "He told me he couldn't manage without you."

"Really? He said that?"

"Yes. Just now. We had lunch together."

"Oh."

John nodded, still smiling. "Hey, where's the laundry?"

"I can show you." Gayatri pushed back her chair and stood, all smiles.

"No, no, it's okay." John held up his hands. "I know how busy you are. Just point me in the right direction."

"Sure." She hurried over to the door, and John stepped back outside. She followed him out and said, "Follow the path behind this building. The first building you come to is the laundry."

"Thank you, Gayatri. Will I see you in the evening meditation?"

Gayatri's face reddened even more. "Yes, of course."

"Great. See you later. Oops, I'm sorry, I forgot we're not supposed to be talking."

Gayatri smiled and waved away his apology. "It's okay. I won't tell anyone."

John winked, then turned away to follow the path. As he turned the corner, he looked back to see her still standing at the entrance, a big smile on her face. Following her directions, he headed behind the building, along the stone path lined by low cut hedgerows, past a small orchard of fruit trees on the right, and on the left, some disused sheds until he came to another longer stone-walled building. Rows of washing lines filled with white clothing fluttered in the breeze in front of it, and he could hear the hum of machinery through the wide-open doorway. The building looked as if it must have been a garage for farm vehicles at one stage but was now filled with banks of washing machines, tumble dryers, and a couple industrial clothes presses.

There were four women working away, all with their backs to him, but there was no sign of Maruti.

"Excuse me," he called loudly enough to be heard above the hum of the machines. All the women turned around, a mixture of expressions on their faces—surprise, annoyance, indifference. "I'm looking for Maruti."

One woman pointed to an open door at the end of the shed, then turned back to the bundle of white clothing she was stuffing into a washing machine.

John walked through the shed to the open door and poked his head inside. Maruti was standing with a clipboard in one hand and a pencil in the other, counting a pile of shirts on a rack of shelves that took up the entire back wall.

"No rest for the wicked."

Maruti looked back over his shoulder and half-smiled. "You seem to be doing alright."

John shrugged and walked inside.

"I didn't see you at lunch." Maruti continued, writing a number on his clipboard.

John leaned against the wall. "Yeah, Atman wanted to see me."

Maruti's eyebrows lifted in surprise. "Really? Why?"

John glanced out the door and saw one of the women watching them. "Hey, can we go somewhere a little more private? I have lots to talk about."

"We're not supposed to be talking."

"You're not supposed to be working with women."

"Ha!"

"I'm serious. I need to talk to you about something."

Maruti turned to look back into the laundry, then nodded. "What time is it?"

"Two-thirty."

"Can you come back in half an hour?" He gestured with his clipboard. "I have some work to finish up."

John shook his head and gave a wry smile. "Why don't you take a break?"

"Someone has to keep you in clean clothes."

"Yeah," John sighed. "I suppose you're right. Okay. I'll meet you here in thirty minutes. Wait for me."

Maruti nodded, then frowned, "Aren't you supposed to be doing service?"

John grinned. "I'm skipping that part of the program."

Maruti chuckled and shook his head. "I'll see you soon." He turned away from John and started counting another pile of clothing. John watched him for a moment, then walked out the door. There was something he needed to check on.

He walked back down the path toward the gate, passing the office building and ducking under the window to avoid being seen by Gayatri. Crossing the car park, he noted the Range Rover had returned. Dust covered the sides and back, and the front was splattered with insects as if the vehicle had been driven far and fast. John hurried past toward the gate, slipping outside before the guard could see him.

When he reached the junction, he turned left and walked over to the tree he had sat under earlier. He turned around and looked back at the junction. From his vantage point, he had an unobstructed view of the road, the entrance to the lane, and the ashram fence. John nodded to himself, walked back toward the fence, and looked up at the steel post on the corner. On top of the post were three security cameras, one pointing in each direction of the fence, the other pointing toward the road junction. John grinned. He turned around, and with his back to the fence, faced in the same direction as the camera. He had a clear view of the junction and the tree beyond. John's grin widened, and he shook his head.

"Got you."

Thirty minutes later, John stood behind a fruit tree in the orchard. He was far enough back from the path to avoid being seen by a casual observer but still had a reasonable line of sight to the path. At three thirty-five, three of the women walked past, heading to their dormitory. Five minutes later, one more walked past. John waited until she was out of sight before skirting his way between the trees and stepping over the low hedgerow onto the path.

Maruti was standing in the doorway to the laundry, leaning against the doorframe with his arms folded,

watching John approach, a half-smile on his face.

"What took you so long?"

John grinned, "I wanted to make sure your guardians had left." He peered past him into the laundry. "You are alone, right?"

"Yes." Maruti watched him quizzically, waiting for John to continue.

"I had a weird experience."

"During the meditation?"

John shook his head. "No, it was on the road outside the ashram."

"Outside on the road?" Maruti raised an eyebrow.

"Yeah." John explained what had happened, starting with his anger and irritability during the meditation and ending with his summons to meet Atman upon his return to the ashram.

"Okay," Maruti replied slowly, then placed a hand on John's shoulder. "Let's go for a walk."

Maruti stepped out of the doorway and turned left, leading John along the path away from the laundry, deeper into the property. The stone path ended and became a single file dirt track through the tea bushes and regenerating jungle. This part of the ashram was overgrown and untended, and despite the faint trail they were following, it looked like it hadn't been visited for some time. Maruti kept walking until he found a clearing, where he cleared a patch of ground in the shade of a tree, sat down, and crossed his legs, waiting for John to join him.

"Don't worry, no-one comes here. It's my secret haven." He waited for John to make himself comfortable on the ground. "So tell me what he said."

"Well, he held my hand, looked into my eyes, and told me he knew I had an experience. When I asked him how, he said he had seen me."

"Seen you?"

"Yes. He hinted that because of his meditation, he can see things."

Maruti nodded, plucked a stalk of grass, and twisted it between his fingers as he stared across the ashram grounds.

"The thing is," John continued, "I went and checked. There's a security camera pointing at the spot where I was sitting, so that's how he saw me."

"Ha," Maruti scoffed. "You're a suspicious one, aren't you?"

"Yup."

"But then,"—Maruti looked back at John—"how would he know you'd experienced something? All he would have seen is you sitting under a tree."

John studied Maruti's face, wondering what he was thinking, but the old man's expression gave nothing away. Eventually, John nodded.

"I've thought about that. I think he's bluffing."

"What do you mean?"

"I think he just threw it out there, gambling there was a good chance I'd agree. Think about when people visit fortune-tellers. Half the time, the fortune-tellers say something vague, the person qualifies what they said and feeds them more information, which in turn, provides the fortune teller with more material."

"Hmmm," Maruti nodded, still watching John.

"I've been in three meditations, then I sat under a tree for some time with my eyes closed. Chances are, I might have felt something or thought about something, and all he has to do is say I have, and I will find ways to agree."

Maruti remained silent.

John continued, reinforcing his theory. "Look, please don't take this the wrong way. I know you're a resident here, and it's not my intention to offend you, but I feel I can be honest with you."

Maruti half-smiled. "It sounds like you are about to insult me."

"No, not at all." John quickly shook his head. "What I mean to say is most of the people here think he's some sort of superior being. If he tells them they have experienced something, do you think they will contradict him? Even if they haven't, they'll think it's their fault, not his. That they are doing something wrong."

"Hmmm."

"So, isn't it just psychology and manipulation?"

Maruti nodded slowly and plucked another stem of grass, breaking it into pieces, still silent. Eventually, he looked up.

"But you felt something."

"Yes," John sighed. "That's the only hole in my theory."

Maruti sighed loudly. "Look, John, I'm no expert, but you need to focus on your own experience. Did you feel something? Did it help you? Do you think if you explore it further, it will be useful? If the answer is yes, then continue. If not, forget about it and try something else. Everything else is noise."

John thought about that for a moment. "But what if I imagined the whole thing?"

"It happened, right?"

"I think so."

Maruti turned and looked directly at John, his eyes wide and intensely focused.

"What happened was a mystical experience, John. It will happen to you more and more as you progress. Don't dismiss it." He continued staring at John, then blinked, smiled, and looked away.

John still had so many questions, but he wasn't sure how far he could push his new friend. Leaning back on his elbows, he looked at the sky. A solitary wisp of white was the only thing he could see in the vast expanse of blue above him. Suddenly, he felt very small.

"When I came here almost four years ago, I was just like you," Maruti said after a while, still gazing out into the trees. "I didn't want to come here. I thought these people were all cracked in the head." He shook his head. "I was a surfer and wanted to spend all my time down on the coast." He paused, and a slight smile spread across his face. "There's something magical about being out on the board, surrounded by the ocean, no distractions, no noise. Nothing else matters." He turned to look at John and shrugged. "But Matilda insisted. She really wanted to come here, and I would have done anything for her." His smile faded, and he looked away.

John didn't know how to respond, so he remained silent, hoping Maruti would continue.

After a while, the old man chuckled. "My name was Will then. William Carruthers." He lapsed back into silence.

"So, what happened? Why did you stay?" John prompted when it seemed he wouldn't continue.

Maruti sighed. "At first, it was because of Matilda. She loved it here. The lifestyle, the practice, the people we met. She loved Atman, too, and he was fond of her."

John sat up and picked up a pebble from near his leg, flicking it into the undergrowth.

"Then she got sick..." Maruti shrugged and sighed again.

"You... didn't think about leaving... I mean after...?"

"No." Maruti shook his head. "Where would I go?"

John stared at the ground, filled with a deep sadness. What would he do if suddenly Adriana wasn't in his life anymore? He felt a lump in his throat.

"That's not why I'm telling you this."

John looked up to see Maruti looking at him.

"The thing is, the longer I stayed here, the more I followed the teachings, the deeper my own meditations became. The experiences I had surpassed anything I ever felt while surfing." He smiled, but it was tinged with sadness. "It helped me a lot when Matilda passed."

John reached out and placed a comforting hand on

Maruti's knee, smiling with just his mouth, then took his hand away.

"I don't know why you have come here, John." He shrugged. "I don't need to know. But if the universe has conspired to put you in this place at this time, there has to be a reason. You must have a need for the things you'll learn here."

John chewed his lip and squinted at the sun. Perhaps Maruti was right. He did feel... different. He couldn't really put his finger on it, but there was a change.

"Don't think about things too much, John. Go with the flow. Do the meditations. Allow the energy to guide you."

John nodded thoughtfully. The old guy was right. He was here. He should just get on with it and make the most of the situation, but he couldn't shake off the nagging doubts he had about Atman.

"But... I don't think he is everything he claims to be."

"Atman?"

"Yes."

"Why?"

John exhaled. Where should he start?

"Okay, the security is crazy. There are cameras everywhere, and I mean everywhere. I've followed the fence in places, and it's all monitored. They lock the gate at night, and the guards are under strict instructions not to let anyone out."

"Safety."

"Oh, come on, Maruti. Safety from what? The locals? I've never felt unsafe or threatened the entire time I've been in this country. Wild animals? Maybe that's why there's a fence, but cameras?"

Maruti shrugged.

"He has a bodyguard at the house, at least one. The guy

looks ex-military, short hair, fit. Not like all the other students."

Maruti nodded. "Max. Ex-French Foreign Legion."

"No way!"

"Yup, him and Georges."

John shook his head and started laughing.

Maruti looked at him, puzzled. "What's so funny?"

"It's..." John stopped laughing and shook his head. "I've had experience with men from the *Légion étrangère*. Huh. The world is a strange place." Maruti stared, and John shrugged. "A long story, Maruti. For another time and another place."

His explanation seemed to be enough for Maruti, who nodded and looked away.

"So why does a man who claims to spread love and acceptance need ex-Foreign Legion bodyguards and security cameras everywhere?"

Sighing, Maruti placed his hands on the ground and pushed himself to his feet, looking down at John, who hadn't moved.

"Forget all that, John. It's not important. He's human like the rest of us. Not perfect, but he's a good teacher. He's helped me a lot, has helped many others... He will help you, too. He does have..." Maruti looked up at the sky as if searching for the right word. "A power... something... call it what you will but use it. Forget all the external trappings. They are not important. He has his journey. You have yours." He smiled down at John. "Now, more importantly, we should make sure we get something to eat before the next session."

After a quick meal in the dining hall, John muttered something to Maruti about an upset stomach and rushed back to the room. Bolting the door from the inside, he retrieved his cell phone from under the mattress. He stood by the window, keeping an eye out while it booted up, then waited for the phone to find a signal. Once it showed a couple of bars, he dialled Adriana's number.

"Hi."

"*Bom Dia,*" John replied with a grin. "What's it like being back at work?"

Adriana sighed, "I'm a bit jet lagged but it's okay. How's it going there?"

"Good, so far. I mean, I'm hungry all the time, and my knees and ankles hurt from constantly sitting on the floor, but otherwise, it's good."

"Are you learning anything?"

"Hmmm, not sure yet." John decided not to mention his meditation experience. "Too early to say... it's only the first day."

"Yes, that's true. You'll still be settling in. Maybe you should have packed some food if you are hungry all the time?"

"Ha!" John laughed. "You should have seen the dragon who checked me in. There's no way I would have got anything past her. Listen, I'll have to go for the evening session soon. Are you in the office? Can you look into something for me?"

"Sure."

"There are two guys here who work for Atman. Georges, you've already met, but there's another guy, Max, his bodyguard."

"And...?"

"They are both ex-Foreign Legion."

Adriana was silent for a moment, and when she replied, her voice was different. "You mean like in...?"

"Yes." John didn't say anymore, neither of them wanting to relive their experience in Oman when two ex-legionnaires hunted them down and tried to kill them.[1]

"But, so what?" Adriana said after a pause. "That means nothing."

"No, I know, it's just that... I think it's weird Atman has them working for him."

"John," Adriana sighed. "Maybe you're too negative? I mean, most bodyguards have some sort of military or police service."

"Yes, I know." John puffed air out through his lips. "But the security here is over the top. There are cameras everywhere, and the entire property is surrounded by a huge fence... with barbed wire on the top. I can't get near Atman's accommodation without the bodyguard turning me away."

"Maybe—"

"Yes, I've thought of all the possible reasons, but I don't

know," John cut her off. "I just feel there's more than meets the eye."

"So, what do you want me to do?"

"Just see if you can find out more about Georges and Max. There must be some record of their service."

"Okay," Adriana replied but didn't sound enthusiastic.

"There's one other thing." John told her about the Sri Lankan girl he'd seen in the middle of the night, and Adriana was quiet. "It could be nothing," John said after a pause. "But these so-called spiritual organizations are notorious for abuse."

"Yes..." Adriana sighed. "I'll do some digging. Oh, John, I'm sorry, this was supposed to be a good experience for you."

"No, no, it is," John reassured her. "It may all come to nothing. I would just be happier if we looked into it rather than ignoring it."

"Hmmm... yes... okay."

John spotted movement along the path. "Hey, I have to go. Someone's coming. Message me with any news."

"Okay. Be careful."

"Always." John ended the call and stepped away from the window. He powered down the phone and slid it under the mattress just as the door handle rattled.

"John?"

"One sec." John moved over to the door and unbolted it. He suddenly had an idea.

---

1. See No Escape: John Hayes #4

Maruti popped his head in, "How are you feeling?"

"About the same. My stomach's a bit dodgy. Must be something I ate."

"The lunch?"

"Yeah, maybe." John moved away and sat on the bed.

"Hmmm." Maruti watched him for a moment, then stepped inside. "I've got something that will help." He walked into the bathroom. John heard him rummaging around, then he came out with two black tablets in his hand and a glass of water. "Here, take these."

"What is it?"

"Activated charcoal." Maruti passed him the water. "Drink plenty of fluids. You'll be fine by morning."

"Thank you." John felt a little guilty at his deception. He popped the tablets into his mouth, washing them down with the water. He passed the glass back to Maruti, then leaned back against the wall.

"Maybe you should skip the meditation. It's no fun if you are unwell."

"Yeah," John agreed and sighed theatrically. "Perhaps you're right."

"Stay here and rest. I'll let Gayatri know."

"Thanks."

Maruti walked out, the door creaked shut again, and John laid back on his bed to wait.

At around six-fifteen, he sat up. It was already quite dark, the sun almost set. John stood and walked over to his cabinet, pulling out the darkest clothing he had, then changed out of his white clothes. For a moment, he looked at his bed, contemplating if he should stuff the pillow under the covers to make it look like he was sleeping, but decided against it. If they caught him outside, he wanted to stick to his excuse of going for a walk after feeling better. Faking a sleeping body in his bed would only make him look suspicious. John stood by the window and listened for a while but couldn't hear anything, so he eased the door open and stepped out. He closed the door behind him and stood on the top step, waiting for any sign of anyone still around, but it was quiet and still. Stepping down, he walked slowly along the dormitory block, stopping at each window and peering in, but the rooms were all empty, so he continued toward the women's dormitory block. He wasn't sure what he was looking for or even if he would find anything, but he had to satisfy his curiosity.

Reaching the women's block, he stood still and listened. Once he was convinced there was no-one around, he did the same as he had with the men's accommodation. Again, all the windows were dark, all the doors locked. John stopped at the end and stood with his hands on his hips. What now? The office? He thought for a while. The front door was covered by the camera over the gate, and the carpark was floodlit, so there was nowhere for him to hide. He could check the windows on the side and rear of the building. Maybe he'd get lucky, and one of the windows would have been left open.

John kept to the shadows as much as he could, passing the meditation hall, then the dining hall on his right. Nearing the office, he stepped off the path into the tea bushes. He ducked down, keeping the office building between him and the car park, and made his way slowly forward. The sun had set, and he was grateful this part of the ashram was well-tended, so he didn't have to worry about his footing.

Reaching the office, he stepped over the hedgerow onto the path, then crossed to the first window. It was closed, and he tried to pry it open with his fingertips, but it held fast. He pressed his hands and face to the glass, trying to get a glimpse of the interior, but it was too dark, and he couldn't see a thing. He moved to the next window but again had no success.

"Damn," he cursed under his breath. He had to find another way in. He checked his watch. He still had around an hour before the meditation session ended, and he didn't want to waste the time, but there was a limit to what he could do in the darkness. He clenched his fist and thumped his thigh. He hadn't really thought it through.

Suddenly, the lights in the carpark went out, and the ashram was plunged into darkness. John frowned and waited for his eyes to adjust to the light. He heard a motor start up, then the lights came back on again, and he remembered the generator shed he had seen when he arrived. He stored the information away for later, stepped back into the tea garden, and made his way back toward the accommodation. Next to the dining hall, he stopped and looked at the building. Would there be anything useful in there? He thought for a moment, then turned around. Very unlikely. There wasn't even decent food there.

Increasingly dejected, he made his way back to his room and sat down on the step, gazing out across the tea garden and the jungle beyond. He hoped Adriana had more luck because so far, his search had all been a waste of time.

Unless...

45

John stepped off the path and moved into the undergrowth just before the stand of trees that served as a natural division between the students' area and Atman's bungalow. He couldn't approach via the footpath since the security camera covered it, so he needed to find a more indirect route.

Skirting left, he followed the line of trees until he was far enough away from the path, then walked into the trees. He had to move slowly, careful of his footing and mindful of the noise he would make. The night was completely silent, and every move he made sounded like a herd of elephants forcing their way through the jungle. Pushing all thought of snakes, spiders, and anything else the jungle might hold to the back of his mind, he crept forward. Barely able to see more than two feet in front of him, he moved with one hand outstretched, carefully placing each foot. It took almost ten minutes before he was through the trees and looking up the gentle slope toward the corner of the bungalow.

Light from the verandah shone out over the tea bushes, but where John stood was still in shadow. The trees gave way to manicured tea bushes, none more than waist height, care-fully trimmed and uniform in appearance. The going would be much easier but afforded little cover. Standing in the shadow of the trees, observing the well-lit bungalow, he waited for signs of movement. Atman and hopefully, Georges would be in the meditation hall. That left Max, Duminda, and anyone else who worked or lived in the bungalow.

John watched for five minutes but saw no-one, so he continued moving along the edge of the trees, keeping the slope to his right. There were easily defined paths between the bushes, allowing access for the harvest, so John could pay more attention to the bungalow than where he put his feet. He skirted the left side of the bungalow without seeing anyone, then moved toward the rear. Spotting a gap in the trees to his left, he slowed and saw a wider paved path that ran to the rear of the house. This must be how Atman and Georges reached the meditation hall. He would check the path later.

Returning his attention to the house, he saw that the path opened into a large and well-lit paved area in front of a double-door garage. Both doors were open, revealing an ATV parked in one space and the other space empty. A movement on the rear verandah catching his eye, he crept back into the shadows as Atman's cook, Duminda moved to the top step. There was a flash of flame, then the red glow of a cigarette.

John waited as Duminda finished smoking, tossed the butt off the verandah, then turned around and went back inside. Still no sign of Max or anyone else. John checked his watch. He had time and wanted to get a better look.

At this distance, he couldn't see any security cameras, but just in case, he crouched below the level of the tea bushes and moved closer, wending his way between the bushes, stopping now and then to shake his legs out as his quads burned from the unusual posture.

There was a rustle off to his right, and he froze, holding his breath. He heard it again, tensing until it moved away. Whatever it was, it wasn't human.

He waited for a moment, regaining control of his breathing, then moved closer until he could clearly see the verandah. Raising himself slowly above the bushes, he scanned the verandah and cursed. Even at the rear corner, there was the small black dome of a camera set into the ceiling. John sat back on his heels. This place was more secure than most banks. There was no way he could approach without being seen. What was Atman so concerned about that he needed so much security?

He raised his head again and studied the camera. If he moved to his left, closer to the path, it was possible the corner pillar would obscure its field of vision. He wasn't a hundred percent sure, but it was worth trying. Slowly, he moved at a crouching walk through the bushes and again raised his head. Not enough. He moved another three feet and looked up again. Yes, the camera on this end was obscured by the post, but when he looked to the right, he was in the line of sight of the camera at the other end.

Damnit. He sat back and ground his teeth together. What a complete and utter waste of time. He was no closer to finding out anything, and there was no way he could get into the bungalow, which was as secure as a fortress. He glanced at his watch again. There was about half an hour before the meditation ended. He considered his options. The only thing left to do was to explore the new path he'd found, the one he assumed led to the meditation hall.

Again, he got into a crouch and made his slow, laborious

way back through the tea plantation, keeping low until he reached the trees, where he straightened up and shook his legs out. His thighs would be sore tomorrow. He took a last look back before following the edge of the pathway until he was out of sight of the bungalow, then stepped onto the path.

It was well surfaced and just over a vehicle's width wide, but unlike the paths near the dormitory, it wasn't lit. He followed it, keeping to the edge until he saw the glow of light from the meditation hall. Parked behind it was another ATV. Now he knew how Atman moved around the property. John observed the building for a minute until he was sure there was no-one outside, then moved quickly past into the darker part of the path beyond. It continued behind the dining hall, then curved left toward the parking area at the entrance. John didn't need to go that far but wanted to inspect a building he could see just ahead on his right.

In keeping with the other buildings, it was low, long, and looked to have been converted from a farm building into smaller accommodation similar to the dormitory where John was staying. There were three doors along the front, with windows on either side of each door.

John walked closer and peered in the first window. The room held two beds and connected internally with the adjoining room but appeared to be unused. He moved to the next one, also empty. There was a faint light coming from the third window, and when John looked inside, he could see an oil lamp burning in front of a small altar. There were two beds, one in use, but the other held only a bare mattress. John scanned the room, narrowing his eyes to see in the faint light from the oil lamp. There were photos pinned to the wall, what looked to be family photos—a Sri Lankan family. There was little else to give a clue who the occupant was. Was this where the Sri Lankan girls were staying? In which case, why was only one bed in use? Had the other girl left?

John reached for the door handle and pressed down. It was unlocked. He eased the door open and was about to step inside when he heard a shout. He spun around and saw a figure approaching from the direction of the carpark. Shit!

Turning, he sprinted away just as a powerful flashlight switched on. He heard another shout and dove over the hedgerow into the bushes, scrambling on his hands and knees to keep out of sight and put as much distance as possible between him and the security guard.

46

John lay panting in his bed, with the thin cover sheet pulled over him. The palms of his hands were scratched and cut, as were his knees, and his heart pounded away in his chest. He breathed in deeply, slowly bringing his pulse rate under control, straining his ears for any sign someone was coming to get him.

After a few minutes, when his breathing was back to normal, he heard raised voices, and through the thin curtain, he could see the flicker of flashlight beams. The voices got louder, but he couldn't understand what they were saying... they were speaking Sinhalese or Tamil. He pulled the sheet higher, tucking it under his chin. Angling his head, so he could see the window, he watched the play of light as the men outside checked the rooms. He tensed when he heard the rattling of doors and voices getting closer, waiting for them to reach his room.

The door handle rattled up and down, then a figure appeared at the window, followed by a powerful beam of light, the thin material of the curtain doing nothing to block it out. John closed his eyes and remained still, hoping they wouldn't spot him, but the figure at the window called out and was answered by another voice further away. He heard footsteps, then the door handle rattled again.

Fuck it. John cursed inwardly, thinking fast. He didn't want them to come inside. He had stripped off his dark clothing and stuffed it under his pillow. Hopefully, they wouldn't see it, but if they saw his hands and knees, they were bound to be suspicious.

The door handle rattled again, then one of the men pounded on the door.

John exhaled loudly. He couldn't ignore them now. Assuming he was being watched from the window, he made a show of waking up and rubbing his face.

"What is it?" he called out, still lying on the bed.

"Sir, please open the door."

"Wait," John replied and sat up.

"Hey!" John heard another voice, vaguely familiar. "What are you doing? He's not well."

John grinned as he recognized Maruti's voice. He might just get away with this.

"It's okay. He's been here the whole time. He has food poisoning," Maruti continued.

John could hear a discussion in another language, then the light dimmed as the flashlights were turned off. John could hear muttering and footsteps as the two men moved away, then a key slipping into the lock, and the door opening.

John remained on the bed, halfway between sitting up and lying down, the sheet still wrapped around him as Maruti walked in.

"What's going on?" John asked, faking a sleepy voice.

"Oh, there's been an intruder, apparently."

"Intruder?"

Maruti closed the door and walked closer as John laid back down. "Yeah, one of the guards spotted them breaking into one of the buildings."

"Wow. So, now I know why we have a big fence... except it didn't work this time."

"Huh... Anyway, how are you feeling?" Maruti asked, looking down at John from his position beside the bed.

"Better, I think. That activated charcoal seems to have done the trick, but I fell asleep. Must be the body's way of healing."

"Good." John could see Maruti nodding in the dim light from outside. "You should be back to normal in the morning." He stepped away toward the bathroom. "I just have to turn the light on to get changed."

"Sure." John closed his eyes as the light came on and breathed a silent sigh of relief. His heart rate slowly returned to normal as he listened to Maruti getting ready for bed.

"I would suggest you take another couple of tablets in the morning before the meditation. Just to make sure."

"Thanks. Will do," John replied.

"Good night."

"Good night."

"By the way, you've got leaves in your hair."

John grinned as the light switched off.

47

By the time John reached the meditation hall in the morning, Maruti was already in his regular spot, legs crossed, eyes closed, back straight, unaware of anything going on around him.

John took a cushion and sat down, stifling a wince at the twinge from his bruised knees and his sore quads. Rather than watch the other students as they came in and made themselves comfortable, John closed his eyes and drew his attention inward, breathing slowly and deeply. For the first time in a very long time, he had slept soundly—no dreams, no nightmares, no faces from his past haunting his sleep— and had awoken refreshed and strangely eager to sit and meditate. There was nothing more he could do about investigating Atman, so he might as well make the most of the time and see how Atman's teachings—if that's what was helping him—could benefit him. As he exhaled each deep breath, he could feel his body relaxing and a feeling of... was it peace? He wasn't sure what to call it, but it filled his being and felt good, so he let it continue.

When he heard a noise from the stage and the rustle of movement as the students all around him stood, he was reluctant to join them, and learning from Maruti's example, remained sitting. He heard Atman's voice, but it seemed like distant noise, so he focused only on his breath and the incredible feeling of warmth and... joy? He felt his face smiling and sank into the feeling. He could hear nothing around him, couldn't feel his body, and his breath was so soft and shallow, it was as if he wasn't breathing at all.

He flinched when someone touched his forehead. He tried to open his eyes but couldn't, then his spine went stiff as a bolt of energy shot up from the base of his spine into his head. He gasped... then there was nothing.

John blinked his eyes open. The hall was empty. There was no-one on the stage, and the room was silent. What the hell had just happened? John felt a tingling in his fingers, shook his hands out, and shifted position. The ache in his knees came back, and he groaned as blood rushed back into his feet. Sensing rather than hearing anything, he turned his head to see Maruti sitting in his corner, grinning at him.

"There you go." He chuckled.

"What?" John shook his head.

"See, I told you. Forget everything else. This is what it's all about." Maruti unfolded his legs, placed his hands on the ground, and pushed himself to his feet. Looking down at John, still sitting, shaking the pins and needles out of his toes, Maruti smiled. "You feel good?"

"I guess so." John frowned. "I mean..." In fact, apart from the usual discomfort from sitting so long, he felt fantastic as if nothing could touch him, and all was right with the world. "Yes, I feel good."

"Sure beats roaming the jungle at night." Maruti winked

and headed toward the door. Turning back with his hand on the door handle. "Now, let's get some breakfast before the hyenas finish everything."

48

By the evening of the fifth day, John had started to fit into the ashram's routine. His body had adapted to the long hours sitting on the floor. It still hurt, just not as much. He was no longer hungry all the time and was actually enjoying the meditation sessions. They weren't all good or filled with experiences, and he still had periods when he was distracted, irritated, bored, or even fell asleep, but overall, he felt, slowly but surely, it was paying off.

His sleep was better than it had been in months, and he no longer felt restless. Maruti had given him a few pointers but pretty much left him to himself, telling him only he could do the work. In fact, during the day, outside of the meditation hall, John hardly saw him, the rostered periods of service keeping him busy when he wasn't meditating.

John had barely spoken to anyone else either. The other students kept to the request for silence, and whenever John tried to strike up a conversation, they ignored him. He had seen little of Sarah, the segregation of the sexes rigidly but subtly enforced. In the end, John gave up fighting the system and went with the flow. There was nothing else he could do, and besides, he was enjoying the solitude.

John hadn't quite given up his suspicions about Atman but had to admit that under his tutelage, his meditations were progressing well. Judging by the way the other students reacted when Atman walked onto the stage each time, they were also receiving some benefit.

Perhaps John had been wrong all along? Adriana had been in touch but hadn't uncovered anything. They had avoided calls, limiting themselves to texts to preserve the phone battery since John still hadn't figured out how to charge the phone without Maruti noticing. Even though John felt he could trust the old guy, the phone was his only link with the outside world, and he was still reluctant to take the risk. But he would need to do something soon because the battery was running low.

John was back in his room just before the evening meditation, and as had become his habit, he turned on the phone to check for any updates from Adriana. He stood by the open door, keeping an eye out for his roommate while the phone searched for a signal. It buzzed almost immediately, and when John glanced at the screen, his heart did a little skip.

Call me as soon as you can.

49

John poked his head out the door, looking both ways to see if anyone was coming, then dialed her number. The phone was answered on the fourth ring by a breathless Adriana.

"Are you running again?" John quipped.

"No, no." Adriana paused for breath. "I was at the other end of the office when the phone rang. I guessed it might be you, so I didn't want to miss the call."

"All okay?"

"Yes, all good. And you, everything okay?"

"Yeah," John sighed, "Same old routine. I was just about to head off to the evening session when I saw your message."

"Yes, so..." Adriana paused, gathering her thoughts. "Where do I start? Um... okay. First, I can't find out anything about Georges and Max. Apparently, when you join the *Légion étrangère*, you are given the option to change your name."

"Oh."

"Yes, it's to stop people like me from making inquiries.

We don't even know if Georges and Max are their actual names, and without a surname, it's even more difficult."

"Okay. It was worth a try."

"But I do have good news. I've found a local guy, a journalist who's done some work for us in the past."

"Here, you mean, in Sri Lanka?"

"Yes. He's based in Colombo, but he's agreed to do some digging around. He said he knows of Atman but hasn't paid him much attention so far."

"Okay, good." John thought for a minute. "See if you can get him to find out about the Sri Lankan girls who are here, where they came from, etcetera. It would be interesting to find out what Atman has told their families."

"Yes, will do. He told me some interesting things, though."

"Really?"

"Yes. It's hard to find any scandals involving people like Atman."

John frowned. "Why's that?"

"Well, apparently, these Ashrams are often used for money laundering by corrupt politicians. So, with that comes significant protection."

"Huh, now why doesn't that surprise me?" John scoffed.

"Yes, well, it seems the politicians launder their illegal money by making anonymous cash donations to the ashram. Ashrams, or Religious Trusts as is their correct name, are allowed to take cash donations without reporting who the donor is. So, they record it as a donation on their books, legitimizing the money. Then the Trust takes a commission and transfers the money back to the politician."

John frowned. "But how do they transfer it back? There has to be a reason for the payment."

"Well, this is where it gets clever." Adriana sounded

excited, and John smiled. He knew how Adriana immersed herself in a story. "These guys are very tricky. One way is to inflate the expenses and give the politician the difference."

"And there's very little actual expense here because we're doing all the work for free."

"Exactly. Another thing they do is hire the politician or one of his businesses to do work for the Trust, consultancy or something equally vague, and pay an inflated amount."

"Huh. If I was to start my career all over again, I think I would set myself up as a religious leader. Easy money."

Adriana chuckled. "What is it they say on TV? 'But wait, there's more.' Listen to this. They buy a property like an office building or blocks of apartments in the name of the Trust, then allow the politician to collect the rent."

"Wow."

"And at election time, the Trust buys votes by giving out free food, clothing, even televisions to the poor, telling them it's from the politician, but on the books, they show it as a charitable donation."

"The things that go on in this world of ours." John exhaled. "So, now we know how he gets the money for his Range Rover."

"Well, we don't know that Atman is doing it, but apparently, these things are common practice."

"Hmmm, it wouldn't surprise me, though. It doesn't matter how holy a person makes themselves out to be, inevitably, greed gets the better of them. It would explain the security. He must have piles of cash at the house."

"But you are benefitting from the program, aren't you?"

"Honestly?" John chewed his lip for a bit before replying. "Yes. I am. Look, I have to admit, he's a good teacher, and..." John paused to formulate his thoughts, "I suppose how he runs his finances is up to him. It just irritates me that someone who purports to be 'a man of God' is actually no different from any other businessman." John shrugged. "But that's just me. I never believe in these people."

"Sorry, John. I shouldn't have pushed you to do this."

"Why are you sorry? It's not your fault. I'm actually enjoying it. Well, not the food, but being here is like a... disconnect. It's helping me unwind, I'm sleeping better, even my liver is getting a rest."

Adriana laughed. "As long as it's not a waste."

"Nothing is a waste, my darling. There's something we can learn from every experience."

"Wow, now *you* sound like a guru."

"I'll be setting up my own ashram soon." John chuckled.

"I did like the Range Rover."

"That will be the first expense." John smiled at the sound of Adriana giggling at the other end of the phone. "I miss you."

Adriana's voice changed. "Me, too." John heard her sigh. "But you're halfway through... almost. It won't be long now, and I promise you a large gin and tonic as soon as you're back."

"Oooh, my mouth is already watering. And a juicy steak, medium rare."

Adriana chuckled again.

John checked his watch. "Hey, I have to get going. They don't like it if we're late."

"Is the dragon still giving you trouble?"

"Gayatri? No, now she's my best friend."

"Really? The John Hayes charm did its magic?"

"Well, of course." John grinned. "Actually, if I'm honest, it's more my perceived closeness to Atman that did the trick."

"Good. The charm is only to be used on me."

"Don't worry. I'll be using it all on you as soon as I get back."

"I can't wait. I love you, John."

"Love you, too. Speak soon. Let me know what he finds out about the girls."

"Yes, will do. Bye."

"Bye." John ended the call and stared blankly out the door. He wasn't surprised. This sort of thing had been going on for centuries, one of the reasons religious organizations had so much wealth. If Atman *was* doing what Adriana said —and John's gut told him he was—it nothing new, just on a smaller scale.

John powered down his phone and slid it back under the mattress. Stepping outside, he closed and locked the door, then walked toward the meditation hall, deep in thought.

The thing is, he wondered, should he do something about it?

50

John watched Atman walk onto the stage and take his seat. He looked around at the other students, their faces bright and glowing in anticipation of their next lesson. All were standing with their hands either on their chest or pressed together in *namaste. How many of you would still stand here if you learned Atman is laundering money through the ashram? Would you still think he's god-like? Would you still afford him the same respect? Or would you ignore it?*

Atman looked up and smiled at the crowd, placing his right hand on his chest. He nodded, then gestured for everyone to sit. John watched the others as they settled, then moved to sit down. As he arranged himself on his cushion, he looked up and saw Atman was looking directly at him. The guru smiled broadly at John, and John immediately felt guilty.

To be fair, there was no proof Atman was doing any of the things Adriana had mentioned. It was all conjecture. Perhaps John was a little too suspicious, too cynical. He smiled back, then closed his eyes, eager to break eye contact, worried Atman could see what he was thinking.

John took a series of slow breaths and scanned his body for tension, relaxing each body part one by one until he was comfortable. He tuned in to the instructions as Atman led the occupants of the hall through a series of preparatory breathing exercises. John followed along for a while, but his mind kept wandering, struggling to focus on the exercises. When Atman moved on to a guided meditation, asking the students to visualize light in different colors and balls of energy, all John could see were suitcases filled with bundles of cash and stacks of dollar bills piled on a bed.

The more John fought his wandering mind, the more irritated he became. His body tightened up, and the discomfort in his legs and hips made its presence felt. He ground his teeth together and shook his head. Taking a deep breath, he tried once more to relax, again scanning his body from the top of his head, but by the time he had reached his midsection, he was so annoyed with himself, he gave up.

Opening his eyes, he looked around at the people in front and next to him. They all seemed so calm and relaxed, several with huge smiles. John exhaled slowly, placed his palms on the floor, and pushed himself back, so he was leaning against the rear wall. Unfolding his legs, he shook them out, then rubbed his calves, helping the circulation.

Giving up on the meditation, he closed his eyes again and imagined what he would do once he had finished the retreat, what he would eat, what he would drink. He visualized Adriana at the arrivals' hall in Lisbon Airport... holding her in his arms. His irritation faded, and he must have drifted off to sleep because not long later, he heard the instructions, 'Slowly open your eyes.'

John waited until Atman got up to leave, then stood with the rest of the students. The middle-aged man, sitting to John's left, an Australian John had gathered from the few words spoken at the beginning of the retreat, gave John a questioning look and a thumbs-up. John nodded and smiled, returning the hand gesture. There was no point in telling him he slept instead of meditating. The man looked pleased, then looked toward the front as Atman left by the side door. Gayatri walked to the front of the stage, holding a piece of paper in her hand and wearing her reading glasses.

"Before you go," she called out. "I have an important announcement to make."

The students quietened down, all turning to look at her.

"As you all know, when Atman feels you have made excellent progress, he will choose a spiritual name for you." She smiled and looked around the hall, "I remember when he gave me my name." Her cheeks visibly flushed. "It was a rebirth. The best day of my life."

There was a murmur in the crowd, and several of the students exchanged excited glances.

Gayatri gestured for quiet, then continued. "Atman is very pleased with the progress of some of our senior students, and I have here in my hand a list of those Atman has chosen to proceed to the next level."

Again, an excited murmur rippled through the crowd.

"I will call the names of the chosen ones. We will hold a ceremony for each of you at the house where Atman himself will initiate each one of you individually."

There was an audible gasp, and Gayatri paused, looking over her reading glasses until the hall was quiet. Once the hall was silent, she looked down at the paper in her hand and began to call out names. The names meant nothing to John. The enforced silence and the segregation of the sexes meant he hadn't met or talked to anyone else other than Maruti and a couple of the supervisors who ran the service roster.

Excited shouts and fists pumped in the air gave away who had been selected. There was only one name he recognized, and even though he couldn't see her in the crowd at the front, he heard her shriek of delight when her name was called. Sarah.

———————

51

"So, what goes on in this naming ceremony?"

Maruti looked up from the book he was reading. He raised an eyebrow and studied John for a moment. "Are you feeling left out?"

"Ha!" John scoffed. "No. I like the name I've got. I'm just... curious."

Maruti looked back at his book and turned the page. "Nothing much, to be honest."

John waited for him to elaborate. "Well?"

Maruti sighed and laid the book down on his chest.

"You have to bathe and change into a fresh set of meditation clothes. Then you get called into a room. You have to sit down in front of Atman. You do a meditation together, then he blesses you and tells you the name he has chosen for you." He picked his book up and started reading again.

"That's it?"

"Pretty much."

John scratched his head and turned to look out the window. He thought for a while, then looked back at Maruti.

"Why?"

"Why what?"

"Why does he change your name?"

Maruti sighed again. "He says it brings forth certain qualities that will help your progress."

"Do you believe that?"

Maruti laid his book down again and sat up. "You're not going to let me finish my book, are you?"

John grinned. "No."

"Okay," Maruti sighed and rubbed his face. "It doesn't matter what I believe, and besides, you are asking someone called Maruti, who obviously isn't Indian, whether he believes in changing his name."

"Well, do you?"

Maruti grinned. "No."

John chuckled. "Then why did you do it?"

Maruti shrugged. "It's just easier to go along with it."

John waited for him to elaborate.

"Look, it means so much to everyone else. I have to live with them, spend every day with them, so why be the odd one out?"

John pursed his lips and wrinkled his brow. "You puzzle me, Maruti."

"In what way?"

"Well... you don't seem to buy into anything that's going on here, yet you've stayed."

"I like it here." He gestured at the room "Rent free, free food, warm climate... what's not to like?"

"Is that the only reason you're here?"

Maruti made a face as if considering John's question seriously, then grinned. "Yup."

John sighed theatrically, then matched Maruti's grin.

"I don't know if you are having a joke at everyone else's expense or..."

"Or what?"

"Or you are the most enlightened one here."

Maruti burst into laughter and slapped the bed. It was so infectious, John started chuckling, too. Maruti's laughter subsided, and his face became serious. He fixed John with that intense gaze, and John's grin faded from his face.

"Do you know what is true, John?"

John shook his head.

"We have to be up at four-thirty." Maruti laughed again as he reached over and switched off the light, plunging the room into darkness.

52

"John, John."

John felt a hand on his shoulder, shaking him. His eyes opened with a start, and he realized his heart was pounding away. He tried to sit up, but a pair of hands gently pressed him back down again.

"It's okay, you are safe," said a familiar voice. John frowned and took a deep breath, and as his eyes focused in the faint light of the moon, he recognized Maruti's face, looking down at him.

"What... what happened?"

"You were dreaming, John."

The dream came flooding back. He had been on the platform of the London Underground. People were rushing toward him, screaming in terror, and he could hear gunshots. One by one, people collapsed to the ground, and as the crowd cleared, he saw a man walking toward him, the gun in his hand pointed at John's head. John tried to move, but his feet were stuck to the ground, and when he looked down, he was standing knee-deep in blood. He looked at the man again and recognized him. It was Sunil Patil... no it was Bogdan Kolisnik... no he was wrong... it was Surya Patil, wait it's... The face kept changing, morphing from one to the other and back again, each face laughing at him, getting closer and closer until the barrel of the gun was touching his forehead—then he woke up.

"I remember now. I... I'm sorry, Maruti. I woke you up." John could see the white of Maruti's teeth as he smiled.

"It's okay. It was a bad dream. We all have them."

John took a deep breath and exhaled slowly, feeling his heart rate coming back to normal.

"Do you get these dreams often?"

"Yes."

He could see Maruti nodding slowly.

"Something from your past?"

"Yes."

"Hmmm. The subconscious can do some funny things to us, John, but remember, it's not real. Keep doing what you're doing here, and it will clear out."

"Is it that easy?"

"Did I say easy?" Maruti chuckled. "Just keep doing the work. Think of it as exercise. The more often you do it, the fitter and stronger you get. But you have to do it."

"Yeah... thanks."

"Let's try something. Close your eyes and relax."

John did as he was told.

"Now take a full breath, as deep as you can, and when you can go no further, hold it for a count of three, then slowly exhale."

John inhaled, and as he exhaled, he felt his body relaxing.

"Good. Do it again."

John inhaled slowly until his lungs were completely full, held his breath, then as he started exhaling, he felt Maruti's hand on his forehead.

That was the last thing he remembered.

53

On the day of the naming ceremony, the late morning meditation was canceled and unfortunately, so was lunch. Word was sent out that Atman wanted everyone to fast, their stomachs to be empty, so they would be better able to receive the energy he would pour into them with their new name.

John grumbled to Maruti that it wasn't fair that he had to starve when he wasn't part of the ceremony, but Maruti only shrugged. He'd been through it so many times before.

All the service assignments were canceled as well, giving everyone a free day. They were told it was a sacred day and to spend their time in silence, meditating and praying. Instead, John sat with Maruti in the sun on the step outside their room, watching as one by one the students walked past the dormitory on their way to Atman's bungalow to receive their new names.

A few nodded and smiled at Maruti as they walked past, but most walked with their heads down, eyes downcast, ignoring those watching them—John and Maruti not the only ones sitting out on the steps—but their pious postures did little to hide the excitement they were clearly feeling.

The students were called in fifteen-minute intervals, the next heading up when the previous one returned, the procession taking most of the afternoon. John watched for Sarah, the only other student he knew, but it was late in the day, the sun low in the sky, when he finally saw her approaching along the path toward the bungalow.

"Congratulations, Sarah," John called out, despite not believing in the whole affair. She looked up in surprise, then blushed and smiled. She walked closer, looked around to see if anyone else was listening.

"Thank you, John."

"You deserve it, Sarah. You've worked hard for it," Maruti added.

Sarah's smile widened. "That means a lot to me, Maruti, coming from you."

"You will always have my blessings, dear."

Sarah's eyes welled up, and she sniffed.

"Go on, you don't want to be late," Maruti urged, a gentle smile on his face. "It's your day."

Sarah nodded, smiled again, and continued on her way.

John sighed. "Sometimes I wish I believed in something so much."

"It matters that they believe in it," Maruti replied, his eyes on Sarah as she disappeared into the trees. "It's their faith that makes it work."

"Hmmm."

Maruti turned to look at John. "The human mind is extremely powerful, John. With faith, it can realize anything."

John nodded thoughtfully. "I agree, but sometimes, in

the wrong hands... no, minds is a better word... in the wrong minds, it can wreak havoc on the world."

Maruti narrowed his eyes.

John hadn't intended to say more, but Maruti wouldn't stop looking at him, obviously waiting for him to elaborate.

"I've seen people commit unimaginable cruelty on their fellow human beings because of their faith in a distorted, corrupted belief."

Maruti nodded slowly. "That explains your dreams."

John shrugged and looked away.

"Keep doing your meditation practice, John, and look within. That will help you more than anything else." He reached over and slapped John on the shoulder, then stood. "Now, come on. I think Sarah was the last one. Let's go get something to eat. I've done enough fasting for one day."

54

Later that evening, John was standing in the open doorway of the room looking up at the stars when Maruti called out from inside the room.

"John, your mattress is buzzing."

John frowned, wondering what he was saying, then swore under his breath. He mustn't have turned the phone off properly the last time he checked it. Damn. If it was buzzing, it meant Adriana was messaging him. He turned around and stepped back into the room.

"You should check it," Maruti said without looking up from his book. "It might be important."

John stared at the old guy for a moment, then grinned sheepishly. "I didn't want Gayatri to get her hands on it."

Maruti shrugged and turned the page. "Makes no difference to me."

John walked over, bent down, slid his hand under the mattress, and felt around until his fingers touched the phone. He pulled it out and looked at the screen.

Call me asap!

"I have to make a call. It's my partner."

"Partner?"

"Ahh, girlfriend."

"Lucky man. Go for it. I'm not listening."

John nodded and dialed Adriana's number, walking to the open doorway as it connected.

"What's the matter?" he asked as soon as she answered.

"I'm fine, thanks for asking."

"Ah... yeah, sorry." John ran his fingers through his hair. "I saw your message and got worried."

"It's okay, I'm teasing." Adriana chuckled. "I have some news for you."

"Yeah?"

"Vidu did some digging around for us."

"Vidu?"

"The Sri Lankan journalist I told you about."

"Okay, yes, I remember."

"The Sri Lankan girls. They are from the same village, Kaluwila," Adriana struggled with the unfamiliar word.

"How did he find that out?"

"Well, apparently, it made the local newspaper when they were chosen to be in the ashram. It seems it was quite an event."

"Okay."

"So, he contacted the parents, and this is where it gets worrying."

John felt a disturbing sensation in the pit of his stomach.

"Both girls would phone home once a week. It was their routine, but this week, one of the girls didn't call." John clenched his jaw as Adriana continued "The other girl told her parents her friend left the room one night, and she hasn't seen her again. The ashram told her she'd gone home, but that was a week ago."

"Shit." John exhaled loudly and rubbed his face. He glanced back at Maruti, but his attention was still on his book. Turning back to face out the door, he asked, "Have they gone to the police?"

"Yes, but the police have fobbed them off, saying she's probably just a runaway. Vidu says they won't investigate anything to do with the ashram."

"Why not?"

"Connections."

John clenched his fist, closed his eyes, and took a deep breath.

"John?"

"Yes, I'm here." John sighed. "It doesn't look good."

"Maybe she has just run away?"

"Yeah, I hope that's all it is, but my gut says otherwise."

"Vidu will keep looking around."

"Okay. I'll see what I can find out here."

"John, please don't do anything stupid."

John stayed quiet, his mind racing.

"John?"

"Yes, sorry, I'm thinking."

"Promise me you won't do anything stupid."

John hesitated before replying. Stupidity was relative.

"I promise."

"Good."

There was silence, neither saying anything then, "I love you, John."

"Love you, too." John frowned, his attention not on the call.

"I'll message tomorrow if we find out anything else."

"Okay, I'll do the same."

"Bye, John. Sleep well."

"You, too. Bye."

John ended the call and turned around. Maruti had put the book down and was watching him from the bed.

"Something wrong?"

"How many days ago?"

"Six."

Maruti nodded slowly. "She might have just run away."

John rubbed his face and paced up and down the gap between the two beds. He paused and faced Maruti.

"Okay. If she ran away, then why? She's a young girl. Ran away with a boy? Anyone else here missing?"

Maruti shook his head.

"Could there be someone outside?"

Again, Maruti shook his head. "It's unlikely. They haven't been out of the ashram since they came here. No-one goes out."

John started pacing again.

Maruti sighed. "John, please stay still. You're making me dizzy."

John stopped, then started again.

"I know what I saw, Maruti. She was coming from the house, and she looked upset. If she ran away, it's because something happened here." John stopped and leaned on the door frame, looking out. He heard a sigh, then the sound of Maruti getting off his bed, and felt a hand on his shoulder.

"Let's go and ask her."

John frowned and turned, "Who?"

"Isuri, of course. The other girl."

"Of course." It was so obvious, John didn't know why he hadn't thought of it before. He stepped outside, and Maruti followed him, pulling the door closed behind him.

"Follow me."

"I know the way."

Maruti stopped and looked at John for a second." Ah, yes, I forgot about your nocturnal activities." He started walking again, and John hurried to catch up.

"Does she speak English?"

"Of course." He looked at John as if he'd asked a silly question. "We are in Sri Lanka."

John ignored him. "Will she talk to us?"

"Why not?"

"Well, no-one seems to talk to anyone here."

"Don't worry about all that." Maruti waved dismissively with his left hand. "She'll talk to me."

They made their way along the dimly lit pathway, Maruti turning right at the meditation hall, then stepping off the path and following the wall of the building until it joined the path Atman used to access the hall. It was close to lights out time, and there was no-one else around, everyone back in their rooms. Maruti slowed as he reached the small dormitory block John had inspected earlier in the week and turned to make sure John was still with him. He smiled, then stepped toward the last door and knocked.

They heard movement inside, then the curtain twitched. Maruti moved, so his face was in the light, and smiled. The curtain moved again, followed by the sound of a bolt being drawn, then the door opened slightly.

The young girl peered out, looking from Maruti to John and then back again. "Uncle?"

Maruti smiled. "Hello, Isuri. I wanted to talk to you about Nihinsa."

Isuri's eyes darted to John, then looked over his shoulder, up the path, and back again.

"This is John. He's a friend."

She nodded.

"No-one else knows we are here."

She nodded again, swallowed, then stood back and opened the door wider.

Maruti nodded at John, slipped off his flip-flops, and stepped inside. John did the same, then closed the door behind him.

Isuri was checking the curtains, then nodded toward the empty bed. Maruti sat down and nodded to John to do the same.

John sat and looked around the room as Isuri moved to sit on her bed. The sweet smell of incense filled the room, and in one corner was an altar with an oil lamp burning in front of a small statue of Buddha.

"Did I disturb you?" Maruti nodded at the cushion on the floor in front of the altar.

"No, Uncle." She shook her head, glanced at John nervously, then back at Maruti, and smiled for the first time. "I hadn't started yet."

Maruti turned to John and smiled. "Isuri meditates until late in the night." He smiled at Isuri again. "Your practice is good. You can teach me."

"No, Uncle." The girl smiled shyly. "I am just a student."

Maruti hesitated, then nodded toward John. "John is worried about Nihinsa. He wanted to talk to you about her."

Isuri's smile faded. "She's not here."

Maruti nodded, his face solemn. "We know." He turned to John. "Maybe you should explain?"

John took a deep breath. Where did he start?

"I saw Nihinsa on the night she disappeared."

Isuri's eyes darted to Maruti, then back to John. "Where, sir?"

"Please call me John. It was around one-thirty in the morning. She was coming back from the house." John nodded in the direction of Atman's house. "I couldn't sleep and saw her from my window."

Isuri looked down at the floor and was quiet. When she spoke, her voice was soft, almost inaudible.

"Atman Sir asked her to meditate with him. He has a room there. It's very powerful. He said she was having some..." She looked at Maruti as if he knew what she was trying to say.

"Blocks?" he prompted gently.

"Yes. He said he would help her. He said she was very close to realising her Buddha-nature, but something was holding her back."

"What time was this?" John asked quietly.

Isuri looked up again. "After lights out."

John nodded slowly and glanced at Maruti.

"Had she gone before?"

"Yes." Isuri frowned. "She had been going for a week, but..."

"But what, Isuri." Maruti leaned forward, so his face was at the same level as hers.

She looked up, looking first at John, then Maruti. "I don't think it was helping her."

"Why?"

"Because she seemed unhappy. We used to laugh and play together, you know, when we weren't in the hall, but she stopped."

John clenched his jaw. His instincts had been right all along.

"I thought she was sick, but she wouldn't talk about it." She looked at Maruti. "What's happened to her, Uncle? Is she okay?"

Maruti reached forward and placed his hand over hers. He smiled, and John was struck by how gentle he seemed.

"We don't know, Isuri, but we will find out."

56

"**I** should have spoken to her," John muttered, shaking his head as the two men made their way back to their room in the dark. "Maybe I could have helped her."

Maruti placed a hand on John's shoulder. "John, you had no way of knowing what was going on. We still don't."

"Come on, Maruti. Do you honestly believe nothing has happened after hearing that?" John gestured back to the room they had just left.

Maruti gestured with his hand for John to lower his voice. "Let's wait until we are back in the room to discuss this."

"Why? No-one will believe me, anyway. They all think the sun shines out of his..."

"John," Maruti growled.

John closed his mouth at the uncharacteristic tone from Maruti. They walked the rest of the way in silence, John's mind whirring away, trying to think of what to do next.

Even once inside the room with the door closed, neither of them said anything for a while. Maruti went into the bathroom, and John could hear water splashing as he sat on the bed, his back against the wall. When Maruti walked out, John stood up.

"I'm going to confront him."

Maruti looked at him, drying his hands with a small towel. "John, sit down." He tossed the towel onto his bed and sat down, looking up at John, who hadn't moved. "John?"

John scowled and sat down.

"John, it's nighttime. There's nothing you can achieve right now. You won't even get into the house."

"I can't sit around and do nothing, Maruti." John clenched and unclenched his fingers. "Not when I feel something has happened."

"I'm not saying, do nothing, John. I'm just saying wait until morning. If you are going to confront him, do it with a clear mind, not an angry one. Right now, you don't have any proof that something has happened."

"Maruti, I can't believe you're saying that. You're as bad as the rest of them."

Maruti's face twitched, but he said nothing as John continued.

"The cult leader invites a young girl to his room at night, repeatedly, and she withdraws into herself, clearly unhappy, then she disappears." John spread his hands and gave Maruti a look as if to say the conclusion was obvious.

Maruti's face remained impassive, but John could see a vein pulsing in his neck. His eyes remained fixed on John's, and this time, John refused to look away.

"All I'm saying," Maruti said eventually, "Is wait until morning. I will come with you. We'll ask him what he knows and see what he says."

John felt his anger ebb away. Maruti was right. There

was nothing he could do now. He exhaled slowly, releasing the tension from his body.

"Good. We have to be calm about this. We would look very stupid if all that happened was, she felt homesick and ran away."

John looked up and glared at Maruti. "Not as stupid as we will look if he's assaulted her, and we did nothing about it."

57

It took John a long time to get to sleep. He lay awake for hours, staring at the ceiling, replaying the events of that night—the night he saw Nihinsa on the path and had done nothing about it. After a while, he removed his phone from beneath the mattress, typed a long account of the conversation with Isuri, and sent it to Adriana, asking her to find out if anyone had seen the girl in the nearby town of Ella. She would have had to have caught a bus or the train. Someone must have seen her.

After turning off the phone, John lay back, feeling a little better now he had taken some action, but it didn't last, the guilt slowly increasing again. He should have stopped her, mentioned it to someone... Wait, he had. He'd told Maruti. John rolled onto his side and stared at his sleeping room-mate. His breath was slow and deep, and John envied the ability of the man to sleep soundly. Why hadn't Maruti said anything that morning?

John lay back and closed his eyes, visualizing the conver-sation. Maruti had said nothing. Why? Had he known what was going on and turned a blind eye? What was wrong with these people? Were they were so obsessed with finding 'The Truth' that they couldn't see the actual truth? John shook his head as if he was having a conversation and sighed. Maybe it was all a misunderstanding. Maybe the girl would turn up. Maybe Atman was the great saint all believed he was. But that was a whole lot of maybes.

One thing was for sure. If something bad had happened, John could never live with himself if he stood by and did nothing. Saint or no saint.

Eventually, exhaustion got the better of him, and he drifted into a fitful sleep, filled with visions of crying girls and dead bodies on subway platforms. When the alarm sounded at four-thirty, it rang for a while before he could even be bothered turning it off. When he opened his eyes and looked across the room, he could see Maruti had already left. John closed his eyes again. He was not in the mood to sit in the hall, striving for inner peace, when the man on the stage could be the devil incarnate. Fuck him. He was going back to sleep.

The sound of the door opening woke him. He blinked his eyes open and turned his wrist to look at his watch—seven-thirty.

"Good morning, sleepyhead."

John sat up and saw Maruti standing in the doorway, his usual smile on his face.

"Taking a break this morning?"

"Yeah," John muttered and rubbed his face with both hands. "I wasn't in the mood."

"And you slept badly."

John looked up in surprise.

"I heard you."

"Sorry." John looked down again. He felt a hand on his shoulder.

"It's okay. It will get better."

John nodded. "Thanks."

"Have a shower. We'll get something to eat, then go up to the house."

John looked up. "You haven't changed your mind?"

Maruti looked puzzled. "Why would I do that?"

John shrugged and pushed himself off the bed.

"Give me ten minutes."

"I'm not going anywhere, my friend."

———

58

J ohn and Maruti sat opposite each other and ate silently, deep in thought.

John rehearsed his conversation with Atman, planning what to ask, anticipating responses, going back and forth, but in the end, he gave up. He had no idea how it would go, so what was the point in stressing? He would play it by ear and trust in his intuition. It hadn't let him down in the past.

Looking down at his empty plate, he realized he hadn't tasted his food or even realized he had finished. Nodding at Maruti, who was still finishing up, he stood, took his plate to the kitchen hatch, and left it on the counter. Ignoring the service roster, he turned to look around the hall.

He spotted Sarah sitting alone at a far table. Ignoring the disapproving looks from the other women, he walked between the women's tables and stood beside her.

"Hi, Sarah," John's voice sounded unreasonably loud in the unnatural silence of the hall, most still observing the instruction to stay silent.

Sarah looked up with a start, stared at him for a second, then looked down at her plate again.

John lowered his voice so the others couldn't hear.

"I haven't seen you since the naming ceremony. How did it go? What's your new name?"

Sarah pushed her plate away, stood, and rushed out the door without looking back.

John frowned. That was strange. He looked around, but no-one else seemed to have noticed.

Maruti walked over. "Let's go."

John frowned deeper, took a deep breath, then nodded. "Yeah, let's go."

They took the path through the dormitories, and as they passed Sarah's room, John noticed the door was closed, and the curtains were drawn.

"Have you spoken to Sarah since the ceremony?"

Maruti shook his head, "Uh-uh."

"Hmmm."

"Why?"

"Just wondered. She was acting strange this morning."

"Maybe she had a bad night." Maruti shrugged as they passed through the trees and into the open ground beyond. He looked at John, and his eyes twinkled. "Like one of yours."

"Huh."

As they climbed the slope toward the house, a figure appeared at the top of the steps.

"Max?"

John nodded. "The welcoming committee."

At the bottom of the steps, they stopped and looked up at Max, who stood legs apart, hands clasped in front of him.

"Yes?"

"We want to speak to Atman."

"Do you have an appointment?"

John sighed. "I didn't know we needed one. I thought he was available to all of us."

"No."

"Max, it's important," Maruti spoke up.

Max looked at Maruti for a moment, his face expressionless, then nodded. "Wait here."

He walked back into the house as John looked at Maruti and shook his head.

"Friendly guy."

Maruti smiled. "He's not so bad."

John turned and looked out across the tea plantation toward the jungle beyond. The morning light was soft and warm, and the bushes glistened with dew.

"Beautiful view from here."

"Yup."

John looked at Maruti, who had his eyes closed, his face tilted toward the sun. Before he could say anything, he heard footsteps on the verandah. John turned to face the house and saw Georges standing on the top step.

"Please come in."

"Good morning, Georges." John nodded at him. "I haven't seen you for a while."

Georges said nothing and moved away from the step, gesturing toward the front door with his right hand.

John exchanged a glance with Maruti, then jogged up the steps.

"Shoes."

John stopped in the doorway and looked around, "I'm sorry?"

Georges looked down at John's feet.

John noticed Maruti slipping off his flip-flops, so he did the same, then followed him inside.

Max watched from the entrance to the hallway in his now-familiar stance, his face blank.

"Please sit down," Georges said from behind them. When John turned to look at him, he gestured toward the sofas.

Maruti took a seat closest to Atman's armchair, and John sat at the other end of the same sofa.

Georges walked over and sat opposite them. He glanced at John, then faced Maruti.

"What can I do for you?"

John cleared his throat. "We want to speak to Atman."

Georges turned slowly and stared at John. John returned his gaze, neither looking away nor filling the silence. He'd said enough.

Eventually, Georges replied. "He's busy right now. Perhaps I can pass on your message?"

John leaned forward, leaned his forearms on his knees, and glared at Georges.

"I know you are doing your job, Georges, but you're wasting our time. We have come to speak to Atman, and it is very important. It involves the safety of the students, and if anything bad happens because of your delay, it will be your responsibility."

Georges' left eyelid twitched. His face remained devoid of expression, but he took a breath, then looked at Maruti.

Maruti nodded.

Georges looked at John again. "One moment, please."

He stood up and walked toward the hallway, Max stepping aside to let him past, then stepping back again.

John exhaled loudly, then shot Maruti a look. Maruti smiled and made a calming gesture with his hand.

John closed his eyes, took a deep breath, and leaned back against the sofa, resting his head on the backrest. He could feel his heartbeat increasing and exhaled, slowing his breathing. He needed to remain calm.

A few minutes later, he heard movement and opened his eyes, looking toward the hallway. Max had stepped aside, and a smiling Atman walked out, Georges close behind him.

"John, Maruti." He beamed. "Good morning."

John and Maruti stood up as he walked over and took John's hand in both of his, a broad smile on his face. His white clothing was crisp and fresh, his hair damp and slicked back, and he smelled of... rose water. Despite John's suspicions, he couldn't help himself and smiled.

"Good morning, Atman."

"I missed you at the meditation this morning, John. Is everything okay? Are you unwell?" He locked eyes with John in that peculiar way of his, and his smile faded. "Something is troubling you." He smiled again and patted John's hand with his. "Don't worry, there is nothing we can't fix." He let go of John's hand and looked over his shoulder. "Max, please bring my friends something to drink." He looked back at John. "We have fresh watermelon juice from the garden." He winked, then moved closer to Maruti.

"My old friend."

Maruti held out his hand, but Atman ignored it and instead embraced him. "You should come up here more often." He released Maruti, holding him at arm's length. "I don't see enough of you."

"You are a busy man."

"Never too busy to see you, my friend." He let go of Maruti and moved to his armchair, sitting down and crossing one leg over the other.

Max walked in with three glasses on a tray.

"Have some juice. It's sweet."

John took a glass, as did Maruti. When Max offered the last glass to Atman, he waved him away.

"I'm fasting today," he explained to Maruti and John. "Now, what can I do for you?" He nodded toward Georges, standing on the other side of the room. "Georges mentioned something about safety."

John took a long pull on the watermelon juice—it was very sweet—while he gathered his thoughts. Licking his lips, he held up the glass. "Very good. Thank you."

Atman smiled.

"Isuri and Nihinsa, the Sri Lankan girls."

Atman smiled wider. "Ahh, my two little angels."

"Well, only one is still here."

"Yes." Atman nodded. "Nihinsa was feeling homesick, so she went home for a while." He looked at Maruti. "It's tough for the young ones."

Maruti nodded but remained silent.

Atman looked back at John, "The attachments we form in this life are hard to break, but we must because they prevent us from reaching our full potential." He nodded at Maruti. "Maruti understands this, but he learned the hard way."

John took a breath. His gut told him Atman was lying, but the guru's words and his body language seemed to indicate otherwise. Either John was very wrong, or the man was a consummate actor.

"She hasn't gone home."

"What do you mean?" Atman looked genuinely surprised.

"Her parents have reported her missing."

Atman's eyes darted to Georges, then back to John. It was fleeting, and John almost missed it.

"How do you know this?"

John cursed himself. He didn't want to give too much away.

"It's not important. The thing is..." John paused before delivering his bombshell. "I saw her the night before she dis... left."

"Really?" Atman tilted his head, eyebrows raised but still smiling.

"Yes, on the path." He jerked his head in the direction of the dormitories, then fixed his eyes back on Atman, wanting to record every reaction. "Around one-thirty in the morning. She was coming from here."

"Yes, we have been doing some intense *sadhana* together." Atman nodded, his expression now serious. "Sorry, John, *sadhana* means spiritual practices. It's a Sanskrit word."

John nodded, not that he cared what it meant. He only wanted to know what had been going on.

"She's been having some difficulties with her meditation, so I scheduled some extra time with her."

"Why at night?"

Atman smiled and spread his hands, "You've seen how busy I am, John. I don't even have time for my own practice. The night hours are the only time I'm undisturbed."

"She was crying."

Frowning, Atman uncrossed his legs and leaned forward. "What night was this?"

"About seven, eight days ago. The last time she was seen."

"I remember. We had been working on past life regression." He shook his head. "It was very tough for her, the poor thing. You've no idea what she has been through in her previous incarnations." Atman sighed and looked down at the floor. "Anyway," he said, looking up, "That's one of the reasons she wanted to go home. Her parents had been with her in previous lives, and she had a breakthrough that night. She has some issues to resolve with them."

"But she hasn't reached her home."

"Yes," Atman exhaled loudly and leaned back against his chair. Steepling his fingers in front of his chest, he nodded slowly, his forehead creased. "That bothers me. I wasn't aware of this."

There was silence for a moment, Atman staring at the floor, Maruti and John watching him. After a while, Atman looked up.

"Don't worry, John. I will look into it. We will make some inquiries." He nodded to himself. "Yes. We have connections with the police. They will investigate, and I'm sure they will find her before too long." He smiled at John, then Maruti. Looking back at John, he said, "Leave it to me. Now, how is your practice going?"

"What do you think?" John asked as soon as they were through the trees and out of sight of the house.

"It doesn't matter what I think. It matters what happened."

"Oh, for f... sake, Maruti! Stop talking in riddles like you're Yoda." John clenched his fist, took a deep breath, and exhaled. "Sorry, I'm a bit..."

"I know," Maruti smiled and placed a hand on John's arm. "Yoda?" he chuckled. "Well, Yoda thinks Atman isn't being one hundred percent truthful, but as I said, we need to find out what actually happened."

"I'll see if Adriana has any leads."

They neared their room, and John stood back as Maruti fumbled in his pocket for the keys, then slipped the key in the lock.

"Hmmm."

"What is it?"

Maruti looked over his shoulder. "I thought I'd locked

the door this morning, but..." He shrugged. "I guess Yoda is getting old."

John pushed past him, opened the door, and stepped inside, pausing in the doorway. He scanned the room carefully. Nothing seemed out of place, but the hair on the back of his neck was tingling. Maruti stepped in beside him.

"Someone has been in here."

"How do you know?" John asked, still looking around the room.

"I can feel it. The energy is different."

John rushed forward and thrust his hand under the mattress. He felt around, and when he couldn't feel anything, he lifted the mattress and flipped it up against the wall.

"My phone is gone."

Maruti stared at the empty surface of the bed then looked at John. "Did you see Georges when we left the house?"

John frowned, then shook his head. "Only Max."

Maruti nodded slowly. "There you go."

"Fuck," John swore and rubbed his head. He glanced across at Maruti. "Now tell me that nothing bad has happened. They've just shown their hand."

Maruti sat down on the bed, his hands on his knees, his shoulders slumped.

John sat opposite him and studied his face. He suddenly looked old, almost as if the light had gone from his face. John tried to imagine how the old guy must be feeling. He reached across and placed his hand over Maruti's.

"I'm sorry. I've been a bit insensitive." He sighed. "I've been so focused on proving myself right, I forgot this is your home, and he's been your... mentor... or teacher for the last four years."

Maruti closed his eyes, and John watched his chest expand as he filled his lungs with air, then deflate as he exhaled. He opened his eyes, straightened up, and smiled. He was back to his old self... almost. "It's okay, John." He shrugged, "I've never been in awe of him like the others here. I told you from the beginning, don't forget he's not God. It's just..." His smile faded slightly, and he sighed. "Disappointing."

"Yeah." John squeezed his hand and sat back. "Humans never fail to disappoint." He chewed his lip, wondering how much he should say. "Maruti... several months ago, I was in Syria."

Maruti looked up in surprise, then nodded as if something made sense.

"That's why you're not sleeping?" It was more of a statement than a question.

"Yeah," John sighed, "One of the reasons, anyway, but that's not why I'm telling you." He took a deep breath. "When I was there, I..." His voice caught as the memory came flooding back. "I went into a house the Islamic State fighters had taken over." John hesitated. "There were about fifteen, sixteen, women, young girls, children..." He looked up and held Maruti in his gaze. "Sex slaves, Maruti. Yazidi women captured from their villages and held prisoner."

A shadow passed over Maruti's face.

"Raped continually for months... some of them years. The youngest was twelve. The oldest was fifty-eight. She had five grandchildren, Maruti. Five grandchildren!" John shook his head. "That sight is engraved in my brain... I can still see their faces..." He trailed off and looked out the open door. After a moment, he said, "I never want to experience anything like that again." He turned back to face Maruti, and when he spoke, his voice was forceful, determined.

"So, if something like that is going on here, if that guy," —he jabbed his finger in the direction of the house—"has done anything to that girl, I'll personally cut off his balls and stuff them down his throat."

John jumped up, fire burning in his gut, and walked over to the doorway. He stood with his hands on his hips, staring out across the tea plantation into the jungle beyond. Images of the IS house in Idlib flashed before his eyes. He took a deep, slow breath, counted to five, held it for two, then exhaled for five. He repeated the process until the anger receded, and he felt a semblance of calm.

Turning, he looked back at Maruti, who was sitting forward, his forearms on his knees, staring at the floor.

"I've seen the worst excesses of human behavior, Maruti, often committed in the name of some unseen god or belief. Perhaps now, you can understand why I have been so cynical about this place from the beginning."

Maruti nodded and looked up. He studied John's face for a while. "It's not been all bad, has it?"

John pursed his lips and gave a reluctant smile. "No... it hasn't. In fact, don't tell anyone, but I was starting to enjoy it." He took a deep breath. "The meditation is helping, and... I know... if I keep up the practice, it will benefit me lifelong."

"Good." Maruti nodded and half-smiled. "I'm sorry, John, that you've had your faith in humanity destroyed again."

"Why should you apologize, my friend? You've been nothing but kind to me. Look..." John paused and moved back to the bed and sat down. He leaned forward and looked straight at him. "Maruti, despite experiences,"—he gestured back toward the house—"like this, I've learned people will surprise you, and it's often the ones you least expect. Never lose faith in the goodness of human beings, whatever happens."

Maruti looked back at John, a strange look on his face, a glint in his eye. After a moment, he grinned.

"Perhaps you should be living in that house, John?"

"Ha," John scoffed. "Shoot me before that happens." He shifted back until he was leaning against the wall and stared at the wall above Maruti's head.

"Is there anything on the phone you don't want them to see?"

"No. Anyway, they won't know the passcode. It will take them forever to get into it. But I can't get hold of Adriana without leaving here."

"Hmmm."

"But I'm not too worried about that. I can always go out and buy another phone from the town."

Maruti was shaking his head.

"What?"

"You won't get back in."

John frowned, waiting for him to explain.

"It's happened before." Maruti sighed and shook his head. "I never connected the dots. There was a young English woman here, maybe two years ago. Pretty thing, bubbly..." Maruti trailed off, smiling at a distant memory. "Matilda was very fond of her. Abbie was her name, from London." He looked up at John. "Anyway, one day, she just ups and leaves, without a word to any of us. That evening in the hall, an announcement was made that she'd stolen from several of the students, and if she ever made contact, we were to have nothing to do with her." He shook his head sadly.

"The thing is not one student admitted to anything being stolen." He looked up at John again. "She wasn't the type, John. I even asked the guards, and they said they'd heard nothing about any thefts but were under strict instructions not to let her back in."

"Do you think..."

Maruti puffed his cheeks and blew out air. "I hope not."

The thought hung in the air, and they both lapsed into silence.

"John, if you leave, they will say something like that about you. They've searched your room, taken your phone. It won't take much for them to spread rumors about you. However, while you are still here, there's not much they can do about it."

"Yeah." John chewed his lip. "I need to speak to Adriana." He glanced across at Maruti. "Do you know Abbie's full name?"

"No, but her record will be in the office on the computer. There's also a phone there."

"Can you get me in there? I mean, without Gayatri knowing?"

Maruti grinned, the spark back in his eyes.

"People don't call me Yoda for nothing."

60

J ohn waited while Maruti locked the door of their room. "Probably not worth doing that anymore."

"Habit," Maruti replied and slipped the keys into his pocket. "We'll have to wait for Gayatri to go to the meditation."

John glanced at his watch. "We still have half an hour, but there's something that's been bothering me. We'll go there first."

Maruti raised his eyebrows but followed John as he set off along the path.

John stopped outside Sarah's room. The door was closed, and the curtains were still drawn. He frowned, looked to make sure Maruti had caught up, then stepped forward and knocked on the door.

There was no response.

John tried again, and this time called out, "Sarah, it's John and Maruti. Are you inside?"

"What do you want?" her muffled voice replied.

John stepped closer to the door, "Sarah, I'm..." He glanced at Maruti. "We're worried about you."

"I'm okay. Go away."

John sighed and looked away from the door. Maruti gave him a questioning look, then stepped forward.

"Let me," he said. John stepped back, and Maruti said gently, "Sarah, it's Maruti. Open the door. I want to see you."

There was no response, and John was on the verge of walking away when they heard the door unbolting.

It cracked open, and Sarah, with puffy red eyes, peered out through the gap. Maruti placed his hand on the door.

"Sarah, dear, what's the matter?"

John heard a sob, then she moved away from the door. Maruti looked back at John, his face creased in a frown, then pushed the door open. Sarah was sitting on the bed, her head in her hands, her shoulders shaking as she sobbed bitterly. Slipping off his flip-flops, Maruti stepped inside, sitting down beside her. He placed an arm around her, but she pushed him away. Maruti looked up at John, clearly at a loss as to what to do next.

Moving inside, John saw a chair in the corner and pulled it closer, sitting down in front of her. He said nothing, both men silently watching as she cried. Eventually, her sobs subsided and Maruti pulled a handkerchief from his pocket and handed it over.

She wiped her eyes and blew her nose noisily into the cloth.

John gave her a moment, then cleared his throat. He had a gut feeling something had happened. It had been gnawing away in his subconscious, but he needed to hear it from her.

"Sarah, we are here to help you," he said gently. He glanced at Maruti, then asked, "Did something happen... up at the house?"

Sarah nodded, sniffed, then started crying again.

Maruti placed a hand on her shoulder, and this time she

didn't push him away.

John took a deep breath. He needed to remain calm.

"What happened, Sarah?" he prompted.

Sarah sniffed, wiped her nose again, and stared at the handkerchief in her hands, twisting it and untwisting it.

She still didn't reply, and John glanced over at Maruti. He was also watching her hands.

"Sarah?"

Without looking up, she said, "He... he..." She sobbed again.

John clenched and unclenched his fingers and looked around the room. He saw a water bottle and glass on a shelf. Standing, he filled the glass and handed it to her.

Sarah took it, sniffed, and looked up. "Thank you."

John smiled. "We are here to help you, Sarah. We'll keep you safe."

Sarah nodded and looked at Maruti. She smiled for the first time, although her eyes were still wet.

John sat down again and waited for her to sip the water. "Whatever happened, Sarah, it wasn't your fault."

She nodded and took another sip of water.

"But you have to tell us because we, Maruti and I, want to make sure nothing like this ever happens again to anyone else."

She nodded again, took a deep breath, and straightened up, looking at Maruti.

"You've always been so kind to me, Maruti."

He smiled and squeezed her shoulder. "You are like my daughter, Sarah."

Sarah nodded and swallowed. "Okay," She took a deep breath. "This is what happened."

61

John stood outside and waited for Maruti to close the door and come down the steps. John had never seen him look so dejected. Maruti hesitated and looked back at the room.

"I think I should stay with her."

"I've been thinking about that. She doesn't have a room-mate, right? Is there anyone among the women you can trust?"

"I don't know." Maruti thought for a moment, then shook his head. "I mean, I need to think about it. They all love Atman."

John reached out and placed his hands on Maruti's shoulders.

"I know this is a tough time for you, but I need you to behave as if nothing is wrong, that we don't know anything. Just for a little while."

Maruti frowned, then nodded.

"I want you to go to the meditation as normal." John glanced at Sarah's door. "I told her to lock the door, so she'll be okay. Maybe tell Gayatri you bumped into Sarah, and she said she's not feeling well, but make sure you are seen in the hall."

"What about you?"

"Don't worry about me. I'm already the black sheep of this family. I missed the morning session, so my absence is probably expected." He shook his head. "There is no way I can sit in there, knowing what we know now."

"I'm going to struggle."

"I have faith in you." John squeezed his shoulders. "Now, how was Yoda going to get me into the office?"

"Well... with my key."

"Huh. Obviously." John held his hand out. "Okay, give it to me."

Maruti pulled the keys out of his pocket and selected one of them. "This one."

"Any alarm?"

"No."

"How about the computer? Any password?"

Maruti told him.

"Thanks. Now, go on up to the hall like usual. I'll hang around until Gayatri has left, then go in to check the records and make a call. I'll meet you back in the room, okay?"

"Yes. Be careful."

"I'm always careful."

Maruti nodded and started walking toward the hall.

"Hey, one more thing." John jogged toward him. "Do you know the combination to the safe? I want my passport and wallet."

"No, only Gayatri knows it."

"Damn. Okay, I'll worry about that later." He looked at his watch. "You'd better go. You'll be late."

62

John gave it fifteen minutes to be safe, then slowly made his way toward the office. Once he was in sight of the guardhouse, he paused and waited. He could see the guard through the open doorway, staring at his phone. A cable went from the phone to an earpiece, suggesting he was watching something, but John waited to see if the guard checked the security feed on the screen in front of him. After a couple of minutes, with the guard not once looking up from the phone, John moved forward as quickly and silently as he could and slipped the key into the lock in the office door. The door opened silently, and John slipped inside, closing it behind him. He locked it from the inside—it wouldn't do for anyone to surprise him, although he expected everyone to be at the meditation hall.

Moving quickly through the front office, he opened the door at the rear and walked into another room with a row of filing cabinets and a clunky desktop computer on the desk that took up the center of the room. John walked behind the desk and peered out the window. It looked out into greenery. Unlikely anyone would see him at the desk. Pulling out the chair, he sat down and moved the mouse. The screen flickered on, and John typed in Maruti's password. He scanned the screen and then opened the document folder. Staring at the screen, he drummed his fingers on the desktop. It would take too much time for him to go through all the files—time he probably didn't have. What was the best way to do it?

An idea struck him. Opening the web browser, he signed into Google Drive, then clicked on the document folder and started uploading the files to his account. It took a couple of minutes to select everything he thought might be useful. Waiting for the files to upload, he emailed Adriana with his Google login and password, asking her to look for a former student named Abbie and why.

Satisfied, he reached over for the phone, picked up the handset, and dialed Adriana's number from memory. While the phone connected, he noticed an unusual clicking sound. At first, he thought nothing of it, then just as the phone started ringing at the other end, he slammed the handset down, disconnecting the call. He stared at the handset, his mind racing. What was that sound? He frowned. Was the phone bugged? No, he shook his head. He was getting paranoid. He picked up the handset again, then immediately put it back. Now the thought was stuck in his head, he didn't want to take the risk.

John checked the computer screen again, then pushed his chair back. There was still time. He opened the desk drawers and looked around inside but found nothing of interest, only old pens, a stapler, and other cast-off stationery items.

Standing, he took a quick look out the window, then walked to the filing cabinets. He gave them the quick once over but guessed there would be enough information in the files he was sending Adriana, so he walked into the front office. He checked through the desk drawers, but the only interesting thing he found was a well-read romance novel with a bare-chested man on the cover.

"Well, well, well, Gayatri." John grinned. "You are human after all."

He looked around the office again to see if he had missed anything, and his eyes fell on the safe.

"My passport," he muttered. He had to get Gayatri to open the safe for him. John chewed his lip, staring blankly at the large steel box. Something was niggling away in his subconscious, and he turned to look at her computer. What was it? Closing his eyes, he took a deep breath, relaxing his body, stilling his mind, did it twice more, and then his eyes snapped open. Reaching out, he picked up the computer keyboard and slowly turned it over.

"Ha! So much for security, Gayatri." Taped to the underside of the keyboard was a list of handwritten passwords. John ran his finger down them and stopped, not believing his luck. He memorized the six-digit number, then strode across the room and knelt in front of the safe. Punching in the code, the keypad beeped, an LED turned from red to green, and something inside the door whirred and clicked. The door swung open.

John reached inside and pulled out a handful of Ziplock bags, searching for one with his name on it. Finding it, he removed his wallet and passport, stuffing them in his pocket. Spotting a phone in one bag, he rifled through the rest of them, ignoring the newer iPhones and Samsungs. He didn't want a modern smartphone that he wouldn't be able to unlock. He needed something old-school, like... He stopped and ripped open the bag in his hand—an old Nokia. Pressing the power button, he waited for it to come on, hoping it had enough battery life left. The screen glowed green, and he checked the battery indicator—half. Good, that was plenty. He read the name on the bag. "Sorry, Eric, but I'll need this."

John tossed the bags back into the safe and closed the door. Standing up, he stared at the phone. He wanted to call Adriana, but... He glanced at his watch. It was better to do it elsewhere. Walking back into the rear office, he checked the screen—one minute remaining. It was the longest minute of John's life., but once done, he logged out, cleared the browser history, and shut down the computer. Stepping back from the desk, he looked around once more, ensuring everything looked as he found it, then walked out. He did the same in the front office, then stood with his ear to the door. It was quiet outside, so he opened it slowly, glanced quickly at the guard hut, then stepped outside.

He turned to lock the door, and just as he removed the key from the lock, he sensed rather than heard someone near him. There was a stinging pain in the side of his neck, and the glossy dark green paint of the door was the last thing he saw.

63

The throbbing in his temples woke him. He blinked his eyes open and winced as the harsh white light burned into his eyes, so he closed them again. Cracking his eyelids open, he allowed his eyes to adjust to the light before opening them fully. Where was he? What happened? His mouth was dry, his tongue thick, and when he moved his head, it felt heavy and slow.

He turned his head and looked around the room. He was lying on a bed in a room similar to the dorm rooms, but this one was bare of any decoration, only peeling white paint and a bare fluorescent tube in the ceiling. There were two doors, one to the outside and another in the end wall, slightly open.

John sat up, and a wave of nausea overwhelmed him as the throbbing in his head intensified. He groaned and lay back down again. What was wrong with him?

Closing his eyes, he remembered leaving the office and locking the door, but how did he end up here?

The door opened, and Gayatri walked in with another

middle-aged lady John had seen once or twice in the dining hall.

"Good, you are awake. How are you feeling?"

John frowned and tried to sit up again.

"It's okay, stay there. You need to rest."

"What happened? Where am I?"

The other lady took his wrist and felt for his pulse, her eyes on her wristwatch.

"This is Uma. She's been taking care of you."

Uma smiled but kept her eyes on her watch.

"Uma was a nurse before she came here," Gayatri continued.

"Where am I?"

"This is our sickbay, John. You collapsed." She looked at Uma. "Poor thing, he doesn't remember." Looking back down at John, she said, "The guard found you in the carpark. You were lying on the ground. The heat must have got the better of you."

Uma let go of his wrist and moved out of his field of vision, then John heard water pouring. Gayatri moved closer and placed her hands under his shoulders.

"Here, sit up now. You need to rehydrate."

John sat up and felt Gayatri adjusting the pillows behind his back as Uma held a glass of water to his lips. John drank eagerly, the cool water easing the harsh dry feeling in the back of his throat.

"Thank you," he murmured. "Can I have some more, please?"

"Of course." Uma had a kind face and smiled readily.

John drank again, emptying the second glass, then wiped his mouth with the back of his hand.

"Now rest," Uma said gently, with a hint of an antipodean twang. "I've kept some vegetable broth here."

She gestured toward a table John hadn't noticed before. "Have it whenever you feel up to it, but don't rush. You can stay here as long as you like."

John had no intention of staying, but he nodded and smiled. "Thank you."

"Uma will be in the next room overnight, John, so if you need anything, just call out."

"Thank you, Gayatri." Then he frowned. Overnight? He turned his wrist and looked at his watch. "Eight-thirty? I've been here all day?"

"Yes, John, we were very worried about you, but Atman said you would be okay." Gayatri's face lit up, "He sent you healing, and see, you are already feeling better."

"Yes, it's a miracle."

"It is. We are all so blessed."

"Yup."

"Okay, Gayatri." Uma placed her hand on Gayatri's arm. "I think we should leave John to rest now. Let him heal."

"Yes, yes, of course." Gayatri walked to the door and waited for Uma to follow. "Good night, John." She flicked off the light.

John waited for a minute, then swung his legs off the bed, the movement sending another wave of nausea running through his body. Closing his eyes, he breathed slowly until it passed. He remembered something and raised his hand to the side of his neck. There was a tiny swelling, like a mosquito bite, still tender to the touch.

He hadn't collapsed. Someone had jabbed him with something.

Shit. He felt his pockets. The passport, wallet, Maruti's keys, and the phone were gone. *Bastards.*

By now, his eyes had adjusted to the darkness, and he reached out for the mug of vegetable broth on the side table, and took a sip. It was lukewarm but tasty, but he quickly changed his mind. What if they had put something in it? Maybe he was paranoid, but right now he didn't know who he could trust. The water was already making him feel better, so that would have to be enough. He wasn't planning on staying a minute longer than necessary in this room.

He stood, steadying himself against the wall with one hand, and walked to the door. It was locked. He moved to the internal door, gently eased it open, and peered out. Uma was sitting in the next room, her feet up on another bed and a book in her hand. John pushed the door shut.

He could just walk out, but she was bound to protest and report to Gayatri, who in turn would report to Atman. He turned his attention to the window. That's how he would leave. Let them think he was in the room for as long as possible. It would probably be a couple of hours before she looked in on him again.

Crossing the room, he moved the table out of the way and unlatched the window. He opened both panes fully, took a breath, and hoisted himself onto the windowsill. Resting his butt on the sill, he was strangely out of breath. What the hell had they given him? Once his breathing was back to normal, he swung his legs out, then eased himself to the ground, careful not to make a noise. He stood for a moment, still a little lightheaded, then reached back inside and pulled the window shut.

Turning around, he took a deep breath and looked across the dark expanse of the estate.

Now, what should he do?

64

The sickbay was simply two rooms in the same building where the Sri Lankan girls stayed. John got his bearings, and it didn't take him long to make his way back to the men's dormitory, despite still feeling unsteady. It was almost nine, so there was no-one around to see John walking around, the doors to all the rooms already closed. John hurried down to the end and twisted the handle to his room. The door didn't budge. He tried again. Damn, it was locked. John knocked on the door.

"Maruti? It's John." There was no reply. John knocked again, harder this time. "Maruti."

He moved over to the window and cupped his hands around his face, peering through the glass. The room was dark, the curtains closed, but through a gap in the curtain, John could see the room was empty.

Where had the old fella gone? An uneasy feeling formed in the pit of John's belly, but he pushed it down, not allowing it to spread.

John moved across to the next room and pounded on the door. He heard a grumble inside, then after a minute, the door opened. John didn't wait for the occupant to say anything.

"Have you seen Maruti?"

"No." The man, a tall thin Swede, whose name John couldn't remember, scratched his head. "Why?"

"He's not in his room."

The Swede shrugged. "Maybe he's in the hall, meditating?"

John shook his head. "I doubt it. When was the last time you saw him?"

The Swede rubbed his chin, then turned to look back into the room. John looked past him at his roommate lying on the other bed.

"The morning meditation?"

"Yes." His roommate nodded. "I don't think he came to lunch, though."

"Fuck," John swore.

"Hey, language brother."

But John had already gone.

65

Johhn tried to run, but whatever they had jabbed him with was still in his blood, and the exertion made him feel sick, so he settled into a sort of running walk. He was halfway past the women's dormitory when he stopped and turned back. At Sarah's door, he stopped and knocked.

"Sarah?"

There was no reply. That feeling in John's stomach was growing. Stepping sideways to peer through the window, he saw the room was dark with no sign of life.

As he had with his room, John pounded on the next room's door until someone came to the window.

"Where's Sarah?"

"I don't know. I was told she's left."

"Left?"

"Yes, someone mentioned it at lunch."

"Fuck," John cursed, and the woman inside the room flinched. Ignoring her, John continued toward the meditation hall.

He broke into a run, the anger-induced adrenaline

forcing out whatever drug residue remained in his system. In the hall, he tried the entrance door, but it was locked. He ran around to the rear entrance, taking the steps two at a time, and tried the door handle, but it was locked as well. John stood on the top step and considered his next move.

Where could Maruti have gone?

He jumped off the steps and ran to the dining hall, finding it locked and dark. Where else could he be? John ran to the office, but before he got there, he could see by the lack of light, no-one was inside. Spotting the light leaking out from under the door of the guard hut, John ran over and banged on the door.

The door opened, and the guard, a thin man in his sixties, looked out.

"Sir?"

"Did anyone leave the ashram today?"

"Ah, no, sir." The puzzled guard shook his head. "At least, not that I know of, but I only started at six."

"How can I find out if anyone left before you came on duty?"

"The register, sir."

"Register?"

The guard stepped back and pointed to a large, hard-covered journal on the desk. "Anyone who comes in and out has to be entered into the book."

John held out his hand. "Show me."

"Sir?"

John exhaled loudly. "My friend is missing. Show me the damn register." He growled, and the guard quickly picked up the book and leafed through it.

"Sir, see here, today's date. No-one has been in or out."

John took the book and stared at the blank page. He leafed back through the book, checking each page. No-one had been in or out for days. In fact, the last person to come through the gate was John the day he'd gone out for a walk.

John snapped the book shut and handed it back. "What's your name?"

"Sanhita, sir."

"Sanhita, is there any chance someone could have left the ashram without it being recorded in here?"

"No, sir. Georges Sir is very strict. We must record everyone who comes in and out of this gate."

John exhaled loudly. "Hey, I'm sorry I shouted earlier. I'm just worried for my friend."

"It's okay, sir." Sanhita smiled nervously. "What is your friend's name?"

"Maruti."

"Maruti?" Sanhita's eyebrows shot up, and his mouth dropped open. "Since when?"

"Since lunchtime, I think."

"I'll phone Mr. Georges."

John slowly nodded as he stared blankly across the darkened car park.

"No, wait." He turned back. "Let me check a few more places. We wouldn't want to trouble Mr. Georges so late if it's a false alarm."

"No." He looked over John's shoulder, scanning the carpark, then lowered his voice. "He gets angry if we bother him with small things."

John nodded as if he understood. "Yes, and we don't want that. Tell me, which room is Gayatri's?"

"Number seven, sir."

"Good, thank you. I'll leave you alone now."

"It's okay, sir." Sanhita smiled. "If there is anything I can help with, you know where I am."

John reached over and shook his hand. "I'll remember

that." He took a couple of steps, then turned back. "Hey, if we need to call the police..." Sanhita looked worried, so he held up his hands. "No, I'm sure we won't, but if we did, how soon could they get here?"

Sanhita puffed out his cheeks and looked up at the sky as he thought about it. "Maybe half an hour if it's an emergency." He looked back at John. "But we have to get Mr. Georges' permission first. He deals with the police."

"I'm sure he does."

66

Gayatri wasn't happy when she opened the door. "John, you're supposed to be in the sickbay." She poked her head out and looked up and down the path, "Why are you making so much noise? It's after light's out."

"Do you have a roommate?"

Gayatri frowned. "No."

John pushed past her and walked into her room.

"John, we do not allow men in the women's dormitory," she shrieked from the doorway.

"Come in, close the door, and sit down." John looked around for a chair and sat down.

She glared at him from the doorway. "I most certainly will not."

John sighed. "Okay, leave the door open or close the door. It's up to you. I have something to tell you that you won't want to hear, and you won't want anyone else to hear."

Gayatri stared at him for a moment as conflicting thoughts fought inside her head. Then she pushed the door until it was almost closed, but not quite.

"Gayatri, I'm not going to attack you. I have much more important things to do."

"Oh." A strange look briefly passed across her face, but she moved closer.

"You'll probably want to sit down." John gestured toward her bed, but she shook her head.

"Suit yourself. Maruti is missing, and so is Sarah."

"No..." Gayatri frowned. "Georges said Sarah left the ashram. That's why she didn't attend the meditations today. She had a family emergency and had to leave immediately. "

"He's lying."

"John! Don't make accusations like this. You are new here. Who do you think you are?"

"Listen to me," John growled, and Gayatri flinched. "I saw her this morning. She wasn't going anywhere. She locked herself in her room for her own safety. Now, she isn't there."

"Safety? What are you saying?"

John took a deep breath. "Atman sexually assaulted her during the naming ceremony."

"What nonsense!" Gayatri exploded and pointed at the door. "Get out of my room!"

"No, it's true, and I think she isn't the first."

"This is a disgusting allegation. I'll see that you are removed from this ashram immediately."

"The Sri Lankan girl, Nihinsa."

Gayatri blinked.

"I believe she was also assaulted. She has disappeared."

"Rubbish. She was homesick, and she went home. She's a young girl. It's hard for them to be away from family."

"She hasn't gone home. Her parents have reported her missing."

"I never liked you, John." Gayatri was shaking her head

vehemently, her eyes darting around the room. "From the first day you came here, I knew you were a troublemaker."

John closed his eyes and took a deep breath. It didn't work. He jumped to his feet and crossed to the doorway in a single stride. Grabbing her by the shoulders, he bent down to stare directly into her eyes.

"Why don't you get it?" John growled at her, and she twisted her head away. "Stop protecting the man. He's a sexual predator and a conman, and you turning a blind eye is only enabling him. He should be in prison."

"No, no." Gayatri's eyes were moist, and she wouldn't stop shaking her head, "No, no. You are wrong... wrong... wrong."

John relaxed his grip and guided her over to her bed. She looked up, a hint of fear in her eyes.

"Sit down." He pressed on her shoulders until she sat, then moved away. "I know it's hard to take in, but Sarah told Maruti and me what happened to her. That's why she hasn't been going to the meditations. She's scared it will happen again, and she thinks it's all her fault."

Gayatri's shoulders shook, and she stifled a sob. She covered her ears with her hands and shook her head. John moved closer and crouched down in front of her, lowering his voice, consciously making his tone gentler.

"I'm sorry, Gayatri, but I'm sure there are others. We need to stop him..."

Tears ran down her face as she rocked back and forth, her hands still covering her ears, her eyes closed as if that would make John go away.

"Maruti told me there was a student called Abbie... We think it might have happened to her, too."

Gayatri opened her eyes and looked up, her hands dropping to her lap. "No. She was a thief. Good riddance to her."

"Was she?" John raised both eyebrows. "What if I'm right, Gayatri? What if Sarah isn't the only one? What if it keeps happening, and you do nothing about it?"

Gayatri just looked at John, then looked away.

"Sarah and Maruti are now both missing, Gayatri. I've checked with the security guard, Sanhita. He says no-one has left the ashram for days. They are here somewhere, Gayatri, and I need your help to find them."

67

J ohn realized having your whole belief system destroyed in a matter of minutes was a lot to process, so despite the urgency, he sat back and allowed Gayatri time to digest what he had just told her.

The constant shaking of her head had stopped, and her tears had dried, but she sat in silence, staring blankly at the floor.

John turned his attention to finding Maruti and Sarah. He was convinced they were still somewhere on the property, and the obvious place to check next was Atman's house. Should he just go up and confront him? Ask him where they are?

John chewed his lip as he visualized approaching the house, then Georges or Max spotting him on the security feed and intercepting him before he could get inside. He was sure they would prevent him from speaking to Atman.

He had to find another way.

Gayatri moved, disturbing his thoughts. She stood and walked to the bookshelf in the back of the room. Moving a stack of books on one of the shelves, she reached behind them. John's eyebrows jumped as she pulled out a bottle of *arrack*. She walked back, the bottle in one hand, a coffee mug and water glass in the other, and sat on the bed opposite John. Without a word, she splashed a generous amount into the glass and handed it to John, then half-filled her coffee mug and placed the bottle down on the floor. John waited as she stared into her mug. She sighed, raised her mug, took a large gulp, grimacing as the spirit burned her throat. Only then did she look at John.

"Might as well," she shrugged.

John took a sip, swallowed, then took another larger mouthful. The buzz was instant after a week without alcohol, sending endorphins rushing straight to his brain.

"Has anything like this happened before?"

She took another sip of *arrack* and shook her head. "No... I mean, I don't know, maybe."

"Maybe?"

She sighed and looked down at the floor again, avoiding eye contact.

"I... it..." She sighed again and looked up. "You have to understand, John, I love... loved..." She took another sip, then shook her head slowly. "Love."

John waited.

"If it happened, I didn't notice. I was too caught up in proving myself to him." She looked at John, her eyes red from crying. "We crave his attention, John. He fills us with such joy and happiness, we'll do anything to be near him, to have him notice us, even if it's just a word or two." Her expression changed, and she asked, hopefully, "Maybe it's all a misunderstanding? Could Sarah have made it up?"

"Why would she do that, Gayatri? I saw her. She was

distraught, too scared to even see him again. That's not the reaction of someone making things up."

Gayatri looked away, and her shoulders slumped.

"And where is she now? Maruti? Nihinsa?"

Gayatri nodded and stared into the coffee mug she was holding in both hands.

"If you still have a doubt, consider this. Maruti and I confronted Atman about Nihinsa. Of course, he denied everything, but when I got back to my room, someone had searched it, and my phone was missing."

"You had a phone?"

"You have alcohol."

"Huh."

John pointed to his neck, "Can you see this? It's probably too dark in here. Give me your hand."

Gayatri frowned and hesitated, then slowly held her hand out. John placed her fingertips on the small lump on the side of his neck.

"Can you feel that?"

She nodded, and he let go of her hand.

"I was searching the office. Maruti gave me his keys. When I came out, someone jabbed me in the neck. I didn't collapse. Someone drugged me."

"No, now you are going too far. I don't believe it."

"I took my passport and a phone from the safe. When I came to in the sickbay, my pockets were empty, and I'm pretty sure you and Uma didn't take them."

Gayatri stared at him for a moment, her eyes narrowed, then exhaled loudly. "Okay." She raised her mug to her lips and then stopped. Tilting her head to one side, she asked, "How did you get into the safe?"

"You taped the combination to the back of your keyboard."

Gayatri almost smiled... almost. Her mug continued its journey to her lips, and she knocked back the contents in one go. She gasped and shook her head, then put the mug down on the bed.

"Right. What do we do now?"

68

"I need to get into the house."

"Georges won't let you in."

"Let me rephrase that. I need to get into the house without them knowing."

"How?"

"I have an idea, but I'll need your help."

"What can I do at my age? Why don't we just call the police?"

"Will they come? We have no proof, and besides, I'm sure Georges has them in his pocket."

Gayatri nodded slowly. "Yes." She sighed. "Now that you mention it, I saw the District Chief of Police at the house one day. I thought nothing of it at the time, but now..."She bent down and picked up the bottle of *arrack*. John leaned forward and took it off her.

"I need you sober. Plenty of time for the rest of the bottle once this is over." John secured the cap, stood, and walked to the bookshelf. "Good hiding place," he said as he put the bottle back and slid the books in front of it.

"I'm not a bad person, John."

John walked back and sat down again.

"I never said you were, Gayatri." He gestured toward the bookshelf. "There are worse things in life than enjoying an occasional drink. But we can debate morals and philosophy later. Right now, we need to find Maruti and Sarah."

John explained his plan, and Gayatri seemed to perk up, noticing a few flaws and making suggestions. When they were both satisfied, John stood.

"Let's go. The sooner this is over with, the better."

Five minutes later, John hid in the shadows as Gayatri unlocked the office and stepped inside. A moment later, light flooded out from the office windows. John stayed where he was, hoping Gayatri wouldn't lose her nerve and change her mind. His heart skipped a beat as he suddenly thought of something. Would she phone Atman from the office?

He relaxed when she appeared in the doorway, first glancing in his direction, then walking across the carpark and tapping on the door to the guardroom. The door opened, and Sanhita looked out, his face breaking into a smile when he saw Gayatri. John couldn't hear what they were saying, but it seemed to have worked when Sanhita followed Gayatri back to the office.

John waited until they were both inside, then sprinted for the door. Taking two steps inside, he grabbed the old man by the arms and propelled him to a chair, pushing him down. Sanhita struggled and protested, but the old man's strength was no match for John's. Holding him down with one hand, John removed the scarf he had borrowed from Gayatri from around his neck and secured Sanhita's arms to the back of the chair. He checked the knot, then walked around and crouched in front of him.

Sanhita's eyes widened. "You... why?"

"I'm sorry, Sanhita. I'll release you soon."

"But..."

John placed a hand on his shoulder. "I'll explain later. It's only for a little while. Are you comfortable? Are your arms okay?"

Sanhita frowned, his eyes darting from John to Gayatri and back again. He nodded, "Y-Yes."

"Good." John removed another scarf he had draped around his neck. "I need to secure your legs, okay?"

Sanhita nodded again.

John wrapped the scarf around his ankles and tied them to the chair legs. He tugged on the scarf and looked up. "Not too tight?"

"No." Sanhita shook his head. "Mr. Georges will be furious with you."

"Yes, but let me worry about him." He jerked his head toward Gayatri. "Gayatri will be here with you until I get back, so you are safe, okay?"

Sanhita remained silent but shot a worried glance in Gayatri's direction.

John unclipped a set of keys from Sanhita's belt. "Do these open everything?"

Sanhita frowned.

"I'll take that as a yes."

John searched through the keyring, checking the labels until he found the key he needed, removed it from the keyring, and slipped it into his pocket. Stepping away, he grabbed a pen and a piece of paper from the reception counter, scribbled a number on it, and handed it to Gayatri.

"If I'm not back within an hour, I want you to call this number. Her name is Adriana. Tell her what I've done and to do whatever she can to get the police to come here."

Gayatri stared at the paper, her eyebrows knitted together. "It's a foreign number."

"Yes. She's my partner. You might need to explain to her that the local police may be compromised."

Gayatri looked up. "But..." her eyes were wide. "If you don't come back..."

John interrupted her. "Once you make the call, take my car. It's the Toyota Camry. Sanhita here will give you the keys. Both of you take the car and get out of here until the police arrive."

Gayatri made to protest, and John raised his finger, punctuating each word with a jab in her direction. "Do. Not. Stay. Here."

Gayatri looked unhappy, but she didn't say anything.

"Now, do you have some candles? You're going to need them."

69

John crossed the carpark and stepped into the guardroom, looking for anything that might be useful. Spotting a large Maglite flashlight lying on the desk, he picked it up, hefted it in his hand, then flicked on the switch, sending a powerful beam of light across the small room. Turning it off, he picked up the walkie-talkie from the charger and turned down the volume then unplugged the handset from the phone and tossed it and the walkie-talkie out the door into the bushes. He was just about to walk out when his eyes fell on the key cabinet attached to the wall. He pulled open the door and scanned the rows of keys. Spotting the keys for his hire car, he removed them from their hook, then with a grin, removed the Range Rover key fob, and slipped it into his pocket.

John jogged back across the carpark and popped his head in the office door. Gayatri was kneeling in front of Sanhita, untying his legs.

"What are you doing?"

She looked up with a start. "You frightened me." She

continued untying the scarf. "I told Sanhita what's happened. He's agreed to help us."

Sanhita nodded. "You should have told me from the beginning." He shook his head, "This is bad, very bad."

"Sanhita has granddaughters."

John examined his face, then nodded. The man seemed genuine.

"Okay." He held out his keys. "Here, take these, Gayatri. I've changed my mind and I think you should both leave now. When I shut the power off, they will send someone down from the house to check why the generator hasn't come on. It's best if you're not here then."

"Where should we go?" Gayatri took the keys, then finished releasing Sanhita's legs and stood.

"I don't care, just don't be here."

Gayatri moved around to the back of the chair and started loosening the knot. "But how will we know if you are successful or not?"

John scratched his head. She had a point.

"Sanhita, take your phone from the guard hut before going. I'll call you from here." He checked his watch, "Give me one hour. If you don't hear from me, then Gayatri knows what to do."

Sanhita nodded and shook his hands free.

"Give me your number." John grabbed a pen and wrote the number on the back of his hand. "Okay, now go, both of you."

John followed them out and turned left toward the generator room.

He switched on the Maglite and wedged it under his left armpit, then removed the key he had taken from Sanhita's keyring, slipped it into the padlock, and it clicked open easily. He removed it, placing it on the ground where he could find it easily, then pulled the double doors open. A strong smell of diesel and smoke wafted over him. Turning his head away, he pushed the doors wider to ventilate the room. He waited for a moment, then stepped inside, shining the flashlight around until he found the light switch.

John knew the power supply for the whole ashram came through this shed; he had seen the wires from the power pole in the road outside. When there was a power outage, the generator automatically kicked in, which meant there was an automatic transfer switch somewhere. He just needed to find it.

The generator was a large steel box, which took up most of the room. On the wall to the left of the door was a steel cabinet bolted to the wall. A large cable entered one side, and John guessed it must be the external supply. The five cables on the other side must be from where the power was distributed around the ashram.

He unhooked the latch on the front of the cabinet and swung the door open. John ran his eyes over the rows of fuses and switches inside. One of them had to be the main circuit breaker. In the bottom left corner was a switch much larger than all the others. That must be it. He took a step back and traced a cable leading from the bottom of the switchboard to another wall-mounted box on the right. From that box, a cable ran to the generator itself. That had to be the transfer switch. John took a breath. Only one way to find out.

Reaching into the main panel, he pulled the large switch down, and the room was plunged into darkness. He stepped back and looked out the door. The lights on the path had gone out, and the usual amber glow from the lights around the dining and meditation halls was nowhere to be seen. John counted in his head, and when he reached fifteen, the generator rumbled to life, and the lights came back on. John nodded to himself—halfway there.

He bent down, picked up the padlock, and pushed the doors until there was just enough room for him to move in and out. Once he turned off the generator, he would need to move fast. Stepping back inside, he looked once more at the cables and where they led.

Satisfied he was correct in his assumption, he closed his left eye, waited for ten seconds, then pulled down on the switch in the smaller box. The rumble of the generator ceased, and John was standing in darkness again, but he had no time to celebrate.

Switching the flashlight on, he stepped outside, closed the doors, and relocked the padlock. Turning off the flashlight, he opened his left eye. It had already adjusted to the lack of light, and he could make out the pathway. If anyone came from the house, they would come from the left. He turned right and took off at a sprint.

70

J ohn ran easily along the front path. Both eyes had adjusted to the darkness, and the light colored stone of the path reflected enough moon and starlight for him to find his way. He noticed the flickering glow of candlelight from a couple of windows in the women's dormitory as he ran past. John didn't slow. It felt good to be moving again as he settled into a fast, easy rhythm, grateful for his regular morning runs.

At the men's dorm, someone was sitting on the step outside their room. John didn't see who, and he didn't hesitate, ignoring their shout as he sped past. Reaching the stand of trees, he plunged into the darkness, relying on memory to find his way, then quickly burst out the other side and sprinted up the slope toward the house. His breathing became labored, and his thighs burned as he forced himself faster up the slope. Reaching the bottom step he crouched out of sight and fought to get his breath back.

The house was dark, but he could hear voices inside, and the beam of a flashlight flashed across the living room window. John waited, taking deep breaths, slowing his heartbeat. He needed to be calm for the next step. Straightening up, he raised his head above the level of the verandah and scanned the windows. Candles had been lit in the living room, but he could no longer hear voices.

He took a deep breath and slowly climbed the steps, then dashed across the verandah and pinned himself to the wall beside the window. He was gambling the security cameras didn't work when the power was off, and so far, it looked as if he was right. Carefully, he moved his head so he could see into the living room. A flickering candle on a side table combined with the light from the oil lamp under Atman's photo to light the room enough for John to see it was empty.

John ducked down below the window and moved around the side of the house. He stopped at another window, but the room was dark and appeared to be empty. John checked his watch. It had been almost ten minutes since he'd turned off the generator. It was only a matter of time before they sent someone to check. He needed to get inside before the lights came back on.

John continued down the side of the house, sticking close to the wall. A board creaked under his feet, and he paused, his heart in his mouth, ready to run, but after a moment with no response from inside the house, he continued.

He was halfway to the rear corner of the house when he heard voices. He strained to hear what they were saying. It had the rhythm and cadence of English but was too muffled for him to understand. He heard a door open and close, then the beam of a flashlight shone jerkily across the rear driveway, accompanied by the sound of footsteps jogging down the rear steps. John crouched down so he wouldn't be seen as the footsteps got further away. An engine started up, then light flooded the driveway as one of the ATVs roared past, heading down the drive toward the entrance to the ashram.

John stood and stared after it, but it was moving too fast for him to make out who was driving. Quickly, he turned and crept back to the front of the house. He now had about five minutes, maybe ten minutes max, to get inside the house before the lights came back on.

It took less than a minute to reach the door, and he twisted the handle and pushed.

It was locked.

Shit, shit, shit! John cursed silently. Of course, it was locked. He had to find another way. John tried the window, but it wouldn't budge. John cursed again. He moved to the right of the door and tried the window that opened from the dining area, prying his fingertips beneath the window frame, but nothing happened. He kept moving and stopped at the corner, peering down the side of the house. The verandah ended here, and the ground was lower on this side, preventing him access to the windows.

About two-thirds of the way down, soft golden light from a candle flowed out from a doorway. Steps led from the door down to ground level, and John could just make out the shape of a row of trash cans. He turned to look directly below him. The ground appeared to be level, so he tucked the Maglite into his waistband, took a deep breath, placed both hands on the verandah railing, and vaulted over. He bent his knees on landing, absorbing the impact, but lost his balance and fell onto his side, bruising his elbow on the hard ground. Something scurried off into the bushes, and John held his breath, waiting to see if anyone had heard him.

There was no noise from the house, so he picked himself up and ran in a crouch toward the steps. He stopped, listened, then was about to climb the steps when he heard footsteps. John shrank back against the wall, trying to make himself as small as possible. There was no time to move anywhere, and he hoped the darkness would be enough for him to remain unseen.

A man stepped out and paused on the top step. John recognized the cook and waited, his breath held as the cook removed a packet of cigarettes and a box of matches from his pocket, shook one out, and placed it between his lips. There was a flare of light as he struck a match, shielding it from the breeze with his hands while he lit the end of the cigarette, then tossed the match sideways, narrowly missing John. He took a puff, then exhaled, the smoke just visible in the light from the kitchen.

The cook took another puff, then stepped down into the garden, walked forward, stuck the cigarette in his mouth, and unzipped his pants. As the sound of liquid trickling into the undergrowth filled the air, John slid sideways, climbed the step, and moved inside the house.

71

The kitchen was empty, the benchtops wiped down for the night, and a single guttering candle dripped wax onto the wooden table in the center of the room. John swiftly moved across the room, removing the Maglite from his waistband, and held it up, ready to use as a club. Easing the kitchen door handle down, he pulled the door open. The hallway was dimly lit and silent. To his left were the dining area and living room. He knew those were empty, so he looked right.

Candlelight spilled from an open door near the end of the corridor on the right, but both the doors on the left were closed. There was another door on the right between John and the open door at the end. It was closed, but a faint light leaked out from underneath. John could feel his heart pounding in his chest and consciously slowed his breathing before stepping into the hallway.

He moved slowly, stopping at the first door on the left, the one that had appeared empty when he had looked from outside. He pressed his ear to the door and listened, but the room was silent. There was noise from the end of the corridor, and a shadow moved across the open door. John tensed, waiting for someone to come out, but the shadow moved again, and he heard what sounded like wheels rolling across the floor.

He waited, then moved forward again, this time pausing at the door on the right. Pressing his ear to the door, he listened. There was a rhythmic sound from inside, and he strained to make it out... a voice... chanting? John frowned, trying desperately to make out what it was, then it made sense. He could hear a mantra, one he'd heard years ago when he was in living in India. As he concentrated, he smelt the soft sweet fragrance of incense. He listened for a few more seconds, then decided to move on. His guess was Atman was inside, but he would deal with him later. He needed to find the others first.

Keeping to the right, he moved toward the open door at the end. The interior of the room was reflected in the glass panel of the rear door. John adjusted his position, moving his head so he could see the whole interior of the room. It seemed to be an office. The walls were lined with book-shelves, and a desk was in the center of the room. There was a pair of large flat-screen monitors on the desk, both dark, a candle at each end of the table, and facing the monitors, his back to the door, was Georges. His head was angled down, looking at something on the desk, then his left hand moved, tapping on a calculator, while his right hand jotted something on the paper in front of him. John eased back away from the door.

Where were Maruti and Sarah?

He turned to look at the only door he hadn't checked. With one foot, he stepped across the corridor, placing his foot close to the wall, and slowly transferred his weight. There was no sound from the floor, so he brought his other foot across and slid along the wall toward the door. He again pressed his ear to the door, straining for any sign there was someone inside. He held his breath, conscious it was only minutes before the lights would come back on. All he could hear was the tapping of Georges' fingers on the calculator and the muffled chanting from the other room. John let out his breath and ground his teeth together.

Where the hell were they? All this had been for nothing. He was just about to move back up the corridor toward the kitchen when he heard it. He tensed, thinking it was his imagination, then he heard it again, very soft, almost inaudible—the unmistakable sound of someone calling his name.

72

J ohn eased the door open and slipped inside. As the
door clicked shut behind him, the lights came back
on, and for a moment, it blinded him. He shielded
his eyes with his left arm, holding the Maglite high
with his right hand, ready to defend himself, then he heard
a familiar voice.

"John, I thought it was you."

John dropped his arm and held his finger to his lips. On
his left, lying unconscious on her side on the bed, was
Sarah, her arms and legs secured with plastic zip ties.

"They've drugged her," Maruti whispered from his position on the floor directly in front of John. His arms were tied
behind his back, and his ankles bound together in front of
him, but he was smiling.

"We have to move fast," John whispered. "Max will be
back soon from the generator room." He placed the flashlight on the bed and knelt down in front of Maruti, "Are you
okay?" he asked as he examined his restraints.

Maruti nodded and whispered, "Sorry, John."

"What for?" John murmured, looking at the zip ties

around his ankles and wrists. "Damn it," he cursed and looked around for something to cut them off.

"I did something stupid. After the meditation, I came here and told Georges I knew about Sarah."

John looked back at Maruti. "And?"

Maruti smiled and shrugged his shoulders. "You can see what happened."

"Indeed." There was a small cabinet at the foot of the bed. John stood and walked over, gently sliding the top drawer open. It was empty apart from a set of prayer beads, candles, a packet of incense sticks, and a box of matches.

"And Sarah?" John slid the drawer closed and checked the two beneath it, both also empty.

"They brought her in later like that."

John nodded. "They drugged me, too." He looked down at her. "If they drugged her in the early afternoon it should wear off soon." He turned and scanned the rest of the room, but it didn't seem to be in regular use. The walls were bare, and apart from the bed and the small cabinet, there was no other furniture.

"You cut the power, didn't you?" Maruti asked.

John nodded.

"I thought so."

John glanced over at Maruti, and the old man winked. John couldn't help but smile, the old man's calm demeanor almost infectious.

"You don't seem worried."

"Will worrying help?"

He had a point.

"What's in there?" John whispered, pointing to a side door.

"Bathroom."

John heard the ATV returning. Shrinking away from the

window, he pressed himself against the side wall as the twin beams of the ATV headlights briefly flashed through the room. John's heart rate accelerated. Time was running out for him. He looked down at Maruti, who appeared to be unaffected, his face calm, his posture relaxed.

Once again, John scanned the room, his eyes lingering on the bathroom door. Bending down below the window, he moved to the bathroom and opened the door. Directly in front of the door was a washbasin and vanity unit. John pulled open the drawer of the vanity unit, and his eyes lit up. Lying beside a flattened tube of toothpaste and a well-used toothbrush was a safety razor. John grabbed it and turned around, grinning at Maruti as he held it up, but the old man shook his head.

"Someone's coming."

John's grin disappeared, and he held his breath, listening for any sound. He heard nothing from outside, but Maruti was staring intently at the door. John slid the safety razor into his pocket, stepped back inside the bathroom, and closed the door.

ohn stood with his ear pressed up against the door. The room outside was silent, but then he heard raised voices and footsteps and the sound of the door opening. It was then he remembered he'd left the Maglite lying on the bed.

Clenching his fists, he cursed himself for his stupidity and moved away from the door, positioning himself to the side, ready to jump on whoever came through the door. There was a muffled discussion outside, but by now, John's heart was pounding so hard, he couldn't hear clearly. He narrowed his focus on the door handle, waiting for it to move. The voices continued, then he heard the door outside close, and the voices died away. John waited for a moment, then let out the breath he had been holding and unclenched his fists. He took another deep breath, exhaled slowly, then pressed his ear to the door again. It was silent.

He eased the door open and looked out. Maruti sat watching him, his face expressionless. John looked over at Sarah, who had rolled over onto her stomach, her head turned to one side, eyes still closed, her breathing deep and regular. John walked out and looked around for the flashlight, but it was nowhere to be seen.

"Looking for the flashlight?" Maruti whispered.

"Yeah."

"It's under Sarah."

John gently lifted Sarah by her shoulder and removed the flashlight. "Fuck." He exhaled. "That was lucky."

"Hmmm."

John crouched down in front of Maruti. Pulling the safety razor from his pocket, he rubbed the blade back and forth across the plastic strip of the zip tie. At first, nothing happened, then he felt the blade catch, so he rubbed harder until the plastic split. Dropping the razor, he tried to pull the zip tie apart, but it stayed fast.

"Fuck it," he growled under his breath and redoubled his effort with the razor until the plastic snapped. It was taking too long, but John had no other way of getting him free.

"Slide forward," he whispered to Maruti, and once he had done so, John began working on his wrists. It took just as long, but eventually, the zip tie snapped, and Maruti shook his arms out and rubbed his wrists.

John moved to Sarah, starting first with her ankles. A door slammed in the corridor, and John paused at the sound of raised voices. He glanced across at Maruti, who was again staring at the door, then turned his attention back to Sarah.

"It's too late, John."

"What?" John looked over his shoulder at Maruti, who was still on the floor.

Maruti returned his gaze and nodded toward the door.

John dropped the safety razor and grabbed the Maglite, but before he could get to his feet, the door opened.

74

"John, what a pleasant surprise."

John lowered the flashlight and slowly got to his feet. His initial urge to assault whoever came through the door faded away. He didn't know why, but despite everything that had happened, he couldn't bring himself to hit Atman.

Atman stood smiling in the doorway. His eyes flicked to the flashlight in John's hand, then turned to look at Maruti.

"My friend, I'm sure you won't mind if I speak to John for a moment." Without waiting for a reply, he reached out and placed a hand on John's arm. "Come."

John frowned and glanced over at Maruti, who shrugged.

Atman stepped back and pushed the door open wide to reveal Georges and Max in the corridor. John hesitated, tightening his grip on the flashlight.

"Why is this girl tied up?" Atman asked. "Untie her immediately and make sure she's comfortable."

"Yes, sir," Max replied.

Atman shook his head and turned to John. "Sometimes,

you just can't get good staff." He turned around and walked out the door. "Come with me, John."

John wasn't sure what to do. The moment he should have acted had passed, and now he was outnumbered and... confused. He looked again at Maruti, but he was watching Max, who had entered the room and was cutting the zip ties on Sara's wrists. Unable to do anything else, John turned and followed Atman out the door. Georges' bulky form blocked the corridor to the left, so John turned right and walked toward the living room.

Atman was standing before his framed picture, a stick of incense in one hand and a lighter in the other. He lit the incense stick, watched it burn for a moment, then shook out the flame, so only the tip smoldered, and placed the stick in the stand.

"Take a seat, John," he said without turning around.

John walked over to the sofa and sat where he could see the hallway where Georges stood, leaning against the wall with his arms crossed.

Atman moved to his armchair and sat down. He crossed his legs, smoothed the material of his pant leg with his hand, then cocking his head, looked at John.

John waited for him to say something, but Atman remained silent, and John tired of waiting.

"You said you had to talk to me."

Atman spread his hands wide. "What is there to say?"

"How about why you abused your position and sexually assaulted Sarah?"

Atman frowned. "She told you this?"

"Yes."

"And you believe her?"

John blinked and glanced at Georges, then back at

Atman. "Of course, I believe her. She was crying her eyes out in her room."

Atman shrugged.

"What sort of reaction is that?" John struggled to control his temper. "Are you telling me she's lying?"

"I'm not telling you anything, John. You need to find your own truth."

"Oh, come on! What sort of bullshit answer is that? Something has happened. She's terrified, withdrawn, and," —John pointed toward the hallway—"you've drugged, kidnapped, and kept her tied up on a bed."

"Yes." Atman turned to look at Georges. "That is unfortunate." He directed his gaze back at John. "What can I say, John?" He shrugged. "Staff."

"You mean ex-Foreign Legion bodyguards."

"Ha!" Atman slapped his thigh with amusement. "Impressive, John. You've done your research." He again looked at Georges, this time with a combination of raised eyebrows and a smile. He gestured with one hand at John as if telling Georges, 'See. Isn't he good?'

Georges didn't react, his face a blank mask.

Turning back to John, Atman smiled. "I'm sorry, where are my manners? Can I offer you something to drink? Tea, coffee, juice?"

John closed his eyes and counted to three. It didn't work.

"No, I don't want anything to fucking drink. Stop avoiding the questions and tell me the fucking truth!"

Atman looked at John with a hint of amusement, not at all the reaction John expected. He wanted to lean over and slap him across the face.

"John..." Atman paused and brushed an imaginary speck of dust from his knee. "Your passion and determination are admirable qualities. With the correct focus, you will go far…" He looked up and locked eyes with John. "But you must continue to look within if you want to find the truth you are seeking. Stop focusing on the external world."

"And you stop talking bullshit!" John shouted, unable to control himself any longer. "A woman was sexually assaulted, here,"—John pointed at the floor—"in this house, and you're telling me to look within?" John turned his finger on Atman. "I'm looking within, and my gut tells me you're a cheating motherfucking bastard, taking advantage of vulnerable women. If there is a hell, you will rot in it!"

John sensed Georges moving closer just as Atman made a gesture with his hand for him to stay still. John turned and glared at the big man.

"You're just as bad. You're enabling him. Is this what the *Légion* taught you? Where's your honor now?"

Georges' eyes had narrowed, and John could see a prominent vein pulsing in his left temple. John kept staring at him, challenging him to come closer, but Georges remained where he was, halfway between the hallway and the sofa. A movement behind him caught John's eye as Max appeared and took Georges' place in the corridor entrance.

"John," Atman spoke up, "Look at me."

Reluctantly, John turned back.

"You need to understand, John, that this experience,"—Atman gestured with his hands to encompass the room—"is deeper than what you see with your eyes, what you hear with your ears."

John shook his head in disbelief.

Atman held up his hand. "Please wait before you pass judgment. These doubts you have, the accusations you make, are all because you lack faith. You lack faith in the teachings. You lack faith in yourself."

John closed his eyes and shook his head. "Bullshit, bullshit, bullshit," he muttered. Opening his eyes, he stared straight at Atman.

"So, everything is my fault?" He shook his head again. "You are un-fucking-believable. You may have conned everyone else, but you won't con me."

Atman smiled. "John, listen to me, please..."

"Why should I listen to you? You talk in riddles, never giving a straight answer, and now you're telling me it's all my fault because I lack faith?" John took a breath, struggling to remain coherent as he burned with anger.

"Okay." He held up his hand, closed his eyes, and took another breath. Exhaling, he asked, "Nihinsa. The Sri Lankan girl you brought here, promising her and her family enlightenment. They trusted you, believed everything you said, and what happened? You made her visit you at night..."

"Yes, John, I've explained this to you already."

"You invite a young girl to your room at night, and after that, her behavior changes until one day, she disappears." John jabbed his finger at Atman. "She was a kid, an innocent little girl, and you raped her, you bastard."

Atman pointed a finger at Georges and shook his head.

John turned and snarled at Georges, who was standing much closer.

"What?"

Georges glared back but remained silent.

Atman was looking at the floor, his face serious.

"We are looking for her, John. We are doing everything we can to find her." He looked up at John, his expression suddenly sad. "She was like a daughter to me."

"Was?"

"Is." Atman dismissed the question with a wave and took a breath. "John, I've been pleased with your progress here, but there are obviously some things you still need to work on. Nothing you are saying, nothing you are seeing is real. It's all theatre, designed to help you learn."

John opened his mouth, but Atman held up his hand,

"Please allow me to finish. The deeper you go, the more you will understand, John. I know it's hard for you right now, but all will become clear in time." Atman sighed. "Let's talk about Sarah. You're probably not aware, but there is a history of sexual abuse in her life. Coming here has helped her."

"How? By abusing her again?"

"You don't understand, John. Your comprehension is limited, but it will improve."

John was struggling to remain in his seat. He tried to focus on his breath, willing himself to remain calm, but the more Atman spoke, the harder it became.

"There's a reason these things keep happening to Sarah. We are all born with a karmic debt and with lessons we need to learn."

"Fuck off, Atman. Sexual assault is a lesson?"

"Exactly." Atman nodded. "It will keep happening to her until she learns what she needs to learn."

John couldn't take it anymore. He exploded off the sofa and lunged for Atman, screaming, "You're a fucking madman."

75

Time seemed to slow down. John could see Atman watching as he jumped at him, but he didn't move and seemed to smile.

Then John felt a shooting pain in his back and his body went rigid. The pain traveled up into his brain, and he tried to scream, but he'd lost all motor control. When it stopped, he folded in half, and collapsed on the floor at Atman's feet.

"Motherf—" he gasped. What the hell was that? He gasped for breath, forcing down the urge to vomit. He heard footsteps, and the blurry shape of Georges appeared in his field of vision. He had something in his hand, and as John's vision cleared, he could see two wires running from it to somewhere behind John. Georges' finger moved, and John's body went rigid again. The pain was excruciating, but John couldn't do anything about it, couldn't move or make a sound. It seemed endless, like nothing John had ever felt before, and inside his head, he screamed, "Stop, stop, stop."

His body went limp again, and the pain subsided, leaving John gasping on the floor.

"That's enough, Georges."

John opened his eyes. His muscles and joints throbbed, and tears ran down the side of his face. He could see Atman's feet near his face and turned his head to look up. Atman was looking down at him, a slight frown creasing his forehead.

"John, you need to learn to control your emotions. The meditation will help, but you must keep up the practice."

John's eyes followed Atman as he stood up and adjusted his shirt, brushing out the creases from the front with his hand. He smiled down at John.

"Remember, John, I love you all." He turned and walked away. John watched him go and then pressed his hands down and lifted his upper body off the floor.

His body went rigid.

When it stopped, and he could open his eyes again, he saw Georges squatting beside him, the taser still in his hand. He stared at John, but his face was blank, giving no clue as to what he was thinking.

John cleared his throat and tried to spit at his feet, but the saliva dribbled down the side of his face onto the floor, and Georges' finger moved again.

Just when John thought he could bear the pain no more, everything went black.

76

J ohn didn't know how long he had been lying there, but when he opened his eyes, the room was empty, and the incense stick had burned out. Gingerly, he tested his arms and legs. His muscles were sore, but he could move. He pushed himself upright and wiped the snot from his nose with the back of his hand, then wiped his hand on the fabric covering Atman's armchair.

"Fuck you and your sofas," he muttered and with difficulty, got to his feet. He felt a painful tug on his back, at the same time noticing the taser lying on the floor. Reaching behind him, he felt for the wires, and gritting his teeth, pulled on them, crying out as the darts tore free from his flesh. "Bastards," he growled and threw them on the floor, kicking the taser across the room. Taking a deep breath, he straightened up and then staggered across the living room.

The house was completely silent. John paused at the kitchen and peered inside. There was no sign of the cook, and the door to the outside was wide open. He continued down the hallway to the end and glanced inside the office. It was empty. He stepped forward and looked out through the glass panel in the rear door toward the garage. Both ATVs were missing.

John grimaced, then turned and walked back down the corridor and twisted the door handle of the door where Maruti and Sarah had been imprisoned. It was locked, but the key had been left in the lock. John twisted it and opened the door.

Maruti sat facing the door, in the lotus position, his eyes closed, but when John stepped inside, he opened one eye and grinned.

"All okay? You looked zapped."

John blinked. "What?"

Maruti continued. "They've gone. I heard the ATVs."

John nodded. "I saw." He reached into his pocket and pulled out the Range Rover's key fob. "They won't get far, though."

Maruti chuckled, and with the ease of a man half his age, unfolded his legs and sprang to his feet. He nodded at Sarah, who was still lying on the bed.

"She's okay. She came round once but is sleeping it off."

"Yeah, I don't know what they use, but it's nasty stuff."

Headlights flashed across the window, and John rushed over to peer out at the vehicle making its way slowly up the rear path. As it reached the light from the parking area, John relaxed. It was his Camry.

He walked out of the room and down the hall to the back door and stepped outside. The passenger door of the Camry opened, and Gayatri stepped out cautiously, but when she saw John on the top step, she visibly relaxed.

"You're safe!"

"Yes... and so are the others."

The Camry's lights switched off, and Sanhita climbed out.

John nodded in his direction. "Thank you."

"You are welcome, sir, but they got away."

"You saw them?"

"We had parked up on the main road, and we saw the two ATVs go past," Gayatri explained.

"I'll worry about them later. Come inside, Gayatri. Sarah could use your help. They drugged her as they did me."

"Oh." Gayatri's hand moved to her mouth as she hurried forward and climbed the steps.

"The second room on the right," John called after her as she entered the house. Turning back to Sanhita, he asked, "Can you fetch Uma? Tell her we need her nursing skills. Take the car."

"Yes, sir."

"Please call me John, Sanhita."

"Yes, s... John."

"One more thing. Check the gate. Make sure it's locked. Change the padlock if you have to. We don't want anyone surprising us."

77

J ohn sat in Georges' office, his eyes on the monitor showing the multiple security feeds while he waited for the phone to connect. Uma and Gayatri were tending to Sarah in the other room, and Maruti was roaming the kitchen, looking for something to eat.

The phone connected and started ringing, and John pressed it closer to his ear. In the top left of the monitor, he could see Sanhita padlocking the front gate, but there was no movement in any of the other feeds, the rest of the ashram occupants unaware of the recent events.

"Hello?"

John switched his attention back to the phone and smiled. "It's me."

"John, oh thank God."

"Ha, thank someone."

"You're okay?"

"Considering, in the last twelve hours, I've been drugged and tasered, I would say I'm feeling pretty good."

"What?"

"Yes, thanks for recommending this meditation retreat."

"John, I'm so sorry."

John chuckled. "I'm teasing you."

There was silence for a moment.

"What happened? Where are they?"

"I don't know." John rubbed his face with his free hand and sighed. "They left. I don't know how long ago, but they're roaming the back roads of Sri Lanka in a pair of ATVs."

"ATVs?"

"Yeah, I hid the keys to the Range Rover."

"John!"

John could hear the amusement in her voice, and he smiled.

"Anyway, Sarah is safe, and so is my roommate." His smile faded. "But I still don't know what happened to Nihinsa, the Sri Lankan girl."

"Oh, no."

"Yeah," John sighed. "Did you manage to do anything at your end?"

"Yes. When... um... Gaya..."

"Gayatri."

"Yes, Gayatri. When she phoned, I called Vidu. He said he has contacts in the Colombo police and would pull some strings."

"Good. You'd better let him know they fled in ATVs. They should be easy for the police to find."

"I will."

"Thanks." John yawned, suddenly exhausted, the adrenaline long since gone, and his body ached from head to toe. "I need to get some rest. It's been a long day. Let's talk tomorrow, and I'll tell you everything in detail then."

"Okay, John. Take care. I love you."

"I love you, too, Adriana. With every aching cell of my body."

John heard what sounded like a sniff at the end of the line, then, "Goodnight."

"Goodnight, my baby."

The line went dead, and John leaned back in the chair, his eyelids drooping. He stood, wincing as his body reminded him of the tasering, and walked out of the office. Uma and Gayatri were sitting on Sarah's bed, talking softly to her, and when he looked in the kitchen, Maruti was sitting at the kitchen table, munching on a huge sandwich. John shook his head, grinned, and continued to the living room. He stared at the armchair for a minute, then walked over to the large, framed portrait of Atman. Reaching up, he removed it from the wall, turned it around, and propped it against the wall. He stood for a moment staring at the back of the picture, then turned away and sat down on the sofa. Leaning back, he closed his eyes, and in seconds, he was fast asleep.

78

J ohn sat at the back of the hall, his eyes closed, listening to the instructions from the stage, but he was content not to follow them.

A lot had happened in the three days since Atman had fled. A police team from Colombo arrived the next morning, but not before John and Maruti had searched the house. John found his wallet, passport, and phone in the top drawer of the office desk, and in the drawer beneath, he found thick bundles of Sri Lankan rupees, which John gave to Gayatri for safekeeping. A paper shredder in the corner was jammed full of shredded files and papers, but it was obvious, apart from the cash, the office had been cleared of anything incriminating before they left.

There was a safe hidden behind the bookshelf, but John and Maruti couldn't open it, and when the police arrived, they quickly took charge, sealing off the entire house. Clothing that looked like it had belonged to Georges and Max was found in the rooms above the garage, along with two Glocks, ten boxes of ammunition, and, as the police put it, 'recreational amounts' of marijuana.

Atman's room was the most puzzling. It was spartan, with a single bed pushed against the wall on one side, while on the other, a low shelf ran from one wall to the other. In the center of the shelf were statues of the Buddha, Shiva as a seated yogi, and Christ on the Cross. An oil lamp burned in front of the statues, and the ash from incense spilled from the shelf onto the floor. Crystals of all shapes and sizes filled the rest of the shelf space, but apart from a single meditation cushion on the floor, there was nothing of a personal nature in the room. Either Atman had taken everything with him, or as he'd told John that day at lunch, money and possessions really meant nothing to him.

John heard the words, 'slowly come back,' opened his eyes, and adjusted his position on the cushion. Many of the students had left when the news about Atman leaked out, so the hall was only half full, and John could easily see Sarah down near the front. She was getting better every day. The drug had worn off quickly, but the psychological scars of her experience would take longer to heal. John saw her move, then turn to smile at the lady next to her. Sarah had already told them she didn't want to leave, and Gayatri promised John she would look after her.

A movement caught John's eye, and he shifted his attention to the figure on the stage. Maruti sat on a cushion in the center, a broad smile on his face as he looked out over the remaining students. He had resisted taking over, but the long-time occupants of the ashram had insisted. He had made a few changes, though. Atman's armchair was now part of the kitchen woodpile, and Maruti no longer wore white. John looked at him now, wondering where he had seen his outfit before, then smiled when he remembered the photo on the wall of Maruti's room. The picture of Matilda in happier, healthier days and Maruti proudly standing next to her in a tie-dyed sleeveless shirt.

Gayatri sat to Maruti's left, and on his right sat Isuri, no longer in a red sari, but dressing closer to her age, in loose cotton pants and a pink Hello Kitty t-shirt. She looked happier, as did Gayatri.

Gayatri had softened over the last few days, visibly more relaxed, no longer the bossy headmistress, more the woman who read romance novels and hid bottles of *arrack* in a bookshelf. John had even heard her laugh on a couple of occasions, most notably when Maruti was around. She would no doubt deny it, but John sensed a burgeoning friendship between her and his former roommate. Time would tell.

John stretched his legs out and sighed. Things had almost turned out alright.

Almost.

Sadly, there was still no sign of Nihinsa, but police in Hambantota, a small town on the south coast, had found a pair of ATVs abandoned near the port. Of their occupants, there was no trace. The news frustrated John, but he had done as much as he could here. The ashram occupants were safe. It was now up to the police and Adriana's reporting to do the rest.

On stage, Maruti got to his feet, and the other students in front of John did the same. John shook his legs out once more, then stood as the students burst into a spontaneous round of applause. Maruti said something John didn't quite catch and laughed, and the hall laughed with him. John smiled. He would do well. John picked up his cushion and walked to the door, then turned and looked back, catching Maruti's eye. They had said their goodbyes earlier. Maruti nodded and winked. John raised a hand, then turned, placed his cushion on the pile, and walked out the door.

Picking up the bag he had left outside the door, he strolled toward the carpark. The sun was high above, the sky clear, and a gentle breeze carried the scents of the forest across the plantation. John smiled. It hadn't been all bad, but he didn't want to stay longer. There was someone waiting for him in Lisbon, and John couldn't wait to get back to her.

At the carpark, he stopped, removed the car keys from his pocket, and stared at his rental. He tossed the keys in the air, once, twice, then caught them and walked over to the guardhouse.

"Sanhita?"

"Yes, sir... I mean, John."

John held out the keys. "Someone will come to pick up my car."

Of course, John." The elderly guard nodded and smiled. "I will keep your keys safe." His smile faded, and he looked puzzled. "But... how will you go? Will you be okay?"

"I'll be fine, don't worry." John smiled and turned away. He reached into his pocket and pressed a button. Across the carpark, there was a beep, and the lights of the Range Rover flashed. "I can look after myself."

EPILOGUE

A month later, the buzzing of John's phone on the café table signaled an incoming call. He put down his coffee and glanced at the screen. The number was unfamiliar, but he recognized the dialing code. He picked it up and accepted the call.

"John?"

"Maruti?"

"Yes." The old man laughed. "How are you, my friend?"

John smiled with fondness at the sound of his voice. "I'm well, Maruti. Very well."

"They've not found him yet?"

"No, Maruti, not a sign of him, but it's not surprising. After all the negative publicity Adriana's article generated, he dare not show his face anywhere. His other centers have either closed or as you've done at Pramodaya, they've been taken over by the students."

"That's good to hear."

"It is, but I'd still like to see him behind bars."

"I'm sure... but enough about him. Can you sleep a full night yet?"

"Ha, I can, and do you know why? Because you are not snoring next to me."

"John, I'm offended."

John chuckled. "But seriously, yes. I'm sleeping much better."

"Are you still doing your practice?"

"Every morning and evening. Not missed a day since I left."

"I'm happy, John. Proud of you."

"Thanks, Dad."

"Cheeky b... I take it all back."

John smiled, caught the waiter's eye, and signaled for the bill.

"How about you, Maruti? How's it going?"

"It's going well, John. Attendance dropped off for a few weeks, but we are filling up again. Gayatri and I reduced prices and are giving free classes for the locals."

"Wonderful. How is she?"

"Gayatri? She's a good woman, John."

"I know that, Maruti. You make sure you look after her."

"I will. Sarah's much better, too. She's started an outreach program for young women in the villages near here."

"Wow. Your call has made me very happy, Maruti. Thank you."

"You're welcome, my friend." Maruti cleared his throat. "There's something else."

John's smile faded a little, "What is it?"

"Gayatri and I took a trip to Kaluwila."

John frowned, "Kaluwila? You mean...?"

"Yes. We paid a visit to Nihinsa's parents."

"Shit." John swallowed. That Nihinsa had never been

found was still eating away at John. "And?" He wasn't sure he wanted to hear the answer.

"They are okay... considering the circumstances. Kiyomi and Asiri are their names." Maruti sighed. "They're very poor, John, and to be honest, Asiri's health is not good. He may not be around too long."

John exhaled loudly and rubbed his head. "I still hope she'll be found."

"Yeah... but..." Maruti trailed off, not wanting to say the obvious. They both knew the more time passed, the less likely it was that she would be found—alive.

Maruti cleared his throat again. "Anyway, the cash we found in Atman's house?"

"Yes?"

"We used it to settle all Kiyomi and Asiri's debts, and what's left is paying for someone to tend their fields."

"Good. That really is making dirty money clean."

"I thought you would like that."

"Huh."

"But wait, there's more."

John waited.

"The ashram is setting up the Nihinsa Education Trust for the children of Kaluwila and surrounding villages. Sarah has agreed to run it."

"That's fantastic, Maruti. Really fantastic. Thank you."

"Thank you, John. You gave me a purpose again."

"I wish it had been under better circumstances."

"Everything happens for a reason, my friend. Now, keep up the practice, and I'll speak to you again soon."

"Will do. Keep up the good work."

"May the force be with you."

John laughed as the line went dead.

. . .

That night, John's sleep was disturbed for the first time since he returned from Sri Lanka. Disturbed, but in a good way. At first, it wasn't visual, just a feeling. A feeling of warmth and unconditional love, then there was light. Warm golden light radiated from a central point before his eyes, then the point changed color from white to red and expanded, forming a figure. The figure increased in size and seemed to get closer as its form became clearer, then John saw her... the girl from the stage—Nihinsa. She smiled, and John felt rather than heard her speak, two words appearing in his mind.

Thank you.

John Hayes and Atman return in FREEDOM: John Hayes #8

ALSO BY MARK DAVID ABBOTT

For a complete list of all my books please visit my website:

www.markdavidabbott.com

The John Hayes Series

Vengeance: John Hayes #1

A Million Reasons: John Hayes #2

A New Beginning: John Hayes #3

No Escape: John Hayes #4

Reprisal: John Hayes #5

Payback: John Hayes #6

The Guru: John Hayes #7

Faith: John Hayes #8

The Neighbour: John Hayes #9

The Chinese Cat: John Hayes #10

The John Hayes Box Sets

The John Hayes Thrillers Boxset : Books 1-3

The John Hayes Thrillers Boxset : Books 4-6

The John Hayes Thrillers Boxset : Books 7-9

The Max Jones Series

The Mule: Max Jones #1

The Irishman: Max Jones #2

The Hong Kong Series

Disruption: Hong Kong #1

Conflict: Hong Kong #2

Freedom: Hong Kong #3

The Hong Kong Series Boxset :Books 1-3

The Devil Inside Duology

The Devil Inside

Flipped

The Devil Inside : Boxset

As M D Abbott

Once Upon A Time In Sri Lanka

READY FOR THE NEXT ADVENTURE?

The next book is currently being written, but if you sign up for my VIP newsletter I will let you know as soon as it is released.

Your email will be kept 100% private and you can unsubscribe at any time.

If you are interested, please join here:

www.markdavidabbott.com
(No Spam. Ever.)

ENJOYED THIS BOOK? YOU CAN MAKE A BIG DIFFERENCE.

First of all thank you so much for taking the time to read my work. If you enjoyed it, then I would be extremely grateful if you would consider leaving a short review for me on the store where you purchased the book. A good review means so much to every writer but especially to self-published writers like myself. It helps new readers discover my books and allows me more time to create stories for you to enjoy.

ABOUT THE AUTHOR

Mark can be found online at:
www.markdavidabbott.com

on Facebook
www.facebook.com/markdavidabbottauthor

on Instagram
instagram.com/thekiwigypsy

or on email at:
www.markdavidabbott.com/contact

facebook.com/markdavidabbottauthor
instagram.com/thekiwigypsy

Milton Keynes UK
Ingram Content Group UK Ltd.
UKHW010935231123
433129UK00001B/21